THE HAUL

OTHER BOOKS BY GARY PHILLIPS

The Ivan Monk Mysteries
Violent Spring
Perdition, U.S.A.
Bad Night Is Falling
Only the Wicked

The Martha Chainey Mysteries
High Hand
Shooter's Point

The O'Conner Crime Fictions
Warlord of Willow Ridge
Culprits (co-writer)

The Harry Ingram Mysteries
One-Shot Harry
Ash Dark as Night

Three Bullet Opera

THE HAUL

GARY PHILLIPS

SOHO CRIME

Published by Soho Press, Inc.
227 W 17th Street
New York, NY 10011
www.sohopress.com

Library of Congress Cataloging-in-Publication Data

Names: Phillips, Gary, 1955- author
Title: The haul / Gary Phillips.
Description: New York, NY : Soho Crime, 2026.
Identifiers: LCCN 2026009011

ISBN 978-1-64129-664-9
eISBN 978-1-64129-665-6

Subjects: LCGFT: Thrillers (Fiction) | Novels
Classification: LCC PS3566.H4783 H38 2026
LC record available at https://lccn.loc.gov/2026009011

Interior design by Janine Agro, Soho Press, Inc.

Printed in the United States of America

10 9 8 7 6 5 4 3 2 1

To Millard Kaufman, a true teller of tales

"The worst thing you can do with money is not spend it."
—Jackie Gleason

CHAPTER ONE

The End

O'Conner exited the rear of the building, heart rate steady. Smoke and flames from the fire inside were etched onto the darkening sky behind him. Glancing down at his bloodied shoe, he wondered if his toes were severed, if they could be reattached. His burned arm was in bad shape, but he kept going. Fire trucks were arriving in the front.

A steady thrum of cars drove by on the nearby overpasses. O'Conner took one last look back, then got in the SUV he was confiscating. He started the engine and put the vehicle in gear. There was one more motherfuckah to deal with.

Back Then

A merlot-colored Cadillac Deville rounded the corner too fast, tires screeching. The wounded driver wrestled the steering wheel to maintain control as a homeless man with an overloaded shopping cart stepped from the curb, attempting to get to the other side. The Cadillac's headlights captured his horrified face. Fear glued him in place.

The sedan swerved just before plowing into him. The car jumped the curb, grazing a fixed city trash receptacle before crashing into a brick wall, loosening bricks but not penetrating. The homeless man, who was known around the neighborhood as Shoe Dog, rolled his cart closer. He watched as the driver's side door was eased open by the toe of a Ferragamo loafer. The windshield was spider-webbed from the crash. Steam jetted from the crushed radiator and bricks were strewn over the crumpled hood. The car was drilled with several bullet holes.

"Hey, fool, you almost killed me," Shoe Dog said, casually. "Got me a haul from the Crimson Lounge to get to the recycler."

Shoe Dog hooked a thumb over his shoulder toward the bar. He'd raided its dumpster, retrieving numerous empty bottles and aluminum cans. There was no name painted in garish colors on the front of the establishment, no blaring neon announcing the tavern to the neighborhood. There was only an address in relief and a narrow awning over the doorway. The patrons of the bar knew the place. The few of them here at this time of the evening had come outside to see what the commotion was about.

"Ain't that Long Box?" one of the customers said, straining her eyes to see in the gloom. She was referring to the man who was stepping out of the bullet-riddled Deville. She wore a gold lamé top that shimmered under the moonlight. A tall white man in a stylish leather coat with a shock of unruly premature gray hair stood in the bar's open doorway. An ostentatious ring gleamed on his crooked little finger.

"Sure enough," Charlene "Charlie Mack" McDaniels said, adjusting her oversized eyeglasses. "That's his ride."

Charlie Mack was a handsome, solidly built woman of a certain age. In her red-nailed hand, a cigarette smoldered at the end of an ivory holder. She was the proprietor of the Crimson Lounge. That is, she was the owner of record.

"He's not doing too good," she ventured.

"No, he is not," the other woman agreed.

Charlie Mack and the white man exchanged a look.

Anthony "Long Box" Tolles, one of the Crimson Lounge's silent partners, was now leaning against the doorframe of the car, his head resting on the car's roof. He was Black, early forties, with short-cropped hair. He was dressed in black slacks and a powder-blue shirt, open collar. Over this, he wore a dark topcoat with off-white flecks. A red stain from the wound on his side was splotched against the material of his shirt.

Tolles licked his dry lower lip and, pushing off the car, walked unsteadily to the rear, beeping the trunk open along the way. He reached inside.

Seeing the blood along the sidewalk, Shoe Dog said, "You might want to get to a doctor, my man."

"Gonna need that cart," Tolles said. He removed three nylon duffels from the trunk.

"This here's all my shit, son."

"Gonna need your cart, homie. This ain't a negotiation."

Tolles pointed the gun now in his hand at Shoe Dog.

"No reason to get nasty about it."

Tolles took hold of the shopping cart and tried to upend it to spill out its contents. Two large plastic bags tumbled out and an assortment of bottles and cans clattered onto the sidewalk. Amazingly, none of the bottles shattered. The other articles in the cart remained. With effort, Tolles got two of the duffels piled into the cart. He tried to hoist the third bag on top of these, grimacing in pain. He put his gun on the other duffels and, with two hands, grabbed the strap of the remaining bag, swung it up. But he'd put too much force into the effort and the duffel sailed over the cart and landed partly in the dankness of a shop's alcove.

"Fuck it," he declared.

His exertion had left him bleeding more. Sweating heavily, he wiped his face with his open hand. Off he went, pushing the shopping cart and leaving the third bag behind. He hurried down the street, hoping to find a pay phone. As his strength ebbed, so did his coordination. His feet got tripped up and he sagged, the cart wobbling. He regained control as he passed by the Hi Hat Liquor Mart.

Inside, a gangly Black kid was sweeping the aisles. He hadn't heard the crash—he'd been at the counter behind the bullet-resistant barrier with Bora Cho. They'd been listening to the basketball game on the radio as she tallied the day's count from the register. She wrote in the ledger while the kid rattled off total sales of items such as potato chips and sodas. He did the sums in his head as he read through the receipt tape.

"Eddie Harper hits a three," Swashbucklers' announcer Chip Barnes said with his usual verve.

On the tall side for his age, the loose-limbed kid couldn't have been more than fourteen. He looked up as the wounded man passed. Like the Crimson Lounge patrons, he recognized Tolles. The youngster put down his broom and went out on the sidewalk to see where Tolles was headed, slumped forward over the shopping cart. Pushing it seemed to require great effort on his part. Splotches of blood trailed behind Tolles along the sidewalk.

"OC, get back in here," the older woman said in Korean.

The youngster answered in English. "I'm just looking, Mrs. Cho."

"Looking gets you shot," she declared, also in English. She came out from where she'd been stacking cans of diced tomatoes and, outside, put a hand on his shoulder. "Come on so we can close up."

"Okay." OC took a last look at Tolles, who went into the laundromat down the block.

Tolles had seen a pay phone inside World of Suds. Clothes tumbling in dryers around him, he put the handset against his ear. He was giddy to hear a dial tone and slotted in a quarter. The metallic tinkling of the coin in the machine was a psychological buoy to the hunted man. He punched in a number, looking back over his shoulder as he did so.

The dial tone gave way to a ring once before falling silent.

"Hello, hello," he repeated. Tolles violently tapped the switch hook over and over, trying to get a dial tone. No luck.

"Ghot-damitt," he bellowed, slamming the handset onto the cradle, breaking it apart. The three women inside the laundromat looked over at him nervously. Tolles let go of the broken handset, letting it dangle on its cable. He turned, rolling his stolen cart out of there. No sooner had he cleared the doorway than he heard the approach of a fast-moving car as it cleared the same corner he'd driven around. A bronze-colored Impala with tinted windows.

Tolles didn't try to run. He didn't have the energy. He let go of the shopping cart. Gun up, he walked down the middle of the roadway toward the car as it zeroed in on him. He shot at the driver and the Impala swerved sideways, striking a twin set of news racks at the curb. Newspapers ejected from them, fluttering about like flying stingrays.

The car stopped.

People bolted from the World of Suds, leaving their clothes. The top of the head of the vehicle's driver had collided with the windshield. Due to that, being shot by Tolles, or both, he remained immobile. The unhurt passenger got out of the car. He was Black, above average height with a modified high-top fade. He wore baggy jeans, heavy boots and a jean jacket over a T-shirt. A heavy gold chain was around his neck. He was some years younger than his quarry.

"Fuck you, Teaflake."

Tolles fired his gun at the man he called Teaflake until he clicked dry. He dropped the weapon as if it had betrayed him.

"You know how the game is played, Long Box," Teaflake

said as he got closer. Tolles stood his ground, keeping his hands down to better hide his shaking. "Cold rockin', baby."

"Bring it, bitch ass."

"It does pain me to 187 ya," Teaflake declared.

Two blasts from Teaflake's gun. The rounds grouped in Tolles's chest and ended his life.

For a moment, Dimitri "Teaflake" Strock regarded the dead man sprawled across the pavement. With effort, he then lifted the duffels from the cart and put them in the back seat of his car. Across the street from the destroyed news racks, he noticed the lights were on inside the Hi Hat Liquor Mart. No sirens approaching yet. He walked over calmly and strode inside.

"You make sure you don't say shit when 5-0 rolls up, hear me, mama-san?"

Mrs. Cho and OC were standing along an aisle. Teaflake held the gun at his side.

"Figure we all look alike to you Ko-re-ans anyway, huh?"

"Leave Mrs. Cho alone."

"OC, quiet."

Teaflake came midway down the aisle. The kid was shaking, but got himself under control. The older woman held him tight by the shoulders. He was already taller than she was.

"Looks like you just about to get some bass in your voice, boy." Teaflake assessed him and turned to go, adding over his shoulder, "Reach big, young blood. Don't let nobody tell you different."

Teaflake walked out of the store. The other two sagged against each other. A few seconds later, there was the screech of tires outside.

"The fuck," Teaflake said.

He stood in the middle of the street, looking to his right. A car had braked roughly to let him pass. Three people were inside. The driver was white. The young woman beside him some other kind of Asian. Another white boy was in the back. From their expressions, Teaflake knew they'd seen the gun in his hand. There was also the matter of Long Box lying dead on the street. Must be why they'd sped up.

"Palmer," the young woman gasped, gripping the driver's arm tightly.

The driver kept staring at Teaflake.

"Must be nerds from 'SC," Teaflake muttered as they gaped at him. The University of Southern California wasn't far from the neighborhood. They looked like students. Teaflake knocked on the driver's side window, which was partially open, with his Glock. The window lowered all the way.

"We're just trying to get out of here," the driver, Palmer, stammered. The other two nodded vigorously in agreement. The driver was looking around for a rescuer, but there was no such person to be found. Briefly, he locked eyes with OC, who stared wide-eyed out the Hi Hat's window at the altercation.

Teaflake grinned at the driver, no humor in his eyes. "Maybe I oughta snatch your ass to make sure your buddies keep their mouths shut."

"Aw, man, come on, please. Just let us get out of here," the one in the back seat implored.

Teaflake kept dead-eyeing the driver, who wet himself. Holding the gun upright, Teaflake said, "Get the fuck on out of here so y'all can go build your robots taking us hard-workin' folks' jobs. 'Cause I'm feeling generous, you got thirty seconds to get your Radio Shack lovin' asses off this block . . . only I've already counted to twenty-five, mother-fuckahs."

His brief mirthless laugh was drowned out by the roar of their car as it drove away.

Teaflake jogged to his Impala. He pulled the dead driver from the vehicle and gently placed him on the sidewalk. For damn sure there was no sense driving around with a corpse, calling attention to himself and all them ducats in the trunk. Sirens were evident in the distance but getting closer. The car started on the third crank. He backed onto the roadway and was gone.

"OC, go on home," Bora Cho said to the loose-limbed kid in the Hi Hat. "I'll tell the police I hide when the guns went off."

"Okay, Mrs. Cho, okay."

There was no back entrance to the Hi Hat, only a side door that let out into a narrow alleyway. The lock on the front door wasn't much. It was the riot gate that secured the store. OC left by the side door and went onto the sidewalk. Several doors down, Charlie Mack was walking in his direction.

"OC, you best get your narrow butt off these streets," she said to him.

"I am," he answered.

She looked around. "Damn," she said softly.

Two patrol cars from Southwest Division had appeared in the street about two and a half blocks away, lightbars bright as they silenced their sirens and parked. Exiting the cars, the cops' forms were washed in reds and blues. Flashlights snapped on. Tight, bright beams of light swept about. Whoever dropped a dime, OC figured, must have come from nearby, but no one on this block. Anybody who saw Teaflake wouldn't be so foolish to tell the cops. Too many had allegiance to him.

"Never mind what I just said, come here. Quick, boy, quick."

OC ran over to Charlie Mack. The cops were now checking between the buildings, slowing their arrival on this block.

"You scared of a dead body?"

"No, ma'am."

"Figured you wasn't," she said, pressing a folded-over fifty in his hand. "Hustle over to Long Box's body and fetch his keys."

"Keys?" He stared at the money. He'd never seen a fifty for real before, just on cop shows on TV.

"Yeah, not for a car or house. They might be old-fashioned. They called 'em skeleton keys back when I was a whippersnapper like you." Frowning, she glared at OC, her eyes x-raying him. "You know what I'm talking about?"

"Uh-huh, I know what a skeleton key is."

"Okay, hurry, go check. See if you find any. I'd do it myself, but ain't steppin' as lightly as I used to." She patted her middle. "Now get, while the Man is busying creeping and peeping down there, 'cause they'll be along this way sooner than you can say Jack Robinson. You find them keys, keep 'em till I see you next."

"Okay." OC turned to go.

"You keepin' up with your studies?"

"I am." He was already moving off.

"Good."

Charlie Mack hurried back to the Crimson Lounge, heels clacking on the asphalt.

Off the youngster scrambled to Long Box Tolles's body. He was all shot up like in a picture in a *Bronze Thrills* magazine, but in color. OC'd seen a dead body before, his grandmother's. He could see the flashlights swinging around again up the block. The police were getting closer. No time to worry about the inevitable. OC took a knee and put his hands in the corpse's coat pocket. The one on this side, then the other. No keys.

"Shit," he said.

Wiping his palms on his jeans, he plunged his hand inside the dead man's pants pocket. He removed a packaged condom. He smiled awkwardly and jammed it in his pocket. Not because he was going to have a chance at using it, he just didn't want to leave the pack with his print on it. In the other pocket were a couple of other items, but no keys. It was time to go. Then he flashed on this kid Benny he knew. He had this St. Christopher medal he always wore around his neck. His brother had given it to him.

OC sucked in air, as if breathing at this moment would lessen his nerve. He reached inside Tolles's collar. Sure enough, he had two keys around his neck on a thin chain. OC yanked them free, chain and keys, taking away a smear of blood on the heel of his thumb. He gulped and, up again, used his other hand to rub the blood into his skin. The fifty and the keys in his pocket, he made to take off but then had another idea.

He ran in the opposite direction from the searching cops to where Tolles's Cadillac had smashed into the wall. The police hadn't seen the crashed car yet. Could he earn another fifty if he came up with something else for Charlie Mack? Heart in his throat but feeling lucky, OC peered through the windows of the Cadillac. Like with the condom packet, he knew from his studies not to touch the car and leave his prints on the metal or glass. Weren't his on file somewhere anyway? Did they change as you got older? Whatever. He walked to the rear of the car, looking across the trunk. He squinted at a dark object across the way. It was gloomy down here, the only streetlight half a block up. He walked over and, in the alcove of an Arthur Treacher's Fish and Chips, he spotted the duffel bag. Excitedly, he bent to it and undid the zipper, revealing cash.

"Oh shit," he exclaimed, eyes wide.

The money wasn't banded neatly in stacks like in a bank. The bills were crumpled and haphazardly thrown into the bag. Tens, twenties, a lot of hundreds too. Everyone knew the rumors that Long Box had stash houses where hundreds of boxes of paper money were stored. Such was the source of his nickname. Even with his math skills, OC couldn't calculate how much this was. He also just as quickly realized he had no immediate place to hide the stash. Where was an empty dirt lot when you needed one to bury your treasure? Not that he had the luxury of time to do any digging with the cops around.

OC pulled the bag farther out of the alcove, risking more exposure. He considered returning to the Hi Hat with the loot but the flashlights were already at the other end of the block. He sure as hell wasn't going to try and get this to Charlie Mack. She was okay to talk to, and paid him cash for doing odd jobs at the bar, like cleaning up. But having observed her more than once telling a drunk or high customer not to fuck up her place, he had a sense of her.

"I got too much money and sweat invested in this enterprise," she would say, hand under the bar near the pistol grip shotgun she kept there.

If he brought her the money, Charlie Mack would peel him off a couple of hundreds for his troubles and dare him to say different. And anyway, he reasoned, the cops were sure to spot him lugging the bag to the bar.

"Come on, come on," he said aloud. He ran to the now-crooked trash receptacle and pawed through the mound as fast as he could. He came away with sticky hands and a discarded Ralphs paper grocery bag partially torn at the top. He stuffed as many bills as he could in the sack. Various denominations fell to the sidewalk as the youngster breathed rapidly, excited and fearful. The flashlights were getting closer. He could now hear the cops talking indistinctly.

OC scooped out another load of bills from the duffel, pressing the bills with both hands to his chest before jamming them into the trash can as deep down as he could manage. He picked up stray bills and shoved them in his pockets, then pushed the garbage that had fallen out back in place. Somewhere in the mess had been a partially eaten banana and the fruit was smeared on his hands. Quickly, he wiped them off on some newspaper sticking out of the freshly packed trash. The beam from a cop's flashlight shined on the storefront next door.

OC stuffed a few more fistfuls of cash in his pocket and, grocery bag tucked under his arm, took off in the opposite direction. He ran like he'd seen Barry Sanders do with the football on TV.

"Ey, you, stop," he heard a cop yell. "Come back here."

"Oh shit." OC ran faster, willing himself to be like the mutant speedster Quicksilver in Marvel comics. Half expecting a bullet in the back, he whipped around a corner and kept going. The soles of his worn tennis shoes slapping the pavement were like booms of thunder in his ears.

"Yo, check this out," he heard one of the cops say. They must have found the duffel, OC reasoned as he ducked alongside Yolanda's House of Glamour Weaves and Beauty Supplies. Back here, he knew he could get over a cinderblock wall and end up behind the Pep Boys. He'd already tightened the rolled-over top of his paper bag and tossed that over the taller wall first. He jumped up but couldn't quite get a grip. Shaking and sweating and ignoring the pain of his skinned wrists, he didn't see anything around to give him a boost over. Were those footsteps? He had to get over that wall.

OC backed up and, charging full bore, leaped. He reached up like he was hoping to grab hold of a handful of stars from the night sky. One hand latched on the top of the wall. He hung there for a moment, the tip of his foot on the cinderblock pushing him up. Then he swung his body upward to get his other hand in place.

He scrambled over and dropped down, gathered his bag of loot from the ground where it landed. He took to the shadows next to the auto parts store and rearranged an unruly pile of cardboard boxes yet to be flattened for the dumpster.

Like in the forts he used to build when younger, he was able to crouch down behind the boxes and remain unseen. He stayed still for several minutes. He didn't hear any cop. He emerged slowly.

OC took off for home. He was already late to check in, but he had a good excuse to lay on Dr. Apgar. An illuminated billboard advertising Valmont Afro Hair Sheen rose above the Pep Boys. Pictured prominently on the billboard above the depictions of a spray bottle and gel in a beauty jar were a young beatific Black man and Black woman. Their hair was fluffed perfectly. Their faces agleam with the promise of a brighter future.

"The police," he told the aging caretaker of the Herninie Griss Group Home. "There was a shooting."

Twenty minutes later, OC and the doctor were sitting at the kitchen table. He'd been having a cup of tea when the youngster came in. As was his habit, the older man removed his glasses, worrying the stem between his thin lips.

"Yes, I heard the sirens."

Roman Apgar was in his early sixties, a clinical psychologist by training. His once jet-black hair was streaked with white, but he stayed in shape through bicycling and jogging. He was of German and Italian stock. Though the boys in this group home tended to be hard-to-place youth for one reason or another, including those who exhibited self-destructive behaviors, Apgar's pleasantly composed face rarely gave way to anger.

"You know full well I'm already your unindicted co-conspirator," Apgar said, "breaking the rules as it were at Hi Hat."

The boys were allowed to have part-time outside jobs, were even encouraged to do so. But you had to be at least fourteen, and OC wasn't. But he knew that Apgar understood OC was savvy. If the kid didn't cause a ruckus, there was slack to be given in certain matters.

"I know." He also knew not to try and snow the old bird with too much praise like "thanks so much" or some other bullshit.

"Did the police ask you why you were out at this time of night?"

"No, they just wanted to know if I saw anything."

"Did you?"

He'd anticipated the doctor would ask this. It was one thing to lie, sort of, about the police. They hadn't caught him so there was that. But on this matter, he decided to be honest—to a point. "Yeah. Long Box got done in by another shot caller. A dude who will hurt Mrs. Cho, probably have his boys burn down her store and, well, I don't know what all else."

The doctor sighed, setting his glasses down on the kitchen table. "What should we do, OC? I realize this was one bad man doing in another, but still."

The youngster slowly shook his head from side to side. "I can't tell you, Dr. Apgar. You can call the police and tell them I know but I won't talk. They can take me out of here and put me in juvie, Wayside, whatever. Don't make me no mind."

A bemused Apgar regarded his self-assured charge. "You know my goal is to mold you young men into responsible citizens."

"Responsible alive citizens," OC countered.

Apgar sipped his cooling tea. "Well, let's sleep on it for tonight. Perhaps in an upcoming group discussion we will engage with just what is the course to take when the reality is there can be the consequences of confluences."

"Actions and reactions, like what Miss Pancella talks about."

"Your science teacher."

"Mm-hmm."

"Get some sleep, OC."

"Okay, Doc."

They got up from the table. On a nearby built-in sideboard was a stack of much-read comic books, some older issues and other more recent editions. One of the donors to the home, a USC alum, was into literacy and periodically sent care packages of comics and books. Next to them was a 1980s vintage boom box. There were various faded stickers on the casing, some not in English. Apgar depressed the play button and soft renditions of classical music issued from its speakers.

OC looked through the stack of comics. New issues had been added. He was pleased to find a Silver Surfer comic and took it with him as he ascended the stairs.

The Griss group home was a converted neoclassical fourplex, the sort dating back to the 1920s in South Central. At one point in its history, the place had been a brothel frequented by vice cops and local community figures. Or so the lore went among the facility's young residents. OC and a couple of the others had also heard from Benny that the doctor had been part of something called psyops in Vietnam. Benny had explained that meant Dr. Apgar and his buddies came up with ways to trick and confuse the enemy, so they could be wiped out easier. And that he'd used his skills on what they called prisoners of war, the Vietcong our soldiers captured.

"You mean torture?" OC had asked.

"Yeah," Benny had said. "It was called the Phoenix Program."

"How do you know this?" one of the other kids had asked.

"Read it in a book my brother gave me, before, you know, the accident." His older brother had died after being hit head-on by a van while riding his motorcycle.

"What book?"

"About secret stuff the government does. Like how Dr. Apgar drugs our food."

"That's only for guys like Mitchell," OC said. Mitchell liked to start fires and wouldn't take his meds. He'd eventually been sent elsewhere.

On the second floor, in addition to the sleeping quarters and bathrooms, there was a small room used to store cleaning and office supplies as well as a cabinet with an overstock of dry foodstuffs. A larger built-in pantry was downstairs off the kitchen. Walking past the room, OC heard murmuring. He opened the door to see Benny and another kid trying to pick the lock on the cabinet. They glanced at him and went back to what they were doing. Benny was using a butter knife to try to pry the cabinet open.

"Thought you said you could get in it," the kid at Benny's shoulder said in a low tone. It was the one they called Raj, for Roger. He had a lazy eye that was perpetually half lidded.

"All you're doing is making scratches," OC observed.

"You know so much, you do it," Benny said. He offered OC the butter knife.

OC didn't take the knife but went to the shelf lined with office supplies. The youngster shook a paper clip loose from a Lucite dispenser. He straightened it out and inserted the end into the lock. He leaned in to hear better and soon had overcome the lock and opened the cabinet door.

Having set aside the butter knife, Benny moved items around. "Where's the Oreos?"

"They're gone," OC said.

Raj flexed. "You eat them?"

"What if I did?"

"Best be cool, man," Benny said.

"I ain't scared of this little bitch," Raj sneered.

OC and this kid were roughly the same slim build and height. Raj made to put his hands on OC, who sidestepped and stomped the bridge of Raj's foot. He yelped and in a flash OC pressed the butter knife below Raj's widening lazy eye, applying pressure. He also had his forearm on Raj's neck, having backed him against the wall. OC's expression remained neutral, devoid of anger.

"Told you to be cool," Benny repeated. "You about to be all Nick Fury in a minute."

"Fine, fuck it." Raj put up his hands.

OC backed off, holding the utensil at his side. He walked backward toward the door. He exited and went to his room, shared with three others and two double-decker bunk beds.

The others were asleep. Antonio, who slept on the top bunk, was snoring again as usual. OC had the bottom tier of his bunk. He lay on his stomach and put his makeshift weapon in his secret compartment—a single floorboard he'd previously meticulously loosened. He wasn't scared of Raj, but no sense leaving the knife laying around until he snuck it back to the kitchen. He brushed his teeth in the shared bathroom between his room and the one on the other side. Unlike a number of the kids at Griss, OC was attentive to his hygiene. This was even before seeing the film they'd shown him in sex ed class, the one the doctor had to okay him taking at Foshay. It was aimed at the girls about the changes their bodies were going through. Everyone laughed and snickered and had to be shushed by the teacher as the old 1960s-era film played, in grainy and garish colors.

"Control your emotions, control your physical appetites," the female narrator warned at one point. Her words played over the image of a woman in an Army uniform who scowled when a man put more papers on her desk to type up. The part about appetites switched to the image of a woman sitting at a table eating a sundae. This gave way to people at a party dancing, smoking and drinking.

"Sex can be a powerful drive. At all times, control must be utilized, especially when in a fun situation during which your guard may be down due to various factors," the narrator had gravely warned. There'd also been a part where a bank teller was counting a customer's money. One of his bills slipped to the floor but they didn't notice as the customer walked out. The teller eventually came around to get the bill off the floor.

"You need to understand what's right and wrong," the narrator continued.

Hands behind his head, OC lay on his back in his bunk.

He wondered, had the teller kept the money for herself or run outside to give it to the customer? But the people in the film strip were squares, not Long Box Tolles and Teaflake Strock. He smiled, conjuring up a scene with Teaflake dressed like the white customer in the suit and hat, leaving the bank. If he'd dropped a damned one-dollar bill he would have known it and, after strolling back into the bank, would have put his pistol in the teller's grill if she tried to stall him. The smile faded as he further contemplated his new reality.

OC had an overflowing grocery bag full of money. More if he could get to the trash before it was emptied. Though could be the cops had already looked in there. Anyway, he was the richest kid in South Central as far as he was concerned. OC was itching to count his haul. Must be at least, like, five or six thousand? No, more—he'd seen a grip of hundreds when he'd been jamming them into the bag. Probably not enough to buy a house but enough to buy a car and get the hell out of there. He knew how to drive. Well, he'd only been behind the wheel of a car once, but he hadn't crashed. Of course there was the fact he was too young to have a driver's license or a learner's permit, and the fact no car lot would sell him a used beater being underage.

A motorcycle? He didn't want to end up like Benny's brother, but a motorcycle was easier to get than a car. Plus it was cooler. Okay, he best learn how to ride one. That's what they called it, right? They didn't say drive, but that's what it was. You had to always be aware on the machine. You couldn't be daydreaming on one of those things like you might driving a car.

OC shifted. As of late, he'd been thinking about girls

differently than a year ago. Not exactly all nasty like in rap songs but still. If you had money to flash, that got their attention, didn't it? Nobody in Griss could know about the money, that would not be good for him. He could handle himself against any one chump like Raj, but what if two or three of them got together to put it to him? Take him to one of those empty houses off Figueroa and torture him to find out where the money was. Even Benny might turn on him for that kind of long green.

On the other hand, Teaflake didn't know about the third duffel bag. The cops did. Would this be mentioned in the newspaper or on TV? Maybe, maybe not. For sure the shooting would be. He imagined one of those pretty ladies on the news saying money was recovered at the scene. He'd heard stuff like that before on broadcasts. Even if the money was mentioned, the cops hadn't ID'd him. But he figured he best not get too comfortable. Dr. Apgar wasn't going to let up about doing his civic duty. He knew the doc would try to be slick about it, not bugging him directly, but he'd find a way to remind him on the sly.

Rolling on his side, OC was determined to get some sleep and worry about his next steps tomorrow. His stash was safe for tonight. Before school the next morning he'd get back to where he hid those ducats and hide the bag better. There were plenty of places to hide the cash at the Hi Hat. He might even let Mrs. Cho in on his score—she wouldn't steal from him. Her brother-in-law, Soon-Li, that chain-smoking mufu for sure would rip him off.

From his hidey-hole in the bedroom, he removed a flashlight and his battered hardback copy of *Where the Money Was.*

The book was about Depression-era bank robber Willie Sutton. He'd bought it at a sale when the library was discarding old books. His other book was called *The Art of Manipulation*, written in the 1950s about safecracking, which he'd chanced upon when he was walking along King Boulevard nearing a bookstore called The Awakening.

"Do you read books, young man?" the smiling older Black lady had asked him. She was outside the doorway straightening newspapers on a rack. In addition to the *Los Angeles Times*, there was the weekly Black newspaper *The Sentinel*, and the Black Muslim's *Final Call.*

"Yes, ma'am," he'd said. "I've read *The Three Musketeers* and *Pinocchio*, and not the kids' picture book," he added proudly.

"Read anything by any other Black authors?"

"What do you mean other?"

"Dumas who wrote your Musketeers was part Black."

"Yeah?" he said. "I didn't know that."

She invited him inside and suggested several titles as she showed him around the cramped but homey shop. Crystals of various shapes and colors hung from the ceiling in one section, with numerous incenses and candles on a large table. There were books about the true meanings of ancient Egyptian hieroglyphics, aliens visiting Timbuktu and so on. He didn't see any titles about the mysteries of Wakanda, the Black Panther's hidden super scientific African kingdom.

The woman's husband was also there, engaged in an energetic conversation with another person. OC learned they were into something called metaphysics, which she tried to explain.

"Like Dr. Strange in the comics?" he said, trying to grasp her meaning.

The nice lady chuckled. "Not exactly, but I suppose he's on his own version of a spiritual journey." Looking around again, she said to OC, "I'm supposing your book budget is kinda tight."

He frowned at her.

"You don't have much money."

"No, ma'am."

She gave him two paperbacks. One was Dumas's *The Count of Monte Cristo* and the other a science fiction novel by a writer named Samuel R. Delany, *The Jewels of Aptor*. Tapping the cover with her finger, she said, "Delany is a Black man in a field where there aren't many of us as writers. This is kind of like a comic book in words, as it involves a priestess and mutants sort of like the X-Men."

OC was impressed she knew about them. On the way out, he'd seen the book about safecracking on a pile of used books near the side of the door. The title and the name of authors, Clyde Lentz and Bill Kenton, were embossed on the hardback in gold lettering. The sparkling letters stood out to him. He picked it up.

"What's this about?"

She glared at the book. "I'm not sure. Maybe manipulating the mind?" She took him in. "You know what that word means?"

That could come in handy dealing with more than one knucklehead of the group home, OC reasoned. He knew from Dr. Apgar's talks what the word meant. "I do. Give you a dollar for it."

"Sold."

They shook hands.

Only later, when he was back home, did he realize what the book was about. He'd read it several times over. That had been almost two years ago. He had yet to be able to practice on a locked safe, to manipulate the combination dial and see if he could open one. That book had led him to the library to search for additional books about other kinds of locks in the card catalog. It took him going to three branches, but he did find one on how to be a locksmith. OC devoured it, spending money to photocopy some of the pages at a Kinko's. He'd recently acquired the one about Willie Sutton.

Opening the book on its bookmark, OC clicked on his flashlight to continue reading. It wasn't like he'd given deep reflections to being a thief. He supposed if he were to come clean with Dr. Apgar he would say he was interested in locks because they required skill and focus to open. "But wasn't that violating another person's desire to keep what is theirs from thieves?" he could hear the doc respond.

"I wouldn't steal from one of the old ladies with their groceries in those funny little carts they use," OC would say. "Any poot butt could do that."

"You mean using force?"

"It ain't nothing, hitting somebody weaker than you in the head and snatching their purse. I'd knock over like, you know, Fort Knox in *Goldfinger*. It's like the Super Bowl or the finals, the best against the best."

"The challenge?" Dr. Apgar would ask.

"Right."

The doctor would take off his glasses, setting the stem on his bottom lip. "Because it would be taking from the government. Isn't that a manifestation of your anti-authority tendencies?"

OC ended his imaginary conversation with "I couldn't say."

He tried to concentrate on his book, but the money stuffed in the Ralphs paper bag wouldn't leave him alone. Be cool, he told himself. Sutton wouldn't let his excitement get the best of him. There was a lesson to be learned from what happened to Long Box tonight. He wasn't no chump, but Teaflake pushed up on him. Never let 'em catch you slippin', is what them rappers say. A fool slips, then he trips . . . and don't get back up.

If he ever got jammed up, OC was going to be damn sure he was the one left standing.

CHAPTER TWO

Now

On a pleasant afternoon, on a converted tennis court in Hemet, California, O'Conner and his partner—old lady, he would say, but knew better—Gwen Gardner played a doubles game of pickleball against another couple. Gardner served. The ball was returned. O'Conner dashed and hit the ball back over the net after it bounced. The ball looped into the air, then plummeted down close to the net on the side of their opponents. But Jane Grainger-Brill was ready and with an underhanded swat of her paddle, connected. The ball once more cleared the net. This time, Gardner's paddle whacked the ball before it could bounce. The ball rocketed between the other two on the far side of the court, where it struck the ground, unreturned.

"That's game, dang it," Steve Brill declared amiably.

"Nice shot, sweetie," O'Conner said, giving Gardner a peck. They'd won best two out of three. They touched paddles all around, chatting while they put their gear away and gathered their light equipment bags. O'Conner's phone sounded as he walked off the court. Removing it from his bag, he regarded the screen as he turned the alert off. He'd been expecting the call.

"Business?" Jane asked. To her, O'Conner was VP of operations for his girlfriend's chain of auto body shops.

"Just an inventory snafu I reminded myself to attend to today," he said, tucking the phone away. "Traffic is going to be stop and go. Looks like I better get on the road now. Can you guys give Gwen a ride home?"

The couple also lived in Willow Ridge, the housing subdivision here where O'Conner and Gardner owned a townhouse.

Gardner put her arm around O'Conner's waist. It seemed less a gesture of affection and more to reassure herself. She let go and said to the other two, "Let's get brunch." To O'Conner, she said, "Let me know how it goes."

"Of course I will."

"You have to leave now?" Steve asked. "It didn't sound that serious."

"It's not," O'Conner answered. "But what with quarterly reports due, better to see about it now than let it fester." He grinned. "I've got a slave driver for a boss."

"I hear what you're saying," Steve said, also smiling. He put his arm around his wife's shoulders. They regarded each other briefly, having picked up on the shift in their friends' mood.

Hands interlaced, O'Conner and Gardner walked a length away. After a few words to each other, they kissed again, deeper and longer.

"Make sure you charge up the Bat Phone," O'Conner said, face close to hers.

"Does that make me Robin or Batwoman?"

"Makes you whoever you want to be."

"You're goddamn right it does."

After dealing with traffic and alternate routes, O'Conner entered the restaurant amid the welcoming din of conversing diners, ice tinkling in tall glasses and layers of savory aromas. Scanning the dimly lit interior, he was aware he was backlit, exposed. Though, after all these years and having pulled down various scores, he'd mostly been out of the game since a job in Texas a few years ago, he remained keenly aware of his surroundings. An arm went up from a far booth. Tachmann. His call to O'Conner on one of his encrypted phones at pickleball had been prearranged. O'Conner had only been waiting for a time and place to meet. O'Conner walked over and sat down, joining Tachmann and another at the table.

"O'Conner, this is Mavis Joyner," Tachmann said in lieu of a greeting.

Tachmann was white, late fifties, silver haired with a trim mustache. That Tachmann enjoyed the good life was evident given his manicured fingernails and his Hugo Boss suit. In the years O'Conner had known him, he'd wore an ostentatious ring on a crooked little finger, as if to highlight the finger's slight deformity.

"Good to meet you," O'Conner said as they shook hands across the table. Mavis Joyner was Black, thirtysomething, frizzed-out styled hair. Oversized glasses complemented her alert face. Along one ear were several stylish silver and gem studs. Joyner looked quite a bit like the images he'd seen of her online—maybe thinner in the face, he estimated. The beginnings of worry lines, his grandmother would have called them, at the edges of her eyes.

"Same here." Joyner glanced at Tachmann, then back at O'Conner. "Cocktail?"

Joyner was having a martini and Tachmann something clear in a tall glass. Back when O'Conner was moving from one takedown to the next, he wouldn't have been as relaxed as he was now. Some things did change. "Why not."

Joyner signaled for the waiter, who appeared at the booth.

"Vodka tonic, house vodka is fine," O'Conner said, elbows on the table.

"Lime?"

"Sure."

The waiter left. O'Conner took his elbows off the table, settling in the booth.

Joyner again regarded Tachmann. "Not sure how to get into this."

"Be conversational," the older man suggested. "We won't speak in hushed voices, calling attention to ourselves," he said. "And obviously we're not going to be broadcasting either. We are what we seem, colleagues chatting about a business proposition."

Joyner nodded curtly but remained quiet.

"You want something stolen," O'Conner said.

"In a way. But it'll be hard to do. I suppose I see this as a kind of consultation, Mr. O'Conner." There was more confidence in her voice now. "I'll lay out what it is, and you can tell me if it's in any way feasible. No harm, no foul if it isn't."

O'Conner moved his jaw toward Tachmann. "You obviously told him."

"The broad strokes," Tachmann said. "Once I heard, though, knew you were the one for the job, O'Conner. That and the curious fact the three of us have a connection, once removed as it were."

"I did wonder how she knows you, Tack."

"My auntie was Charlie Mack. She pretty much raised me at one point," Joyner answered.

"Huh, I'll be," O'Conner remarked. Studying her, he could see a resemblance.

"I attended her high school graduation," Tachmann said. "We've kept in touch over the years."

Clearly there was more to the ties between Tachmann and Joyner, but O'Conner kept on point. "Go ahead, Ms. Joyner."

"Mavis, if I can call you . . . what do you like to be called?"

"Connie if you like. Just O'Conner or even OC is okay, too."

His drink arrived and they waited while the tumbler was set down. The waiter took their food orders and left.

"I used to work for Palmer Van Noy. You know who that is?"

"Billionaire," O'Conner said. "Though he keeps a low profile, unlike some of those other tech bros."

"Yeah, he cultivates that image." She had some of her drink. "To make it plain, he ripped me off."

As if she were daring him to contradict her, Joyner's head cocked slightly to the side, a mirthless smile on her face.

"I see." O'Conner tasted his drink. Proportioned correctly, he concluded. "And you want revenge?"

"I surely do."

Having some down time between talking with Tachmann and agreeing to this meet, he'd looked up info on Joyner.

"When I heard about you, I watched a couple of interviews with you online." He knew from his brief research Joyner was a software engineer. She was involved in efforts to lend support to other women of color in tech as well as undertakings to bring girls into coding. Being Black and a woman in tech—and less than 5 percent were, he'd learned—she'd no doubt had to deal with plenty of minefields.

"I promise not to get in the weeds, but there's been a lot written and debated about racial bias in facial recognition systems. Leading to the wrong folks being accused or arrested. To put it simply, after a hell of a lot of sweat and gray hair, I developed a generative app that reconfigures and refines such software. Millions in savings could be realized by the user not having to scrap a given facial recognition system. My program can discern and overwrite. Reducing the error rate in some cases to less than four percent."

Frowning, O'Conner said, "You mean this program of yours self-corrects? Like they're training AI to do?"

"My intention is my program is a tool to be wielded so as to make such apps function accurately," she emphasized. "Like how a brother doesn't get railroaded into prison when DNA exonerates him."

"He took credit for this program you invented," O'Conner surmised. "Erasing your work, essentially."

"Like with everything he does, he was calculated," she said. "He acknowledged my work but played it off as if I'd only achieved preliminary results. Employee ingenuity and innovation is encouraged at Magnus-Noy. My contract had economic incentives built in. There are various engineers who have benefited."

"None of them Black women, eh?" Tachmann pointed out.

"You still work there?" O'Conner asked.

"No. I made no attempt to negotiate a new contract or be a freelancer with the firm. Though Palmer offered to sweeten the pot in terms of my percentages going forward. In the spirit of being colleagues."

"I'm confused. If he was offering more in the way of money, why take this big step out of line? Why consider this crazy move, whatever it is you want got? Sit back and keep on being a civilian."

"It was chump change, low-rent buy-off money."

A hard cast took hold of her face and for a moment reminded O'Conner of her aunt.

"Nigger money if I may be so bold," she said. "What I'm owed is white people money." She drank more. "When I brought my breakthrough to him, he claimed he'd already been working on this kind of app."

"That could be true," O'Conner responded.

"For sure plenty of techies are trying to solve all sorts of problems. Everything from trying to get to Mars to doping out fusion in a bottle. But I solved this one. Documenting your technical setbacks and progress is de rigueur in software design. I recorded my efforts up the wazoo. Only he faked me out. He produced his own, not exactly mirroring what I created, as that would be sniffed out. Essentially, he stole my code, modified it, then eliminated his trail. He didn't do this for the money, but the street cred he'll get out."

O'Conner's policy was to approach each job as dispassionately as he could. You had to clinically examine the angles—the weaknesses of the target to be exploited and the deficits on your side of the ledger. Joyner was personally invested in this; she was out for revenge. That was okay with him, but if he took this on, would her need to punish Van Noy be a detriment, tripping him up?

"I'm sure Tack told you I tend to specialize in cash. Don't all you computer types keep your money in Bitcoin and whatnot? Ghostly cyber vapors."

Tachmann chuckled.

She shook her head. "There's one place I'm sure that Palmer keeps cash, and I mean a king's ransom of it. His laid-out survival bunkers."

"In case there's the zombie apocalypse?" Tachmann said straight-faced.

"Given the state of our politics, more like the collapse of society. Civil war."

"The bunkers are where you figure he keeps cash?" O'Conner said. "Not some damn device storing his cryptocurrency keys?"

"He's thorough, I imagine he has those too," she said. "Van Noy's not the only one to brag about his survival shelters. It's something of a status symbol among his crowd, including a couple of players on the Swashbucklers. These things can be blinged out with swimming pools, underground gardens and game rooms."

Tachmann leaned forward. "To state the obvious, if society has collapsed, why do these types think having a bundle of cash will mean anything? It is after all, as comrade Lenin told us, or maybe it was Redd Foxx, merely a means of exchange."

"Like I said, he's going to cover the bases. Cash, gold,

diamonds . . . canned goods. Any humans left, and they will be armed, you better have something to be able to barter."

"Okay, let's say you're right," O'Conner said. "He keeps serious stacks in his expensive hidey-holes. But it's not the money so much that matters to you, but getting back at him, 'cause you're not the only one he's screwed over."

"Let's say you're right," she echoed.

"Beyond such a probability, what do you know about Van Noy that could be useful?"

"Before we get into that, I want you to know I'll be in on this. I'm not a watching-from-the-sidelines kind of gal."

"I don't like civilians on a crew."

Generally speaking, civilians were the weakest links when the squeeze happened. And despite all the planning, the angles covered, damned if there wasn't always some kind of shit coming at you from left field. O'Conner continued, "In this case we're talking about a cat with more money than Jehovah who will pour resources into finding the thieves."

"That doesn't seem to worry you," she countered.

"This isn't a hobby," he answered flatly. "I work with pros. They know the drill. If they get hemmed up because of the job or some other score they pulled, they don't roll over. They don't try and make a deal." This wasn't true in all cases, but he wasn't trying to be nuanced.

"You figure Mavis will be a natural suspect," Tachmann offered.

"Hell yes," he answered.

Still, O'Conner wanted to hear more before he turned her down. Over a year and a half ago, when fires savaged the Southland, a billionaire real estate developer used his two-thousand-dollar-per-hour private firefighters to protect his mansion and some of his commercial properties. As far as O'Conner was concerned, the haves protected their shit in the good times and bad. He was sure Mavis was right—a "have" like Van Noy would squirrel away cash.

And what the hell, O'Conner had a mind to enjoy the spicy chicken egg rolls he'd ordered.

"So, about Van Noy?" he asked again.

"Once I decided I wasn't going to work for him anymore, I sought to reverse engineer his claims. I consciously didn't go public with my assertions. I wanted him to forget about me, as if I'd moved on. Hardly," she stated. "I set out to prove he constructed a falsehood and drag him to court."

Their food arrived. Tachmann speared a brussels sprout with his fork and popped it in his mouth. "Going down one rabbit hole invariably leads to numerous warrens."

Joyner said, "I intended to penetrate his computers, worm my way through back doors to strip away the camouflaged source code, the steganography, hiding files within files, to reveal my original work."

"You mentioned not getting us deep in the weeds," Tachmann reminded her.

"Copy that," Joyner said, smiling. "I made progress, then hit a wall. To do what I needed to do was going to be too much exposure for me. I considered sending what I had to one of the outlets that cover tech, but even if that got an investigation going, it could be many months or years before there was a satisfying conclusion."

O'Conner remarked, "Committing grand theft robbery was your next idea?"

"I considered and dismissed various options."

"How do you figure he'll react to being robbed? Aside from not liking it."

"He's going to want to solve the problem. How did this happen, who did it and so on. But I think, too, he'll not want the embarrassment."

"Among his peers, you mean," Tachmann said.

"Right," she said. "At their precious bro gatherings he wouldn't want to be subjected to the ribbing and whatnot. Who would? He's going to want to keep his responses close and on the Q.T. The fewer that know that he was vulnerable, the better."

"Okay," he said, assessing the information.

She continued. "Palmer has two shelters here in town. One is under the family compound that was destroyed in the Palisades Fire in the Santa Monica bluffs. The other is below Del Norte arena."

"Didn't he have private firefighters to save his crib?" Tachmann said.

"He did," she acknowledged. "But the road to it was clogged with Teslas and Volvos."

"Damn," he said, exchanging a look with O'Conner.

"The arena is the new venue he built for his team," O'Conner declared.

Van Noy was a majority partner of the pro basketballers, the Swashbucklers.

"Yes. One of Palmer's children has severe food allergies. He has special deliveries of prepared meals made to both shelters."

Tachmann asked, "And you found the outfit that does the food prep?"

"Not only that, I even worked there for a spell. Palmer is always boasting about local sourcing. Enlightened," she said. "The place he uses, supplying both shelters, is in Inglewood. Not far from the arena, in fact. It's called Leafy Fields. It's also a microbrewery."

"Of course it is. What'd you do there?" O'Conner asked.

"Line cook," she answered proudly. "Faked my résumé, identity, and altered my appearance. I got to be buds with some of the workers, including one of the women who did the deliveries."

"Am I supposed to be impressed you got nerve?" O'Conner asked.

"I am," Tachmann admitted.

Joyner went into the particulars about the deliveries, including robotic carts used to ferry the containers of the fresh and freeze-dried meals. The two deliverers could only access the loading dock areas.

While he considered ordering another round of those wonderful egg rolls, O'Conner interjected, "If they weren't allowed deeper into the bunkers, then where are you going with this?"

She beamed. "My former coworker on the line likes her rum and cokes. Especially when someone else is buying."

"Okay," Tachmann said. "But she didn't get to see any of the rooms, and not a clue as to what kind of fortifications there are."

O'Conner said, "She saw something she talked about at happy hour."

"From the loading dock area, there was a side door. The kind with a small view window. They both looked through this of course. They could only see part of one machine. My girl said it looked like it belonged in a *Star Wars* show. I was able to get a few other details from her, and my best guess was that she'd seen part of the air filtration systems.

"I determined Palmer had installed this particular model made by a Swiss concern outfit. The company in turn jobs out the manufacture of several key components it uses." She waved a hand, realizing she was about to get into too much detail. "Anyway, I found out enough and was able to articulate a series of rough schematics."

"You have layouts for the one in the hills and the arena?"

"Not of the arena as a whole, but where the shelter is, yes, including of course how it's accessed. The shelter there has two separate entrances. There's always an escape route."

"Impressive," Tachmann declared, smiling paternally at her.

"There could still be variations," O'Conner said, more for his benefit, thinking aloud. "Invariably there's going to be last-minute changes."

"Buzzkill much?" she quipped.

"He's thorough too," Tachmann said.

O'Conner asked, "What do you estimate in the way of loot in one of these end-of-the-world retreats?"

"From what I know of Palmer, I'd say a minimum of twenty-one million. I have no idea why, but numbers divisible by three recur with him."

O'Conner said with interest, "He's superstitious?" He recalled Eddie Harper, a retired power forward for the Swashbucklers, wore number 33 when he played.

"And he gambles. He sometimes hangs out at the

Hollywood Park casino, among others. His security is always with him, of course."

"Let's assume too these bills didn't come directly from the Treasury," Tachmann said. "Your boy Palmer probably acquired an amount of them through his connections. The more black market, the better."

"Is that important?" Joyner asked.

"Pre-circulated money," O'Conner explained. "Makes them untraceable."

O'Conner sipped from his glass. "It's going to take a few weeks to line up everything properly." For certain he would need an explosives expert and someone to handle transportation needs.

Joyner said, "So, it's on?"

The two regarded O'Conner. He remained silent for several moments, the clamor of the restaurant prominent around him. Finally, he tapped his index finger once on the table. "Less than a month from now the arena opens, isn't that right?"

"Wouldn't it be more prudent to hit the shelter in the hills? The day the arena opens, Palmer will be otherwise engaged," Joyner said. "The compound is getting rebuilt, but there's a way in and out via the secondary emergency route."

O'Conner replied, "What's prudent is not taking on one of the richest men in the world. Someone with unlimited resources."

"Which is why you need me," Joyner stated.

"To use your skills to give him a false trail," Tachmann said.

"That's right," O'Conner agreed. He would prefer an

actual target for Van Noy to go after. Maybe before all this was over, there would be one.

Leaning forward, he added, "We're only going to get one chance at this, Mavis. Once he knows about the robbery, he's got to discover the false lead, but he's got to work for it. If it's handed to him, he'll know something's up."

"I understand," she said.

"I hope you do. He'll already be putting every aspect of the construction and maintenance of his overpriced doomsday basements under the magnifying glass. And make no mistake, those builders will also be in on trying to ascertain who knew what and who did they talk to."

Sitting back, he spread his hands. "Maybe your drinking buddy remembers what she said and maybe she doesn't. What is known is, whatever cover you concocted as the line cook, that person is no longer at the restaurant. What about the car you drove, your coworkers saw it?"

"The car was registered in the name of my alias. Afterward I dumped the vehicle."

"Dumped how?"

"A scrap yard, a pick-a-part place in Wilmington."

"Good. Me and Tack don't exist in a lot of ways. You, on the other hand, are a known entity."

"I've taken a break, but I understand that I'll have to retreat more into the background."

"Just the opposite," he said. "You have to maintain your normal activities. If you're asked about the robbery, you shouldn't be neutral. Palmer Van Noy's chickens have come home to roost as far as you're concerned. That's what happens to a mufu who takes credit for the work of others."

"You might possibly be a bit more restrained in your language," Tachmann advised.

"Granted," O'Conner said. "But you get where I'm going with this. What you talk about going forward has to line up with what you've stated previously. Don't go overboard, sure. But by outward appearances, everything is the same as it always was."

"Van Noy's been sued by any number of people he's worked with," Tachmann observed.

"Let's not forget his public fights with several right-wing assholes," Joyner said. "I also have some ideas on how we can plant a false cyber trail leading away from us on the dark web. I have an in to A Minus One."

"Right on," O'Conner said. He was familiar with the left-leaning hacktivist group. They'd conducted cyberattacks on various entities, including the State Department, ICE and the Kremlin.

"For sure they might come in handy."

"No doubt," Joyner said. "So we're doing this?"

She did control the plans. And he wasn't going into this blind.

"Yes," he answered after a measure. "I'm going to have another round of egg rolls while we talk about a bunch of other stuff, including how we stay in touch, and what you need to be doing between now and then. Have you fired a gun?"

"If we do this right, there will be no need for violence," she said.

"I wholeheartedly agree. I expect you've vetted me with Tack, about how I minimize gunplay—otherwise you probably wouldn't have asked for the meet. Be that as it may, this here is a criminal undertaking, Mavis, and there's always extenuating circumstances. I haven't made it to this age by not adapting to shit going sideways."

"Charlie Mack taught me how to handle a gun," she declared. "But isn't your specialty to be in and out and no one's the wiser?"

"I haven't changed," he said.

"I suppose you figure to get the lion's share?" she asked.

"A percentage more than y'all, yes. You object?"

"Just getting my facts straight."

"My end is thirty-three percent of the haul. Guess I got a thing for threes too. Anyway, the rest is divided equally among the heisters."

"My ten percent comes out of yours and his end equally," Tachmann told her. "The freight as it's your idea and his overseeing the execution."

"Understood," she said.

"I put together the string and secure the equipment and logistics, some of that through Tack, our quartermaster. There's going to be a lot of prep and rehearsals. I take it you're not doing freelance work, so you can make the time if need be?"

She agreed.

"No significant other wanting time with you?"

"Sadly, at the moment, no," she said. "You're not asking me this 'cause I'm queer, are you?"

"No, ma'am. I'd ask this of any other square Jane citizen." He recalled her sexuality coming up in more than one interview he'd seen with her on YouTube.

Tachmann worried his big ring back and forth on his

little finger. "Who else you have in mind for this undertaking?"

"Burgess for sure," he said.

"He's still around?" Tachmann asked.

To Joyner, O'Conner said, "He blows up stuff."

They clinked glasses.

After watching Joyner drive away, O'Conner and Tachmann talked next to the older man's car, a Jaguar F-Type.

"I know you're taking a lot on trust with her because of me," Tachmann said. "But I know Mavis, I vouch for her, otherwise I wouldn't have reached out."

"I get it, she's got it bad to want payback on Van Noy. Of course, it's all fun and games until—"

"You get hit in the mouth," Tachmann finished, paraphrasing Mike Tyson.

"Aren't you worried about her doing this?"

"Like you said, she's got her mind made up. I for sure don't want her working with amateurs. I know you'll do right by her, O'Conner."

"You mean not put a bullet in her head after the robbery to take care of a possible loose end?"

"That's not your style. You don't turn on a member of your crew. Unlike some we could name."

O'Conner said, "I'll be in touch."

They shook hands. Tachmann got in his car and left. O'Conner noted a cardboard box of wine on the back seat. He closed in on where he'd left his Cadillac CT5 Sport and stepped between two other parked cars to cross an aisle. Turning onto the aisle at the near end came a white car with a broad yellow stripe along the center of its hood, a lidar unit on the roof. He paused, as did the self-driving vehicle. O'Conner stepped back between the other two cars. The whine of the electric vehicle resumed as it approached again.

O'Conner looked through the windshield, confirming no one was behind the wheel or anywhere else inside. The car stopped once more, its sensors detecting his presence. He stepped farther back. The car finally went on. He noted the insignia on the side of the autonomous vehicle as it went past: Overland. The taxi service Palmer Van Noy had bought recently. The car reached the end of the aisle and turned. O'Conner waited several beats, then got in his car and also departed.

TALES FROM THE CRIMSON LOUNGE

Charlie Mack drifted behind Valerie Gaffney, the bartender, and took a position to her right. Mack's red-nailed hands gripped the edge of the inlaid ivory–topped bar, the veins pronounced on the backs of her hands. Her Remington was within reach. She, Gaffney and the others eyed the two men, the arguing patrons. The altercation had started innocently enough, with each favoring their respective basketball team playing on the recently installed television in the Crimson Lounge.

The fancy TV, made by an outfit called Philips, was called a flat-screen. It replaced the boxy, tube-powered Zenith that had been a fixture in the bar for more than a decade. This modern device was only three inches thick, weighing less than forty pounds. Its screen measured thirty-five inches diagonally. The new set was bracketed in place where the Zenith's shelf had been, over the racks of bottles situated behind the bar. Word of the newfangled wonder at the Lounge had reached beyond the neighborhood. Several newcomers had visited the bar just to see the TV in operation.

What started as the usual back-and-forth trash-talking

had escalated. This increase was due, in part, to alcohol. The heat too was a factor on this late Saturday afternoon. It was November, but this was Los Angeles. Rather than a cold snap having moved in, a high-pressure system had developed off the ocean. As the sprawl of the city was in a basin, the heat settled over its residents like a dome.

One man bolted to his feet, his chair tipping over, banging loudly on the floor. The object of his scorn was already standing. Both of them sweated from the beer they'd been drinking and their rising anger. The one already standing was Billy Lyles, who was dressed in his Department of Water and Power work clothes, complete with a utility vest and heavy boots. He'd worked weekend shift. The other man was in street clothes, a stingy brim pushed back on his balding head. Stingy Brim's eyes were glassier. On the TV, guard Ali Kassan sank a three for the Swashbucklers. They were playing the Bay Area Admirals.

"Look, brah," Lyles said, "you're entitled to your motherfuckin' opinion just as I am. See, that's what makes this country not England or North Korea. But what you're not entitled to is to stroll in here, you clearly not from around here, and loud as you please spout your bullshit on all of us who is down for the Swash."

Stingy Brim weaved slightly, putting a hand on the round table to steady himself. He did his best to focus on Lyles. "I have a high tone is what I have, my . . . man. And you goddamn right I can express who I like, such as the Admirals, and who I think are a bunch of spoiled prima donnas more interested in chasing Hollywood pussy than leaving it on the court."

"Yeah, then how come the Swash is up by eight, huh?"

Stingy Brim swiveled his head, gaping at the TV. "Third quarter, plenty of time left. You'll see."

The husky Lyles inched closer to the skinnier Stingy Brim. "See what, the Admirals get smoked?"

Gaffney side-eyed her boss. Several years ago, Charlie Mack had been going around with a handyman named Hank Dixon. He'd created a hidden compartment under the bar. At the press of a disguised button, the spring-controlled false front would drop, revealing the hog's leg, as Charlie Mack's grandfather would have called it. At that moment, she was reaching under the bar. Gaffney's eyes narrowed as she held her breath. The images on the television changed. It was a nature show about badgers on one of the public broadcasting channels. Gaffney let out air.

"Now look here," Charlie Mack said as she came from around the bar, turning down the sound of the narrator informing viewers how badgers burrow with the remote she'd plucked from underneath the bar top. "I'm all for everyone enjoying themselves in this here establishment. Truth be told, I derive great enjoyment from seeing folks in here. Laughing, making side bets when we have our domino tournaments, catching action, hell, even just sittin' in a corner, crying softly, cuddling some cognac. Well, shit, there's room for that too.

"I like to think of the Lounge as more than a business . . . an oasis, ya dig? An island where we can get away if only for a while from the toils and tribulations of the outside world. But when any one of my customers gets too out of pocket, interfering with my patrons enjoying theyselves, that's a problem. Ain't it, Billy?"

"Look, Charlie Mack, I—" he began defensively.

"Tut, tut," she said, cutting him off. Her raised hand gripped the remote as if it were a torch lighting the way to new worlds. "You were wrong, and so were you, sir." She pointed the remote at Stingy Brim, who offered a weak smile. Her intercession seemed to have sapped his energy.

"Shake hands, go to your neutral corners or get out of my bar. For you, Billy, that means banned for a month."

Charlie Mack knew from overhearing him in here that he was going through a rough divorce. The bar was indeed his refuge at this time. She put a hand on her hip, waiting.

"Fine," Lyles said. He put out his hand.

Squinting, Stingy Brim looked around, finally assessing the crowd, then offered his hand. The game resumed on the flat screen. The crawl announced the Swashbucklers were up by five.

To his credit, Stingy Brim remained in place. He even clapped cordially when one of the players on the Swashbucklers scored a three. But his team lost in a close contest, 117 to 113. Eddie Harper on a pass from Kassan made a decisive dunk at the buzzer. The Admirals' lone supporter was gone by then.

"Homeboy must have been from out of town," a patron opined. He was an older man dressed in baggy khakis and a short-sleeve shirt. While some filed out, he came over to the bar to take a now-empty seat. Gaffney went to the back to take care of some stock and Charlie Mack took her place behind the bar. The Crimson Lounge had three respectable brews on tap. He didn't want one of them, or hard liquor. He ordered his current favorite.

"Gimme another Zima, Charlie. Over ice this time, with a lime."

"Celebrating the Swash's win, Devon?"

He winked. "That and got a hot date tonight. We're going square dancing over to the center."

"Well all right." She smiled at the widower.

Charlie Mack's beeper went off as she set the glass on a coaster before the older man. She turned from the bar as she unclipped the pager from her belt. She recognized the phone number accompanied by the message 911. Emergency. Charlie Mack clipped the pager back in place and busied herself slicing up a few more limes and wiping down the bar. Any given situation demanded a calibrated response. Like the two getting hot over a damn basketball game, grown-ass men getting paid millions to toss a ball through a hoop. Gotta keep your perspective, she understood. Gaffney returned and Charlie Mack excused herself to her office.

She closed the door and sat behind her desk. She didn't use her private line. From a desk drawer she took out a lockbox and put it on the desk near a small framed photo of her younger brother holding his new baby girl. She extracted a satphone after unlocking the box with a key from a crowded ring. She thumbed it to life, then called the already-memorized phone number displayed on her pager's green-lit screen.

Anthony "Long Box" Tolles answered on the second ring. "What took you so long?"

"I was in the bathroom," she lied.

"It's on. My girl let me know Prof gets in at ten tonight. Union Station."

"You sure you want to do this? This way, I mean."

"Charlene," he drew out, using her real name as if talking to a child. "Teaflake ain't gonna see this comin'. You just do your job like we discussed. You just happen to be at the train station seeing a cousin off or some shit and you offer to give him a ride instead of taking a taxi. Easy as pie."

Tolles hung up to forestall any pushback. Charlie Mack put the satphone back in the lockbox and returned the case to the drawer. She picked up her ornately carved cigarette holder and inserted a fresh Virginia Slim.

Sparking the cigarette alight, she took a deep drag and let out a stream of smoke. She studied the dissipating pall, hoping against hope to figure out a way akin to the earlier dustup, solving the problem without resorting to violence. For her sake and the person coming to town.

CHAPTER THREE

Gwen Gardner set the rake aside, lifting the red plastic cup to take a swallow of her homemade lemonade. In her late forties, she was trim in worn cuffed dungarees, a work shirt and a wide-brimmed straw sun hat. Tilting her head up, she regarded O'Conner, who was on a ladder repairing one of the rain gutters, which had come loose from an eave. He descended, portable drill in hand, as Gardner came over to him and put an arm around his waist.

"Hey," she said, giving him a kiss. "Kinda sweaty," she remarked as their lips separated. "Nice."

He smiled, took the lemonade from her hand and sipped. "Kinda tart."

"Don't think I don't know you're being a smartass."

Gwen had another sip and put the cup back on the patio table. She resumed raking leaves and clippings. They'd spent the morning doing yard work and making minor repairs to the exterior of their townhouse. O'Conner put the drill and toolbox away in the detached garage-turned-semi-ADU, the improvements done sans permit. In a corner, covered by a tarp, was a more than two decades old Kawasaki motorcycle. He'd recently rebuilt the engine, but he hadn't taken it out for over a year.

After O'Conner helped Gardner finish the yard work, they sat at the table across from each other. The umbrella in the middle of the table offered partial shade from the early afternoon sun. Gardner kept her hat on, liking the warmth. They were quiet, a middle-aged suburban couple taking in their handiwork as butterflies and bees flitted about the flowers and vegetables growing in more than one garden box.

"I'm going to do the job in about four weeks' time," he said measuredly.

"I halfway assumed you were, since you kept the meet with Tachmann."

"It's a hell of a score, as he'd hinted."

"Care to elaborate?"

O'Conner told her. At this stage of their relationship, there was no pretense about what he did.

Gardner folded her arms. "The millions mean nothing to a man like Van Noy. He'll make that back in weeks, probably."

"True," O'Conner said. He then told her what Joyner said about planting misdirection about the theft. "But a dude like that, with an ego like all those AI lovers have, doesn't appreciate being taken advantage of."

"Much like you," she observed.

He didn't respond, but she was right.

She continued. "Still, seems Van Noy'll put his resources into finding out who stole from him."

"Which is why I plan to give him a different squirrel to chase." Not having who or what the squirrel might be he kept to himself.

"Nothing is foolproof, OC."

"For sure."

"You don't need the money. We don't need the money."

Gardner had inherited Fix & Go, a body shop chain, from her late father. O'Conner had invested monies from past jobs in the business. He was hands-on in the hiring of managers, going over the monthly totals and so on. Gardner owned eight of them outright and had franchised another ten in Arizona and one in Hawaii. One of them had burned in Altadena in the Eaton Fire, and another was smoke-damaged in the Auto Fire in Ventura.

O'Conner kept his name off the paperwork, but after taxes Gardner dutifully routed his share of the profits to certain offshore accounts. Though, like Van Noy, he had other legitimate investments, he also had a fondness for cash—also like Van Noy. He kept stashes from his scores in various locales across the country, should he have the need to go on the run. Though he had to admit he'd gotten used to laying his head on a pillow in his own house at night. Always on the move, always looking back . . . just didn't get him energized like before.

"It's been a few years. I want to know if I still got it."

"These last few years have been good. Van Noy is not one of the misanthropes and gangsters and crooked politicians you've gone up against in the past." Pointing at him, she continued, "Nobody would dare rip off a tech billionaire but you, huh?"

"You know me too well."

"Uh-huh."

"I like to think I'm honest about it. I mean, what about those con artists who sold supposed found originals by famous painters to the one percenters?"

She made a dismissive sound. "They got caught. This is different, you do understand that, don't you? I mean I know I'm one to talk, seeing as how slowly but goddamn surely I've aided and abetted your criminal ways."

"And I love you for it."

"I'm serious," she said, using his real name. "He can disappear you. And me."

"That's not going to happen. You know damn well I'll cover all the angles."

"As your prep."

"That's right." O'Conner paused, looking off then back at her. "I won't try to kid you. This'll be my swan song . . . or is it swan dive?"

"I don't know. That's what's worrying me."

"Those tech guys all think they're smarter than the rest of us."

O'Conner considered he was taking what happened to Joyner personally. Her being related to Charlie Mack and his fond memories of her. He best stay dispassionate.

"You gonna leave your business card?"

"You got jokes."

"You expect this to be as gnarly as what went down in Fort Worth? You're telling me this to be ready if you don't make it back?"

"I'm coming back. This isn't going to be a shootout at the Crystal Q."

That was the name of a massive cattle ranch where his crew had stolen a sizable slush fund from a group of old school, good ole boy GOP types in Texas. After the robbery, the owner of the ranch had also sent hitters to hunt down and eliminate the thieves. O'Conner was among those who went at the killers and prevailed.

He said, "The ones I'm looking to bring in on this, I've worked with them before. We've been in tight spots together. Now Joyner is the outsider, but she's motivated and has useful insider information."

"You've got your mind made up then," she declared.

"It's what I do. Even retirees have to keep busy."

She snorted. "Does anybody retire in your line of work?"

"Sure."

"Could you walk away?"

"I'm saying I can. Afterward."

"Look, honey, I haven't lost sleep about what you do. Truth to tell, it's an attractive quality about you. Now what does that say about me? All of us are a little bent, if only vicariously."

"It keeps the blood flowing."

"You figure this Mavis showing up means something."

He shrugged. "Fate or whatever messes with our lives is telling me to pay attention," he said. "I don't think she was even born when I used to clean up the Lounge."

She put back her head, guffawing theatrically and clapping her hands. "Now we're getting to it. Why yes, you are getting old, sport.

"Underneath all the other stuff you work out on these scores, it's finally occurred to you, you can't do this forever. When you first rode in here on your busted-down motorcycle you were wondering if you could hang it up. Be a square, unclogging the garbage disposal and getting the water heater replaced when it went kaput. But you didn't. You just kept what you do out there separate from this." She indicated the yard, solemnity arranging her face.

"Now you have to make a choice."

"We've rolled this far together."

"That we have, darling. I knew this day would come. Or the day one of your crew sent me word you were dead."

"I hate to admit it, but yeah, what Mavis represents does affect how I'm approaching the job," O'Conner said. "I'm going to be careful, as always. Extra careful if I'm on the real. This is not going to come back on our doorstep. I haven't lived my life looking over my shoulder. But I'm damn sure you can't keep swimming in these kinds of waters."

Gardner rose. "You say this now, until the next someone or something comes along."

"Gwen," he began.

She'd already turned away. "Mavis or not, you won't be satisfied. You'll want to test yourself again."

On into the house she went.

That evening, O'Conner sat at his desk in the study he shared with Gardner, a glass of beer and a bowl of cashews handy. The built-in shelf at his back contained a range of nonfiction books, including the ones he'd read several times during his group home years, along with *The Art of Manipulation*. Another book, acquired in his twenties, was about Adam Worth. He was a German-born Civil War veteran who, in creating an international criminal enterprise, perfected tunneling into banks. Called the "Napoleon of Crime," he was the basis for Moriarty in the Sherlock Holmes stories. The fiction, which reflected his and Gardner's tastes, ranged from thrillers with supernatural elements to the works of Chester Himes and China Miéville. There was also a Marvel Masterworks reprint edition featuring the Silver Surfer. He remembered how he'd wished as a kid that the silver-skinned alien's flying surfboard, which could soar on cosmic winds, would be sent to carry him away.

Interspersed among the books were a few knickknacks, such as a 1990s-era Game Boy Color handheld device, a present from the late Charlie Mack. She'd given him the console before they were available in stores. He'd kept the Game Boy hidden for fear a knothead like Raj would steal it.

Munching some cashews and chasing that with a swallow of beer, he called Tachmann on a secure phone to arrange a matter. After he hung up, he tapped his desk computer awake and went online.

He scanned videos about the Del Norte Diamond, the official name of the arena. This included a video montage of the groundbreaking ceremony with celebrities and Swashbucklers in attendance. There were also segments with Palmer Van Noy. Of medium build, his reddish-brown hair was parted in the middle, big locks looping on either side. His hairstyle made him look like he belonged in one of those boy bands O'Conner remembered from back in the day. Like he had other tech billionaires, O'Conner had seen Van Noy now and then in the news. Besides those times, and what Joyner had said, he had no other impressions of him.

One of the snippets of Van Noy was taken at a press conference, the skeleton of the arena rising behind him. He said, "Naturally, I want to make sure we offer a varied price point that doesn't gouge the audience we want to welcome here to enjoy not only the Swash, but all the Diamond has to offer."

Van Noy's image gave way to his voiceover as there was a cut to a panoramic shot of the rapt audience. The view lifted skyward to clouds rearranging themselves via CGI into pillowy words announcing the time and date of the opening-day ceremony. This in turn gave way to highlights from Swashbucklers games.

O'Conner watched segments of other videos featuring Van Noy, and not just about the arena. Before he was a billionaire, fresh out of college, Van Noy had been in a partnership with two friends from USC, Wayland Wesson and Heidi Chang. The three had begun a start-up, got monies from a few venture capitalists. They were on the rise. Then came a falling-out between the two men as to who didn't get proper credit for certain innovations. Wesson was eventually bought out. O'Conner checked and sure enough, Van Noy and the female partner, Heidi Chang, were a couple at that point.

Later they'd gotten married and had two children. They were now divorced going on six years. Though, according to what O'Conner read, they remained good friends. Thereafter, Van Noy had been linked to a few other women, including a popular host of one of those so-called reality shows. Idly, O'Conner wondered—did you make space for the mother of your children and your girlfriend in your swank survival bunker?

O'Conner returned to their bed at two in the morning. He lay on his back beside Gardner. She was sleeping and remained undisturbed. They'd been cordial to one another earlier. But shit was frosty, as his grandmother would have said.

The mention of Charlie Mack that afternoon had him drifting to when he squirreled away Long Box's money. He used those ducats about four years later when he ran away for good from foster care, winding up in the Bay Area, in Oakland, where he lived for a while with an older woman, Trinity Godard.

Trinity was a lesbian, so whatever sexual urges he initially had toward her were nixed. Trinity's friends ranged from graying lefties to artists to those at the margins of social convention, hustlers and sneak thieves. O'Conner, not the name he was using then, became part of this eclectic crowd and their often informal gatherings. Imbibing white wine, the aging radicals would ramble on about how the Black Panthers had squandered their opportunities, or what it would take to finally have a peace dividend. He didn't find their discussions all that interesting, but they had good weed and always shared.

The child of a professor and an MD, Trinity was a part-time art teacher slash art therapist at a school for learning-challenged children. She was also a part-time counterfeiter. Trinity used her skills to produce fake music concert posters, dutifully distressed as if from the 1950s and '60s. She sold them online through eBay and elsewhere in person, like swap meets. O'Conner had learned from Trinity, and what little money he had he'd invested in Trinity's enterprise. He helped her buy a letterpress and worked with her to produce the posters. Then one day she was gone, up and disappeared, no note, phone call, nothing.

Oddly, this memory of her leaving him didn't discomfort O'Conner. Being a product of the system since before his teens, he'd long concluded despair was a useless emotion. You could cry, but to what end. Best keep your mouth tight and fists up. He also recalled their skeezy landlord, Boley, tried to jack up the rent given he was still a minor.

"You'll get the rate Trinity and me paid in cash and in time each first of the month."

"You'll pay me two hundred more a month, homeboy, or you're out. You ain't about to put the ole' conner on me," Boley had said, his slang for putting one over on someone. As usual, he was working one of his perpetual toothpicks between his uneven teeth. If he wasn't doing that, he was forever sucking on one of his side teeth. Sometimes he did both at the same time. The dotcom boom was on, and rents in next-door Berkeley and across the bridge were skyrocketing. But in that part of Oakland, in the shadow of the Coliseum, there were still plenty of Raiders signs in windows and loaded weight benches on lawns.

Two nights later, O'Conner broke into Boley's apartment on the ground floor. He knew he'd be elsewhere, busy as was usual on a Thursday bingo night at the VFW hall. Finding what he was looking for, he snapped away with the Polaroid camera Trinity had left behind. He left two of the prints where Boley would see them on his kitchen table. No note, no phone call. Thereafter no increase in rent.

The memory of putting one over on that skeeze brought a thin smile to O'Conner as he fell asleep. From the people he'd met through Trinity, he'd found out Boley dealt speed to make extra income. O'Conner had taken snaps of his supply to let the motherlover know he was on to him. Then, as now, it was always about knowing who and what you were going up against, where was the leverage.

• • •

The following day, O'Conner drove to Pacoima, arriving at a rec center in a park fronting San Fernando Road. Inside, he approached the young woman behind the desk. There was an indoor court where men and women who looked more like jogging types were playing basketball. One of the double doors to the court was open. Words of encouragement floated out from inside, such as "good shot" and "sweet layup," rather than the usual trash talk.

"Is Oscar around?" he asked.

"Who?"

"Jeet Silvera."

The young woman continued to stare at him blankly. "I don't know who you're talking about."

O'Conner estimated she wasn't older than twenty-three or so and it could very well be she was too young to know what was what. "Is there an older employee around I could ask?"

Now she let her annoyance show. "No, man."

"How about your supervisor?"

She glared at him. "I am the supervisor."

"Right, thanks."

He left. It had been a few years since he and Silvera had worked together. He'd originally met him through an old-timer thief named Hector Gonzales. A safecracker. But he couldn't ask Hector since he was dead, a casualty of the Crystal Q aftermath. Just one of many who were no longer around. Men and women retired or in their graves. He needed Silvera's skill set to pull this off and he didn't want to burn up time he didn't have trying to find a replacement. The heist of Van Noy's survival bunker had to happen on the arena's opening day.

But you didn't go around asking for a guy too freely because then whoever you talked to got to sniffing, wanting in on whatever it was you were up to. Or worse, derailing a job before it could get going. There was another way he could get to Silvera. He was reluctant, but it had to be done.

Back in his car, O'Conner returned to the freeway, toward Long Beach. Maneuvering along several concrete exchanges, he passed a Swashbucklers billboard. The graphic showed point guard Sthal Casall poised to take a shot beneath the message "get your swash on."

Eventually, O'Conner arrived at an indoor mall and parked. His took the escalator to the second floor and entered an oxygen bar called Second Variety. The name derived, O'Conner understood, from a Philip K. Dick novella. The young pink-haired person behind this counter was more solicitous than the woman at the park.

"How may I be of assistance today, sir?" Taking him in, his blockish hands, thick neck and general air of a working man, they added, "Is this your first time visiting our kind of establishment?"

Gwen had taken O'Conner to an oxygen bar once. In a similar scene, customers were scattered throughout the room behind oxygen concentrator contraptions. Each was outfitted with side-by-side transparent cylinders with a different colored aroma oil in a cylinder. Each station had an oxygen tube leading from the machine and clipped to the nose of a patron as they inhaled the scented, purified air.

"Not here for a fill up, but was hoping to talk to Aesop."

Pink Hair said, "Is he expecting you?"

"Could you let him know it's O'Conner."

"Very well. Have a seat, please."

He waited on a couch next to an older woman and her small dog in her big purse. The dog kept its saucer eyes on him.

Soon, Pink Hair appeared and bent toward O'Conner, hands pressed together between their knees. "Aesop said go on back, Mr. O'Conner. Down that way, last door on the left."

"Thanks."

"Of course." To the woman with the dog, they said, "We're ready for you, Ms. Russell."

O'Conner turned the knob and stepped inside without knocking. Aesop Hong looked up from his desk. He had one of the oxygenators apart, a pair of needle-nose pliers in his hand, a screwdriver on a stack of papers next to him. The room was compact. The desk, a leaning bookcase and Hong's wheelchair took up most of the space. Next to the bookcase was a three-legged stool for visitors.

"Long time, O'Conner." Hong was in his late thirties, his combed-back hair to his shoulders in need of styling. He wore wire-framed tinted glasses. He had on a crisp polo shirt, his tanned arms sinewy and veined.

"Yeah, it has been."

In pictures on the wall Hong could be seen in a suit, an arm extended toward a lone person. These were taken at various times, at his various stage shows. Most of the pictures were taken when he had use of his legs, though there were two of him in his wheelchair. O'Conner recognized the late magician Ricky Jay in one of the photos with a younger, smiling Hong.

Setting the pliers aside, Hong said, "Since you're not the type to drop by to reminisce, what can I do for you?"

"Trying to get a line to Jeet Silvera."

"What for?"

"Like you said, I'm not the nostalgic type."

"Ha," he drawled. "You must be desperate, coming to see me."

"It's not like that. I'll pay for the information."

Hong turned sideways behind his desk, putting his hands on the canted wheels of his chair. He worked the wheels back and forth, scooting the chair forward then backward. "Time is tight on whatever this score is you're lining up. Not only do you want Oscar 'cause of what he brings to the table, but you want the string put together now so as to have the time to do the prepping."

O'Conner knew what was coming. Deep down, he figured this was how this meet was going to go. He supposed he wanted to hear how Hong would sell himself, convince him he was still up to holding his own on a heist. He pushed back.

"Aren't you settled in your new line of work, Aesop?"

"Oh, yeah, I'm the oxygen king."

"You ain't broke."

"You call this living? I'm not sitting around here singing the blues because of what happened to put me in this chair, O'Conner. I went into the job with my eyes open, I knew the risks. Just like you did."

O'Conner calculated there could be a role for Hong to play. He was talking.

"Anyway, it isn't like I'm not mobile. Let's go outside and you can watch me pop them wheelies." He tilted the chair back, arms extended, keeping his balance. "I'm in shape, play in a disabled basketball league. I mean, damn, son."

O'Conner chuckled. He was certain the new arena would be ADA compliant to accommodate a disabled thief.

"You need a diversion, I can take a tumble, no problem. Sneak some shit in my chair, hey, I'm your man. I know you, O'Conner. Whatever this is it's a ribeye steak, not no Bonus Jack. I want a bite, baby. Got to be an opportunity for a man of my abilities. No one looks twice at a crip."

"Get me Oscar and you're in. Not a full cut, but you're in. You'll be working to earn it."

"My man." He came around the desk and they bumped fists.

"Is Oscar in town?"

Hong said, "I know his current situation."

"What does that mean?

"O'Conner, I got this."

"Aesop, I know I don't need to remind you, but this kind of action is all about the quiet as it's kept."

"Ain't it always?"

"Goddamn right it is."

O'Conner let him know a few more details—enough to relate to Silvera but not enough if for whatever reason either of them let slip anything to anyone else. Driving away, he passed civilians out on the sidewalks, going to a lunch or ducking into stores to buy toilet paper and light bulbs. They went about their tasks as the thousands around them did, worried about the rent and what to make for dinner tonight.

O'Conner glanced from the pedestrians back to the windshield, wondering if he could truly be one of them. Or would it always be a facade he put on when in Willow Ridge, making sure to stop at the drugstore to get the Pledge Gwen had asked him to fetch. Coiled inside, waiting for the next opportunity to put together a crew and take down another fat cat.

O'Conner had no delusions he was striking a blow for the downtrodden against the ruling class when he stole. His few memories of homelife included his grandmother Jean watching one of Reverend Frederick Eikerenkoetter's videotaped sermons on a secondhand portable TV at the kitchenette table. Just the two of them in the one-bedroom apartment. The kid slept on a futon in the corner of the main room. Reverend Ike was a prosperity preacher. He dressed well and sported a Black man's version of a pompadour. A colorful, peripatetic speaker, he once upon a time would extol to his far-flung congregants in viewer land the best ways to "think and grow rich." You could also send in money for one of his prayer cloths, he would not forget to mention.

When he watched then it was years past the height of Ike's popularity. On a Sunday night, the public access channel would play reruns of Ike's shows he'd taped years before on local television outlets nationwide. Sometimes, on those evenings as a young kid, he'd stand next to his grandmother as she sat watching the bombastic reverend. There'd be a tin ashtray with several ground-out cigarettes on the table and a bottle of Michelob.

"Honey bean," she'd say, patting his back, "I'm not so foolish as to swallow hook, line and sinker what this man is going on about." She'd wave her hand toward the television screen as she talked, a lit Virginia Slim wedged between her red-nailed fingers. "But you gotta give it to him. He's got style and that's why he had a following. Why all them old ladies sent in their wrinkled dollar bills over and over."

"Isn't keeping your money better?"

She poked his forehead lightly. "You're right, boy, but folks want to believe. Believe bad."

"Is that why you watch, Gram-gram? You believe?"

She laughed. "Like I said, it's not his line of jive I buy, but it's his finesse you gotta appreciate. You know what that word means? Finesse?"

"No, I don't."

She inhaled her cigarette and blew a stream of smoke toward the ceiling. "Well, I don't rightly expect this is the dictionary definition, but it means to be slick, to pull off a trick and not get caught doing it."

"Okay," he said, absorbing her words.

O'Conner never wanted to be a huckster like Reverend Ike, flashy and carrying on, feeding on the spotlight. But even then, a nascent outlook on life was forming in his brain, gleaned from those Sundays watching the preening preacher. Yeah, he'd determined a few years later, laying on his county-issued mattress in the group home. He was going to be a different kind of slick to get what he wanted.

By then, his youngish grandmother, who should have had many years to go, was dead from a brain aneurysm. She'd been carrying a full tray of dirty plates to the kitchen at the Cockatoo Inn's restaurant on Imperial Highway, where she was a waitress. Her knees gave out at the swing door. Plates crashing and breaking around her, she slumped to the floor, back against the doorway. She lasted another week in the hospital on a ventilator. He'd overheard her coworkers discussing the incident at the funeral. The people at her funeral were the working poor, like her, but had passed the hat and gotten together enough money for a cheap coffin and a graveside service. She was the only family he had a relation with, a mother and father only referred to vaguely by her.

"When you get a little older, I'll explain them to you," she'd told him more than once. "It's a complicated, grown-up mess is what it is."

Years later, when he had the wherewithal, he hadn't tried to find his mother or father. They sure as shit hadn't looked for him. No going back. He wasn't going to be anchored by the past. O'Conner was invented. He applied his version of finesse on the thefts he'd pulled. Be foxy, don't get caught. Don't wind up living in a one-bedroom claptrap apartment next to the power lines. When you had your send-off, have the scratch to afford a silk-lined casket with gold-plated handles. Go out like a champ, his grandma would have said.

CHAPTER FOUR

Head down, bent forward, O'Conner came around the counter fast, ramming his shoulder into the bigger man's midsection. The man had unkempt blond hair, was younger than O'Conner and wore a retro bowling shirt. His well-formed chest was evident underneath. He didn't go over as O'Conner hoped. He was too solid. Instead, he got his big hands and muscular arms around O'Conner, who did what he could to stay on his feet. Saggz, the other man in the shop, moaned from where he lay on the concrete floor. O'Conner had kicked him in the face. His head rose, eyes unfocused as he made an effort to rise.

Bowling Shirt drove a looping punch into O'Conner's kidney, causing him to buckle and gasp, dazed. Another one like that and he'd be on the floor, too. Redoubling his efforts, he got his arms around the leg of his opponent and, twisting his body, made them tumble sideways. They crashed into a metal shelf. Parts and tools cascaded on the two as they grabbed and tore at one another there on the greasy floor of Rurric Tool and Truck Rental.

Saggz staggered past them, making his way farther into the place. O'Conner figured Saggz was going for a gun. He better take care of Bowling Shirt but quick. Both of them were on a knee, arms interlocked like Olympic wrestlers. O'Conner willed himself not to succumb to the pain as he reached frantically for a scattered tool. The bigger man struck a glancing blow on O'Conner's jaw, sending pinwheels whirling behind his eyes. Then, something metallic under his fingers. He latched onto it like a life preserver. O'Conner brought it down hard on the bigger man's skull, opening a ragged gash on his forehead. Bowling Shirt gushed out a torrent of fried onion breath, momentarily stunned.

On his feet, O'Conner kneed him in the face, then covered the space to Saggz. He swung what he was holding, a drill, just as Saggz turned, a Beretta in hand.

"Motherfuck," Saggz wailed as he stumbled backward, his mouth bloody from being struck with the power tool.

O'Conner slammed the drill on Saggz's gun hand, making him lose his grip on the pistol. He caught it in mid-flight. "Get over there with him," he ordered, breathing hard and sweating.

Hand on his mouth, Saggz walked over to the bigger man who was now standing, wary eyes on O'Conner. Saggz was older than O'Conner by a few years, average height and, like the last time O'Conner had seen him, was wearing baggy khakis. He was bald on top, one of those men who let what remained of the hair on the back of his head grow so he could put it in a ponytail.

"You knocked a tooth loose," Saggz protested.

"Explain what the fuck is wrong with you," O'Conner said.

Two men in working clothes looked inside through the

glass front door. The door began to push open. O'Conner turned his head to the side, his back to them. "Give us a few minutes, will you, gents? We're in the middle of a business meeting."

The two exchanged a look and withdrew.

"This is a misunderstanding, O'Conner," Saggz said.

"Uh-huh. I come here and ask a simple fuckin' question and the poor man's Travis Kelce here goes apeshit."

From his expression, the bigger man took offense but didn't lunge. "You was looking for Burgess." He spoke as if that explained their hostile actions.

"He owe you money?"

The bigger man glared at him, wiping at the blood on his forehead.

"No, not exactly," Saggz said.

"Not exactly what?"

"That's my business," Saggz answered.

"How about I shoot you in the knee, then work my way up? At your age that might put you on a walker."

Saggz held up his hand. "Take it easy, will you, O'Conner? Me and Tyler didn't mean to get off on the wrong foot. We're sort of wound up is all. You come in here asking about Burgess, well, we kinda figured to ask you what you knew. A lead, that's all."

Tyler continued to put the mad dog on O'Conner. "Why are you looking for him?"

"None of your fuckin' business."

Saggz said, "Look, we ain't the only ones. You're not around like the old days, O'Conner. Guess your ear isn't that close to the ground anymore."

"That give you an excuse to come at me like you did?"

Saggz didn't answer, glancing at Tyler, who'd been the first to swing.

"Make it plain, will you, Saggz, I haven't got all damn day."

Tyler shifted and O'Conner zeroed in on him with a baleful expression, the gun held firm in his knotted hand.

"I don't know what all is involved, maybe he double-crossed him some kind of way, but there's a finder's fee offered on him," Saggz said.

"Who put it up?"

"Kanser."

"How much?"

Saggz didn't answer.

"How much?" he insisted.

"Seven Gs for his confirmed whereabouts."

Tyler spoke. "We could use the payday. Spruce it up around here."

Saggz offered a weak smile.

O'Conner decided the amount wasn't large enough to suggest anything else at play than what was stated. "How long has Kanser's offer been in place?"

"A few days," Saggz answered.

O'Conner mulled this over. Did Kanser want to press Burgess in to do a job or did he want to find him for personal reasons? O'Conner and the explosives expert had both been in on a job Kanser had put together in the past. Could Tachmann have gone to Kanser looking for O'Conner? That didn't seem right, but he would check. He removed the magazine from the gun and ejected the bullet from the barrel. He tossed the gun onto the counter.

"I'm'a leave this outside," he said, indicating the magazine. "Now I don't need to remind you not to call Kanser about our little tête-à-tête, right?"

"Whatever the fuck that is, who the fuck are you to tell us what to do?" Tyler said.

"Understood," Saggz said. "We don't want to get in the middle of whyever you're looking for him."

O'Conner left the rental office and walked across the macadam to where he'd parked his Cadillac. He got in. Behind the wheel, he took a few moments, breathing in and out, trying to recover from the fight. Tyler's blows had him aching. If those two clowns did get a line on Burgess, they'd call Kanser for sure to collect.

"Shit," he said, rubbing a hand over his face. He stared hard at his partial reflection in the rearview. Like he'd said to Gwen, maybe this really should be his last go-round. But putting together the rip-off was still the shit to him. The various pieces, the angles known and unknown he had to account for and still be nimble to come out whole when things went south. Dealing with the knuckleheads you had to corral in this line of work, though. That took a toll.

"Fuck it," he said, starting the car. He would find Burgess, handle Kanser, and Hong would get to Silvera. What was one of Reverend Ike's homilies, "Close your eyes and see green?" O'Conner chuckled as he drove off the truck lot, playing a CD. The unit had been an extra price as part of the trim package. He could remember having an old hoopty with a cassette tape deck in it. And the cassettes housed on a rack inside the middle console. Yet another sign of the years passing him by.

• • •

Back at the townhouse in Hemet, he had a late lunch with Gwen. She said, regarding the bruise on his face, "Everything lining up smoothly, is it?"

"It will."

The two sat in the kitchen nook. This was the first time they had discussed the job since the argument in the backyard. They hadn't been silent with each other but had purposely avoided talking about it.

"I'll be leaving today," he announced.

"Putting the pieces together for the score," she said flatly.

"Yes. After it's over, I'd like to come back."

"Expect me to be waiting by the window, a candle lit and all that shit?"

"Sure."

At least Gwen chuckled. Eventually, she said, "I'm not interested in going around and around about what you do. Clearly the time to object or walk away was when you first leveled with me. Our lives becoming intertwined, the high and low roads." She looked up from her plate at him. "And frankly, it is partly what attracted me to you and continues to do so. The guy who can fix the garbage disposal and plan intricate robberies like they were three-dimensional chase games. A vicarious thrill. Goddamn me."

"Everything's gonna be cool, baby."

"So far so good, huh. Lumps and all."

"It comes with the territory."

"Said the man passing the thirtieth floor after falling off the skyscraper."

"Like I said, you're hilarious."

"I'm a riot."

They continued their meal in silence.

O'Conner said, "Isn't the contract coming due with the Hingle Brothers?" The manufacturer located in Long Beach supplied fasteners for Fix & Go.

"I'm meeting with them next week," she answered.

"All business is always about the bottom line."

"Except if things go sideways with them, a bunch of fools in ski masks won't be coming after us."

"They won't."

"I'm not grabbing my go bag and going on the run, OC. Your ultimate takedown blows back on me. Well, I'm a grown-ass woman and I make my own decisions. But I damn well expect none of this shit if it affects Harley Lynn."

Gwen was referring to her grown daughter, who lived in another state. Harley knew O'Conner was shady, but no specifics. "Van Noy would be dead before I'd let that happen," he vowed.

"Look, it's unrealistic for me to expect you to retire now from your wicked ways, concentrating on your legitimate businesses," she said. She knew about his investment in a business that converted cargo shipping containers to offices and housing, and several other enterprises.

"I could."

"You'd get bored. And I'd be bored seeing you bored. 'Cause I can't see you or me in our rockers on the front porch. Not for some years anyway."

"Gwen, if I make a misstep, if I get . . . got, I've set it up that none of this will blow back on you or Harley Lynn. Of course, you'll have access to my money too."

"All bridges burned behind you?"

"On that, you can rely."

"That's what it's always been about for you, hasn't it? Like when you were a kid and found that loot?" she said. "You used it to escape, on your way to becoming O'Conner."

O'Conner put down his fork. "You were comfortable with money coming up."

Gwen hunched a shoulder. "Like a lot of middle-class white kids, sure, I took it for granted. There were always groceries in the fridge, vacations, the lights and water always on." Gardner shook her head side to side. "I remember when I was twelve or thirteen going over to a girlfriend's house. I was shocked they had secondhand furniture and this dinky little portable color TV. Not the big honking GE model we had dominating our living room."

She cocked her head as if tumbling loose a memory. "Pretty sure it was called an AC/DC model. Those letters stamped right on the front."

"Surely not a switch you could flick for porn on it."

"Surely," she affirmed.

"I do understand this score will be different than the others." A memory tumbled loose for him too. Seeing Dr. Apgar that day in the garage for the first time in years, he said, "I got my third eye open."

"You better."

He got up and, coming over to her, pressed his forehead against hers.

"Keep in mind big money breeds big greed," she said.

"Talkin' that gun moll talk turns me on."

They kissed. He couldn't tell if it was a farewell one or not. After lunch, he washed the plates and got his suitcases, a large one and an overnight one. Gardner stood in the living room, watching him.

"Okay," he said.

"Okay," she also said. "I'm going to luxuriate in a bath with the scented candles. Like I said, your dangerous endeavors are part of you. On the other hand, playing the chick who's all aghast at what her old man does ain't me. Ride or die, they still say that?"

"Hell if I know."

A kiss again, her gripping his shoulder, and then he was gone.

O'Conner maneuvered along with the afternoon freeway traffic heading back to the Los Angeles area, Taj Mahal and Ry Cooder's rendition of the blues number "The Midnight Special" providing nuance to his melancholy. He wouldn't be driving the eighty-five-plus miles back to Hemet later today. He'd already arranged to stay in town and was heading to the Presidium Hotel, LAX nearby. Del Norte Diamond was also in the vicinity. At some point as he got closer, O'Conner exited the freeway. He stopped at a liquor store to buy a pint of vodka.

Upstairs in the hotel after checking in, O'Conner used the bathroom. He wasn't surprised to see blood in his urine, a by-product of his fight at the trucking outfit. Back in the main area of his suite, he went through a series of stretches and forms, working up a light sweat. Gwen, who'd been doing tai chi for years, had encouraged him to try the exercises and he had to admit, they helped to keep him limber. He took a long, hot shower when he finished, working the kinks out of his muscles. Then he ate in the hotel's restaurant and returned to his room.

Propped against the headboard, stripped down to his boxers and athletic tee, O'Conner studied the architect's sketches of the Del Norte Diamond on an air-gapped iPad, having medicinal sips of his vodka in a glass with ice. Tours were being conducted of the facility. With Joyner's help creating false credentials, he was on one tomorrow. Tonight, as he reviewed, he made notes on a yellow legal pad, wearing his reading glasses.

CHAPTER FIVE

The Del Norte Diamond occupied thirty acres of land, less than half a mile south of where the Hollywood Park racetrack once was. A four-point dome covered the main complex. A large diamond, the logo of the Swashbucklers, bore the team's name in stylized script. An additional gleaming kite-shaped diamond served as the single eye on the face of its anthropomorphic pirate bulldog, complete with an eyepatch and head scarf.

Not just a basketball venue, the complex also had a 125-room hotel, four stories of offices and an exterior semicircular parkland with two state-of-the art playgrounds. There were also elevated tracks being finished for the Metrolink light-rail to take passengers to and from the nearby airport. Del Norte, a snack food and energy drink conglomerate, had won the naming rights by ponying up some $500 million toward the facility's total price tag of $2.4 billion. O'Conner wondered how much the luxe bunker underneath the facility had added to the cost. The naming rights weren't permanent.

O'Conner's tour group assembled on the first-floor concourse. Among the gathered were members of several local community groups. The name at the end of his lanyard was

Peter Banner. He was supposedly a suit with a regional school-supply outfit headquartered in Riverside.

Their tour guide, a cheery woman named Dale Deering, the vice president of public relations, was saying, "Working with local betterment organizations, Swashbuckler Enterprises has proudly signed onto a community benefits agreement. This has set in place local hiring policies and funding for afterschool coding programs."

The gathered nodded their approval. Sports complexes meant jobs, but often spurred gentrification and displaced residents and local mom-and-pop businesses.

"And because we are responsive to our community partners," Deering added, "we've moved up the opening day ceremonies to the first Wednesday next month rather than the second, as that conflicted with other planned activities."

A blank-faced O'Conner nodded along with the crowd. He had just learned that there were only three weeks to solidify the crew and get all the prep done. Time was tight before. Now there could be no missteps.

Deering ushered the group onto the basketball court, and from there they ascended into the stands. O'Conner recalled seeing Deering in several of the videos he'd watched. Her presence attested to the seriousness the enterprise saw in its agreements with their community partners. They went into the announcers' and press booths, and back down into the locker rooms and offices of the coaching staff. Deering spoke about the history of the team, which had started in the farm leagues in Fresno in the 1950s before moving to L.A. The Swashbucklers didn't win the title last year but had made it to the second round of the playoffs. This coming season, after some key player acquisitions and retentions, the team was being touted to take it all the way. Before Van Noy bought a majority share, the last time the Swashbucklers had been contenders was more than a decade ago.

"We're now heading to one of the three clubs we have to offer at the Diamond," Deering said. "One of our clubs is members only but this one, the Finale Room, is open to the public. It's a tribute to the days of Bronzeville in Los Angeles. This was a bleak time in our country's history, when issei and nisei Japanese citizenry were interred. Black aircraft workers, many of them transplants from the south, rented rooms in the then–tenant vacant Little Tokyo. More than one jazz joint flowered in those days, like the Finale's namesake and Shepp's Playhouse, a three-story club where you could find the Kawafuku restaurant."

The blueprints Joyner had devised detailed an entrance to the bunker hidden in Van Noy's office in the club. This was a separate suite distinct from the manager's office. Joyner had also ascertained that there was a second entrance and egress to and from the shelter on the grounds.

Deering continued. "The plan is that at times, even in season, when the Swashbucklers are at away games, we'll have live performances in here. Again, in keeping with the name, there will be an emphasis on jazz and blues acts, but pop music too. The Finale is, as you see, an intimate space but can seat up to two hundred quite comfortably." As she talked, she made a sweep of her hand, much like a television game show host revealing the prize behind the curtain.

The Finale Room was finished in 1940s decor. Round

tables fanned out from a raised crescent-shaped stage with inlaid stylized lightning bolts around its edge. The dark wood walls were done in beaux arts details including wall sconces and plenty of chrome railing. There was a bar of marble and brass with built-in stools and, below the large-screen monitors behind the bar, racks for the numerous liquors.

Idly, O'Conner figured that the notion of designing this room as a callback to a Black nightclub of a long-gone era must have been advanced by one of the complex's community partners. Certainly Van Noy wouldn't know anything about this history or acknowledge it, would he? The house lights were up. O'Conner imagined when the club was open, the interior properly dimmed to set the mood, guests would feel like they were stepping into, if not another era, at least the holodeck version.

Deering was keeping the group up front, apparently not inclined to show them the club's back rooms. Standing to the side of the others, O'Conner glimpsed the panel of a junction box not too far along a hallway which he was sure led to the rear offices. While Deering enthused about the musical acts already lined up for the coming year, he lingered by the club's double doors, figuring out the best way to barricade them.

She pointed toward the ceiling, going on about the exposed wood rafters and the Japanese-style hanging lanterns. As heads craned upward, O'Conner took the opportunity to stroll into the hallway. Keeping his phone at belt buckle level and pressed to his body, he snapped a few shots of the circuit panel and the closed double doors.

Feeling confident, he started to walk deeper along the passageway, aiming his phone at the electronic combination lock of the door nearest him on the right.

"Sir, could I ask you to rejoin us?" Deering called out, backlit at the head of the hallway. She held out her hand as if beckoning an errant child.

"Yes, ma'am, my bad, just, you know." He shrugged. "Looking to take all this in."

The group returned to the concourse. As they started toward the escalator, a boxy delivery robot rounded the curve coming toward them, beeping.

"Wonderful, I didn't think we'd see any around today," Deering said joyfully, stepping into the robot's path. It stopped. "Our service robos are the next generation in advancement." She removed a walkie-talkie-like instrument from her belt and spoke into it. "Cliff, I'm going to take control, okay?"

"Okay, Dale," the unseen Cliff answered.

Deering pressed another button on her device and the top portion slid into the radio, exposing a small monitor screen. "Okay, folks, come with me back inside the arena." With military precision, she pivoted and went through an arched tunnel leading to the stadium seating. The delivery robot trailed her like a trained pet.

"To ease congestion at the concession stands, as I mentioned earlier, we've installed touch-and-go monitors at kiosks to facilitate orders. Or you can place your order by using a QR code on your phone. Our robos can bring your food and drink right to you, so you never have to leave your seat and miss the next three-pointer."

Deering looked down to the machine and said, "1-A, Section 122, Row 17."

The orbs in 1-A's head bobbed, light flashing behind them. With a beep, it wheeled over to the next set of steps.

"It can understand voice commands?" one of the group asked.

Deering held her device aloft. "Yes, but you need one of these for it to 'listen' to you."

"What do you call that gadget you're using?" someone else asked.

"An Omnikan," Deering answered, smiling.

The robot began to climb the steps. The bracketed wheels were jointed such that the machine would get to the foot of a step, the front wheels rolling it upward and then gaining purchase on the next step and so on, reaching the next level and row of seats. Its progress earned the 1-A a round of applause as it continued its ascent.

Fascinated, O'Conner clapped too. His eyes shifted to the multipurpose device Deering held.

"During a game, when the prepaid food and drink arrives like this," Deering said, "the Diamond dogs and so on will be bagged and tagged to identify who ordered what. The food can then be passed down by your fellow patrons as it happens now with hot dogs and such to the rightful recipient."

O'Conner asked, "How many of these robots do you have in the arena?"

"Thirty for now."

"You have camera drones too, right, to cover the games?" another in the group asked.

"Yes," Deering said. "Of course, the networks have their own, too, and we will be housing some of theirs as well." She pointed to the announcers' booth overlooking the floor.

"Can you control those too with the . . . Omnikan, you call it?" O'Conner asked.

Eyes bright, Deering said, "The Omnikan can do it all. The device is inspired in part by the communicator used by the intrepid crew of the *Enterprise*. And yes, our chairman is a big *Star Trek* fan. Anyway, let's go out to the plaza to see what our fabulous restaurants and bars have to offer. We've made a commitment to hiring locally and, speaking for myself, I regularly enjoy cuisine in the area."

The tour group landed in Swag Central, the merchandise shop. Inside were all manner of team gear and overpriced knickknacks for sale. There were jerseys with players' names and numbers on them. Headbands, water bottles, soft-sided lunch boxes, snow globes with a miniature Del Norte arena inside of it, baby onesies and more. All of it in the team colors, royal purple and aqua blue. When O'Conner was a teenager, a roughneck might bust you upside your head and snatch your Swashbucklers team jacket. Especially if it was a limited edition, like one signed by superstar Eddie Harper. Nowadays, the former player was often seen selling muscle ache ointments and testosterone supplements on television, among other hustles. He'd even done a stint on *Dancing with the Stars*.

The tour over, O'Conner conducted a personal tour of the surrounding neighborhood, considering how he might obtain one of those Omnikans. He'd occasionally pull to the curb to make notes and sketches on his legal pad. You could burn paper, hell, you could eat it if you had to—and he had more than once when in a tight spot in the past. He knew of one thief who got too used to recording his notes on his phone. He assumed when he hit delete, such was gone for good. Prosecutors were able to recover his backup data and restored enough of his incriminating comments to convict him. That dude was still down on a ten-year bid.

Done with his recon, O'Conner went to Leafy Fields, where Joyner had worked undercover. He went to the modernistically designed establishment to have lunch and nothing more. It cost a hell of a lot more than a meal at Denny's, but he had to admit, the grub was good.

Back in his car, O'Conner went over his notes. He'd worked his way out from the arena in an expanding grid of avenues and streets, residential and business sections, with the sports complex at the center. If the robbery went off as he envisioned, there'd be no need to burn rubber in a getaway. Still, you had to plan for contingencies. Particularly given their target. He put on his sunglasses. His face took on an etched quality, like a portrait captured by a Cubist painter. A commercial jet reflected in his windshield as it ascended from the airport, then crossed the sky. His phone buzzed.

"I got a line on Burgess," Tachmann said, as if he were a genie granting the thief's wish.

TALES FROM THE CRIMSON LOUNGE

OC made another tidy mound with the push broom. He liked cleaning up in the Crimson Lounge on Sunday afternoons when the place was still closed for the day. He had the radio on, playing the oldies station KRTH. He liked stuff like N.W.A and Cypress Hill all right, but rap didn't compare to jams like "The Still of the Night" and "Silhouettes." You could listen to the stories they were telling in one part of your brain and still focus with the other part to get your work done.

OC stood there for a moment, holding the shaft of the push broom in both hands like it was a standing microphone. He swayed his slim hips to "Pretty Little Angel Eyes," imagining he was serenading that cutie Yolanda in his social studies class. The song ended and he retrieved the dustpan. He bent to sweep up his pile of discarded matchbooks, balled-up napkins and the like. Smoking was now banned indoors by the state but as far as Charlie Mack was concerned, it was still the 1980s. The fire department had started to go around and warn bar and restaurant owners to obey the law or get fined. As far as OC knew, they hadn't shown up at the Lounge yet.

Lifting the filled dustpan, he paused, frowning. Amid the trash was some crushed bloody tissue paper. It wasn't the first time he'd come across blood in the Lounge. One time it had been a silky lady's handkerchief with a big smear of red on it that wasn't lipstick. Another time, a piece of gauze and tape, like a wounded customer had come from the hospital itching for a drink to dull his pain. He could tell there was something inside the balled-up tissues. With two fingers, he gingerly picked up the ball and set it aside, then dumped the rest of the waste into the trash can.

"OC, you want a hot link sandwich from Mr. Jim's?" Val Gaffney called from the back. Miss Val was always nice to him.

"Yes, please," he said. "And potato salad too."

"Got it," she answered.

He assumed Miss Val was talking to her boyfriend over the phone about picking up the grub.

The youngster sat at one of the round tables. With the precision of a veterinarian about to operate on a bird's wing, he carefully opened the wad of tissues, revealing two teeth set in a metal bracket. OC leaned closer, examining them. Had whoever owned the fake teeth forgotten about them? Could the teeth have fallen out of their pocket and they didn't notice? Some old person took them out to drink? That didn't seem likely. Whatever the case, should he tell Miss Val or just throw them away?

OC recalled what Charlie Mack had advised him on his first day at the Crimson Lounge. "Maybe sweeping and mopping is not glamorous like building a space rocket, but that don't mean you half-ass a job." She also told him don't be lollygagging. And if he saw anything that looked hinky—that was the word she'd used—put it out of your mind, 'cause it didn't concern him.

"If, though, you can't forget what you might see, come talk to me about it, okay?" she added.

"You mean like a dead body?"

"I don't traffic in no dead bodies, OC," she'd said, annoyed. "I just mean, I don't know, maybe some ladies' underwear, something like that."

"That wouldn't upset me."

"Yeah, I realized as soon as I said it, that was a bad example. Listen, it could be a knife, you see where I'm goin' with this?"

"I do," he said.

"And you for sure don't go telling your Doctor Strange over at the house about anything odd you might see in here," Charlie Mack emphasized. "Or anybody else for that matter. We crystal clear on this?"

"Yes, ma'am, we are."

OC took the "anybody else" to mean not to go talking to the police about finding a knife or a gun. Like he would. Did teeth in tissue paper count as odd or hinky? He took another look, this time noticing that one of the pair was cracked. Was that why the person had taken them out, the tooth got cracked when he was chomping on a handful of chips? Or had they been hit in the face, and the teeth got damaged?

For now, OC thought he better get his work done. He took a few clean cocktail napkins from the bar and, unfolding those, wrapped them around the tissues and teeth. He didn't want to put them in his pocket, so he set the teeth under the bar. By the time he was through wiping down the bathrooms with the Lysol, there was a knock at the front door. Wiping his hands on a rag, he opened the door, letting in afternoon sunlight.

"Young blood," Doze greeted as he stepped inside.

Miss Val's boyfriend was a big man she called Doze, short for his other nickname, Bulldozer. For three years he'd been a linebacker on the Barons practice squad. He'd been elevated to play in a few games but eventually got cut. Every now and then, when the Crimson Lounge had a local band playing, he would be the bouncer on the door. Now, Doze was holding a plastic bag with three Styrofoam containers from Mr. Jim's Bar-B-Que. The tagline heard on the chain's commercials on Black radio was "You need no teeth to eat my beef."

"What's happenin', Doze?" OC said, smiling.

"Hey, baby," Miss Val chimed in as she walked into the main room from the back. They smacked lips, OC checking them out.

Doze set the food on the table where OC had examined the teeth. Miss Val brought over bottles of beer for the two of them and a canned soft drink for OC.

"Thank you," he said, taking the offered Sprite.

Doze and Gaffney sat at another table, OC next to them at his.

"Let's see what's on the news," she said, holding the remote for the new TV. She pressed a button and the new flat-screen television came on instantaneously. The Zenith would have taken several moments to warm up.

". . . to the south, partially cloudy," the weatherman said, standing before an image of mountains outside the city. "We expect early morning gloom for the next few days. Hunter?"

OC bit into his sandwich, savoring the tangy sauce and the spiciness of the hot link sausage.

"Got to dig out this dead pygmy palm or whatever you call them at my Aunt Josephine's," Doze was saying to Gaffney.

"She's been bugging you about that for a minute, hasn't she?" Gaffney gnawed on a rib she held delicately with her fingers.

"Don't I know."

OC watched the news as the couple continued their conversing. The female newscaster, Lannie, was dark haired and dark eyed. At a desk of curved metal and glass, she reported a break-in in Toluca Lake accompanied by stills projected behind her.

"Dang, OC," Doze said. "The way you're scarfin' that sandwich down, looks like your skinny butt could put two of those bad boys away."

The young man bobbed his head. "For sure. Mr. Jim's is way better than what we get to eat at Griss."

"I heard that," Doze commiserated.

". . . the dead man was found behind an appliance parts jobber on Hooper near Slauson. He's thought to be in his sixties. His identity has yet to be determined, as he was found with no identification," Lannie was saying. "The unidentified man was dressed in a car coat and slacks. There were several fresh lacerations to his upper body and bruises to his face. A bridge was also missing from his mouth. Police are requesting that anyone with information call the tip hotline . . ."

"I wonder what happened to him?" Doze said offhandedly.

"Nothin' good," Gaffney added.

"What do they mean, a bridge was missing?" OC asked.

"False teeth," Gaffney said.

OC ate a helping of potato salad, chewing slowly. Old people had false teeth. Could the ones he found be the dead man's? Naw, he dismissed. He wiped his mouth with a paper napkin and closed the Styrofoam container.

"You done?" Gaffney said.

"Yeah, want to save what's left for later." He rose, patting his stomach. "Sure was good."

"Okay, now," Doze eyed OC. "Hey, you want to work a few Barons games? Got a pard'ner of mine handles concessions at the Coliseum. They pay over minimum wage and can always use a go-getter like yourself to help with seating or even work one of the hot dog stands."

"He doesn't have a work permit," Gaffney said. "Charlie Mack and the Koreans pay him under the table."

"Hustler," Doze enthused. "Ain't no problem getting you the permit if you want to be brought on. Save your money like I'm aimin' to do and buy into that fancy car lot action like Tack's doing with Teaflake." He winked at the kid, laying insider information on him.

"You okay to work with Teaflake, Doze?" OC said. Hearing Teaflake's name made him uncomfortable. OC'd seen him around as he also had business with Long Box in the back office here. But he was wary about him, given the neighborhood stories he'd heard. A double-crosser was a snake as far as OC was concerned.

"Doze, you know better than to put other people's business on front street," Gaffney said, arms crossed.

The big man held up his hands as if in surrender. "Okay, like it's all Secret Squirrel. But yeah, I hear you, baby." He laughed good-naturedly.

"Doze, I'd like to work at the Coliseum if I could."

"My man." He put out his large hand and they performed an elaborate soul shake. "I'll let you know when to come down."

"Bye, OC," Gaffney said, wiggling her fingers at OC as he headed for the door.

"See you," he said, stepping outside with the remains of his lunch. Now what was he supposed to do, he wondered, walking along, sipping on his Sprite. Did those teeth belong to the dead man? Had he lost them in the bar, took them out of his mouth and forgot about them? Old people were forgetful and Lannie the news lady said he was in his sixties. At that age, you might forget to put on your pants before you left the house.

OC threw his drained soda can into the overflowing sidewalk trash can. He supposed he should tell Charlie Mack, but what if she had something to do with the dead guy? His talking to her could put him on the spot. What if she worried he was a snitch? Maybe, like the song went, they got stitches, or worse, got a damn ditch. It occurred to him that, while he had no conception of what it meant to be sixty, he'd like to be around to find out. And what about the teeth, the evidence?

"Shit," he whispered. The teeth were in the tissues under the bar. He'd figured to take care of them later, but the news shook him. Once they were found, wouldn't it be obvious he was the one who put them there? He considered doubling back but decided against that. He would be too nervous, lying to Miss Val and Doze that he'd forgotten—what? He didn't have shit to leave behind but the clothes on his back. He had to get those teeth and disappear them, but good. The notion he should go to the cops with the teeth crossed his mind and was quickly dismissed. He could see this 5-0 corn-fed white boy looking at him the way they do around here, assuming of course he gangbanged. Yeah, sure, he'd listen to him telling this fool he found the teeth behind the bar. No, beside the Hi Hat. The cops might believe that.

"You studying rockets in school?"

It was the homeless dude they called Shoe Dog. "Not yet."

"Stay up, young buck." On he went in the opposite direction, tugging a rusty red wagon of junk.

By the time OC got back to Griss, his appetite had returned. He sat in the front room where the chairs were arranged in a circle for the therapy session later today. Putting the barbeque container on a chair, he proceeded to finish his meal while starting a book, an Andre Norton sci-fi novel he pulled off the shelf. He liked her stories. This was one in the *Beast Master* series.

Benny walked in and pointed at the barbeque.

"From Mr. Jim's?"

"Yep. Miss Val bought it for me."

"You got all the luck."

"Huh." They were in foster care. Was that lucky? Better than being on the streets, so maybe luck was just the odds, like rolling dice. You had a hand in it, but you could come up snake eyes.

OC consumed the last of his sandwich. Those false teeth

the news lady talked about wouldn't leave him alone. He hoped he wasn't going to be chased by a giant set of joke teeth, the kind you wound up to clatter, in his dreams tonight. Benny went on, and OC took the empty container into the kitchen. The trash was full and sighing, so he took the bag out and tied it off, then went out the back steps to the garbage cans after putting in a new liner.

He heard a noise, thinking at first it was one of the stray cats who came around. One of them, white and tan, had a tag and was named Doolittle. Sometimes Doc left out milk or sardines for her in a metal bowl. OC followed the muffled sounds to the detached garage. One time, he'd spied on one of the boys who brought a girl in there. They didn't get naked but grinded furiously. There were two warped and weathered boards on the side of the garage, which itself was in need of painting. Putting his eye to the gap between the boards, OC peered inside. Light came in through windows along both side walls of the garage. Plenty of stacked and sealed cardboard boxes, a folded-up rollaway bed and other stuff took up the space, which was used for storage. Among all this stood Dr. Apgar, his back to OC. He was wearing a starched shirt and faded Levi's, the pant legs rolled into neat cuffs.

Dr. Apgar's arms were outstretched and he was mumbling, but OC couldn't tell what he was saying. Turning his upper body to the left, he brought his hands closer together but didn't clasp them. Like he was pretending to be holding on to something. Whatever it was supposed to be, he crouched and took a knee. He then pantomimed placing three of these imagined objects side by side on the garage floor. He turned with his back again to the unseen OC, intoning whatever it was he was going on about. Dr. Apgar then pivoted to the right and repeated the motions he'd done on this side of his body. After his third placement, he once more turned away, now on both knees. He bent forward, hands flat on the floor, head down. It dawned on OC that Dr. Apgar was praying. Before him, on a short stack of boxes, was a statue.

OC had no idea who the statue was, but the figure was sitting cross-legged and had four arms, a different object in each of its hands. One of them appeared to be a rolled-up scroll. He knew that word from Adam Warlock, who'd been in a two-part Silver Surfer cartoon show. The mystic space man was always dealing with a villain who was trying to get ahold of a cosmic cube, or an ancient scroll buried on Mars which contained mathematic equations they could use to take over the universe. In another hand, the small statue held some sort of fancy spear.

OC withdrew. Walking toward the main house, he imagined the doctor was casting a spell, hoping to tap into forbidden mystical secrets and gain superpowers. The idea tickled him. Maybe Doc would be generous with his boys and lay abilities on them too, like a version of the X-Men. For his part, OC reflected as he ascended the stairs, he'd want to be able to fly. Yeah, fly away and never look back.

CHAPTER SIX

Casablanca Furnishings served a mix of clientele in Thousand Oaks in Ventura County. The younger man escorted O'Conner into the back of the furniture store. An odd assortment of chairs, lamps and narrow shelves were crowded in the area serving as an office. The building, designed in the architectural style its name implied, occupied a section of a large open-air mall. Past the street, running behind the businesses, was a subdivision. Green-covered hills towered beyond that. The store carried all sorts of furnishings from sectional couches to patterned silk rugs.

Kanser paced as he talked on a landline phone with a long cord, going on about being shorted on an order of throw pillows. He didn't raise his voice as he insisted that the matter be corrected. Receiver pressed to his ear, he acknowledged O'Conner with a curt nod. Now in his sixties, Kanser had maintained his slim build. He was tanned and dressed in a white suit, open collar. This one was offset with a blue striped shirt and a solid blue pocket square. His mane of white hair was barbered and grew past the nape of his neck.

"That'll be fine," he said, hanging up the phone and

placing it on a metal industrial desk that looked out of place given the rest of the decor. "To what do I owe the pleasure, O'Conner?"

"I'd like you to call off the dogs regarding Burgess."

"Why should I do that?"

"I need him for a job."

"So do I, good sir."

"I'm betting mine is a bigger grab."

"What the fuck do you know? Who's been runnin' their mouth?" The one who'd brought O'Conner in spoke from where he stood at the other side of the room.

"That's no way to talk to our guest, Lanny," Kanser said.

"Yeah, Lanny," O'Conner cracked.

Lanny, about two inches taller than O'Conner, glared at him but kept his mouth shut. His arm was in a cast but not strapped around his shoulder. O'Conner had also noticed a bruise on his face. He estimated it wasn't more than a week old.

"I got this. You can go. And pull the curtain, would you."

Lanny seemed inclined to stay, but he did as requested.

"Have a seat and some tea, O'Conner." Kanser walked around a low stack of rugs to an open area. A couch was positioned before a lacquered driftwood coffee table, both items upon a Berber area rug. Nearby, a stocked tea cart held a decanter of an amber liquid and an electric kettle.

Standing in front of the cart, Kanser asked, "Any particular preference? Chamomile, chai, Earl Grey?"

"Tea is tea to me."

"That's sad, you're a heathen. Earl Grey it is."

Kanser placed tea bags in cups and poured the heated

water. He'd been born Rodney Cox from Toledo, Ohio. As he moved west, O'Conner had been told, he tried on various personas, including dress and mannerisms inspired by David Bowie's various incarnations as well as Marlene Dietrich's. Kanser had certain ways of doing things.

Kanser placed the china cups and matching saucers on the coffee table and sat on the other end of the couch. "Down to business," he said.

O'Conner replied, "First off, I have no idea why, beyond the obvious, you want Burgess. But for some damn reason you spooked him and that's messing up getting my groove on, Kanser."

"Yes, you're wondering if he turned me down, why didn't I just move on?" He sampled his tea, taking in the brew soundlessly.

O'Conner also had some of the Earl Grey. It did not make an impression on him.

"We had a meet about this opportunity and for several reasons, it fell apart."

Recalling Saggz had said the finder's fee was a week or so old, O'Conner said, "This has to do with your boy Lanny, doesn't it?"

"Unfortunately, yes."

"Don't be shy now."

"After the meet, Lanny took it upon himself to go to Burgess and needle him about the job. You see, this would be a nice little payday for him if it went down."

"That hothead would be in on the job? Doing what, besides pissing everybody off? He's not your current boy toy, is he?"

That earned a brief burst of laughter from Kanser. "You know I have better taste that that, O'Conner. For a familial reason I won't go into, I'm stuck with the lad. He's Gen Z and he's entitled. He wants to bust his cherry on a takedown and was rather overeager about stressing this with Burgess."

"You intend to come at Burgess?"

"Of course not. But as I said, Lanny got somewhat carried away and Burgess mistook his eagerness for hostility."

O'Conner conjectured, "So they tussle and Burgess gets away, one step ahead of riled-up Lanny."

Kanser allowed a wan smile. "I just want to talk to him to clear the air. What choice do I have? It's good for business, as you well know."

"What if he's already got it in his head that eliminating you along with Lanny is the solution to his problem?"

"Ole Maude used to advise, don't make an enemy of a guy who can blow up your car," Kanser said.

This was why Kanser'd put up the money, to get the matter settled as quickly as possible, O'Conner concluded. "You've put out overtures through intermediaries?"

"I have, but clearly, Burgess is wary. The silence on his end is not good."

Probably the same people O'Conner had contacted, he figured. He kept still for several moments, considering a few options. He kept coming back to the idea of making Lanny the goat, figuratively tethered to a stake and left in the open to draw the wolf out. Hell, if there wasn't a family tie to Kanser, O'Conner could kill Lanny and let Burgess know. This was not an idea he weighed lightly. He didn't consider himself bloodthirsty. But sometimes there was only one way to deal with a hardhead. Okay, such wasn't an option for the time being. There might be another way to solve this mess.

"Here's what's going to happen, Kanser. I'm going to reach out to Burgess and assure him Lanny's not going to be an issue. Your boy out there doesn't know me, and he won't be able to find either of us. Now, Lanny come sniffing around, then that's on him. Are we understood?"

"I'll make it clear to him."

"Thanks for the tea."

O'Conner left. As he'd expected, Lanny was trying to look busy but had probably been eavesdropping. He walked over to O'Conner.

"So what's up, you gonna make it right with Burgess?"

"For myself, not you. If I were you, and praise the Lord I'm not, I'd take a few lessons from Kanser in the relaxation department. Maybe it's all the high-octane marijuana you youngsters smoke these days. Which you would think would make you mellower, not edgier."

"I'm not a kid, old-timer."

"Bye-bye, Lanny."

As O'Conner turned, Lanny grabbed his arm. O'Conner allowed the momentum to twist him around and he used it to shove the other man backward. Lanny's calves collided with an ottoman and down he went. An older woman and the salesman she'd been talking to looked over, wide-eyed.

"You gonna regret that, man," Lanny growled, jetting back to his feet. "Them dentures in your head are about to get loosened."

"Lanny," Kanser called out. He stood at the head of the hallway that led to the rear area.

That stopped him. O'Conner continued on his way.

Back in L.A., O'Conner walked into the emptied space of a former wholesale restaurant supply concern. The low industrial building was in Frogtown, as the locals called this area northeast of downtown. The lights were on. There was only a desk and three hardbacked chairs in here. Tachmann was waiting inside.

"What do you think? This is not exactly an isolated location, as you no doubt observed driving in. The good news is several of the places around here are rented out to fabricators, set builders, artists and the like. Having construction going on, and people here at all hours, won't be out of character in this neck of the woods."

"Yeah, this will work. What about the lumber?"

"Delivery is set for this Friday. I'll be here to receive it."

"Work your magic so we can get it sooner." O'Conner told Tachmann about the new opening date. "In fact, tell me where and I'll fetch the two-by-fours, fiberboard and whatnot with a truck. The workers can load it. You be there to pay them off."

"Fine by me."

O'Conner didn't intend to duplicate Van Noy's entire bunker, which they estimated to be roughly 2,700 square feet based on Joyner's blueprints. She had told the two this included a living room, separate bedrooms, an exercise room and an appliance-laden kitchen. No—the construction in here would concentrate on the area around the vault.

The windows were high up and barred. Good. O'Conner pointed at a locked side door. "You have a key for this?"

"Should."

Tachmann produced a set of keys and unlocked the door. It opened onto a cleared earthen pathway, overgrown plant life on either side. They walked around, taking in the other industrial buildings. Each calculating possible escape routes. They soon went back inside.

O'Conner opened a battered wooden door to reveal the restroom. He looked in as Tachmann came over, pointing to another section.

"Gonna put in a couple of dividers and make that the kitchen so to speak. Microwave and a minifridge. A few cots too, I guess."

"You'll spoil us."

"Nothing like causing discontent among a crew with crappy facilities. After all, there will be a lady." He smiled.

"Get some free weights, will you?" O'Conner asked. "A few dumbbells too, ten and twenty pounds would be good." Tachmann's quizzical look prompted O'Conner to explain.

"A million in hundreds is twenty-two pounds. Assuming for efficiency's sake Van Noy isn't hoarding lower denominations, being able to carry two stuffed duffels in plain sight and not look like we're overly straining is going to be important to our covers."

"How about I rig up some duffel bags. Figure military standard size. So, like sixty pounds each?"

"Bet," O'Conner said, a faraway look in his eyes.

• • •

Later in the afternoon, and with the set of keys from Tachmann, O'Conner parked at the California African American Museum in Exposition Park. When he was a kid, he used to ride his bike here. He'd see the older ladies wandering around the rose garden or families going into the Natural History Museum on these shared grounds, their little children soon to be wowed by the dinosaur skeletons on display. He liked them too, in those days, he thought as he passed through the doors of the nearby museum.

For those first few years after he'd chanced upon the bag of money Teaflake hadn't seen, O'Conner had been judicious about spending the cash. He couldn't very well show up at the Griss group home with brand new Air Maxes on his feet or a PlayStation console. But he wanted a bike. He'd never had one, not even a used one. Yet before he could buy a bike, he had to solve where he could hide it. Just like he'd moved his stash from the crawl space under an abandoned house to a better hiding place.

"Hello," Mavis Joyner greeted him, interrupting his reverie.

"Hey," he said.

O'Conner told her about the adjusted timetable as they fell in step, passing through the museum's front area, which was wide and airy, allowing light to flood the interior. Their meet had previously been set to go over certain details. They wandered into one of the exhibition areas. In here, the exhibit was about pioneers of the Black press in the last century.

"Do you have your crew together?" Joyner asked softly. It wasn't out of place to talk in low tones in the museum.

"Almost, next couple of days tops."

No sense worrying the civilian. He'd solve the Burgess matter. She didn't, though, strike him as being the nervous type.

"We have a location for our rehearsal hall?" she asked.

"We do. The crew will have a get-together there. I know I asked you about your love life, but any other obligations you have, commitment-wise?"

"Anything I can't turn my back on you mean?"

O'Conner flashed on Gwen. "Yeah."

"No, I'm good." Regarding him, Joyner said, "What about you, playboy? Just a string of broken hearts? Or is it safe to assume thieves like you are all lone wolves?"

"You'd be surprised. Some of them are the picket fence type when not on the clock."

They paused before a wall graphic about Charlotta Bass. She'd been the editor-in-chief of the *California Eagle*, once one of three Black newspapers in Los Angeles, and the most progressive among them.

"That goes for you too?"

Once, not far back, O'Conner would have ignored the question. "Sort of. She and I have an understanding."

"She's a square, as you'd say?"

"Her eyes are wide open. She understands where my money comes from."

"And she's cool with that?"

"She's made peace with it. Can we get back to business?"

"Deflection much?" Snickering, she said, "I got us on the NGO guest list."

Leisurely they walked around, stopping regularly, pretending to take in a particular aspect of the exhibit. O'Conner spoke again.

"What do you know about them Omnikans?"

O'Conner described what he'd seen Deering do with the gadget on the tour.

"Don't know about them."

"I snagged a couple of pictures. I suppose that's not much to go on, but maybe you could do some digging on the quiet like and see about them."

"You want to try and duplicate it, you mean?"

"See, you're already thinking like a thief."

"I gather that's a compliment."

Joyner examined the photos on his phone.

O'Conner said, "Far as I know, these things weren't mentioned or pictured in any of the promotional videos."

"Doesn't mean we can't find out about them. I'm sure Palmer has a personal version of this Omnikan. More sophisticated of course."

"To control the security systems and devices in his bunker?"

"Precisely," she said evenly.

"The wife and mom would have one too," O'Conner estimated.

"You can't try to rip it off, that would be a red flag."

"For sure. But what if it could be borrowed for a while? I'm sure there's all sorts of safeguards built in to prevent its cloning. But I'm also sure he and the wife keep theirs handy in case you're at the grocery store and the vampires swoop in for some spinach dip."

Joyner considered this for a moment. "Probably. Emergencies."

"One for the car and one for home?"

"Why not."

After a few more moments, O'Conner said, "You're right. It's too much of a long shot getting to the ex-wife or the mother."

"No shit."

O'Conner recalled Dale Deering mentioning staff made sure to patronize the cafés and shops in the area where the arena was located. He told Joyner this.

"There's no bodyguards on her because there's no reason for her to be as protected," he added.

"Her version is probably not as sophisticated as what the family has."

"But she can open doors with hers, so that means they can be locked out too."

The two continued walking around in silence, Joyner keeping her thoughts to herself and O'Conner working out his next moves. They paused in front of a battle-worn Speed Graphic camera on a pedestal. Behind it on a nearby wall was a graphic of the crime photographer who'd owned the camera smiling crookedly, the stump of a black cigar jutting from a corner of his mouth. The two continued on.

CHAPTER SEVEN

The following evening, near the back end of a golf range in Rancho Mirage, its sprinklers on, Tachmann met with a burly individual. The burly man's salt-and-pepper hair was cut short and he sported a substantial groomed mustache. The cars they had arrived in were parked nearby. Absently, Tachmann worried the gaudy ring on his crooked finger while the other man approached.

"How's it hanging?" the man said jauntily as he walked up.

Tachmann handed him a thick manila envelope.

"What? No small talk?" the other man said, hefting the package.

"I'm tired and I want to get to bed."

"Not alone, I hope."

Tachmann sighed and started toward his car, which was barely visible through the sprinkler's heavy mists.

Envelope still in hand, the man with the mustache watched Tachmann as he walked away. "You've been spending time away from home lately," he called out.

"Keeping watch on me?" Tachmann said over his shoulder.

"Just looking out for your welfare, Tack."

• • •

Elsewhere that same evening, Lanny Murser was carrying two plastic grocery bags up the stairs to his apartment in Thousand Oaks. On the second-floor breezeway, bags drooping in his hand, he used the other one to pull keys from his pocket. He unlocked the door and went inside. That's when O'Conner, stationed along the inner wall next to the door, smashed him in the nose with a handgun.

"Motherfuck," Lanny bellowed. He staggered, dropping his groceries. Apples and avocados spilled from one of the sacks and rolled across the floor.

O'Conner struck Lanny again, hard in the head, before he could recover. Down he dropped. The thief put a foot on Lanny's chest, putting his weight behind it.

"Open your goddamn eyes," O'Conner demanded. He pointed the gun at Lanny. The injured man's broken nose bled crimson down the lower part of his face. It took him a moment to focus on O'Conner's gun. "The only reason I didn't kill you is because I don't want Kanser getting steamed. But you make sure you stay the fuck away from me and forget my name. You understand me?"

"Yeah," Lanny grumbled.

"Say it with conviction, asshole."

"Yeah!" he shouted.

O'Conner walked out of the apartment and down the steps. He'd staked out the furniture company and tailed Murser here. It wasn't much to get past the locks on the apartment's door.

Back in Inglewood, O'Conner leaned away from the desk in his suite at the Presidium Hotel, his notes and laptop before him. Tomorrow morning, he'd get word around and hopefully would hear back from Burgess. He'd left two messages for Hong but hadn't heard back from him yet. O'Conner would circle back to Hong next.

O'Conner got up, stretched, and looked at his phone. No call or text from Gwen. He went to the window. The yellow underlit arches of the Theme Building at LAX were prominent in the mid-distance. When he was a kid, having run away from a foster home yet again, he'd once made it all the way to the airport. In those days, he'd only seen a picture of the Theme Building in a magazine. To him, it was an old *Jetsons* cartoon come to life. He'd also gone by where the Cockatoo Inn was, where his grandmother had worked and died. By then it was closed for good.

CHAPTER EIGHT

O'Conner stood on a patch of empty land. A sign nearby with a rendering on it indicated a two-story strip mall was destined for this location. He looked north across the east–west expanse of Century Boulevard at the Hollywood Park Casino. The Hollywood Park racetrack had once been there, too. SoFi football stadium, where the NFL Barons played, now occupied the land. The Kia Forum was also visible.

A young OC had snuck into a concert one night at the latter venue, when it was simply known as the Forum. He'd gone to see a show put on by Prince. He wasn't particularly a fan. But he did appreciate that the Purple One opened his show by descending from the rafters in an old-fashioned Thunderbird held in place by metal struts. The more O'Conner heard that night, the more he liked. If the Silver Surfer had swooped onto the stage as Prince and the band played an extended instrumental of "Betcha By Golly Wow!" he would have passed out from giddiness.

O'Conner waited for a break in the light traffic and jaywalked across the wide street. There were no tours at Del Norte today. Nonetheless, people were present, strolling around the exterior. They pointed at the impressive structure, talking to one another about this or that feature. Others were in the park, watching their kids enjoy the playground. Several people shopped in the team store.

O'Conner headed to a side of the arena, hands in his pockets, doing his best to play the curious fan come to see his team's new home. Around the curve, he stopped where he'd calculated the main section of the power plant and control room should be down below. A heavy metal door was inset here—no lock, no keypad. The thrum of the powerful machinery penetrated the soles of his shoes. He put a hand to the door, feeling a steady vibration coursing through his fingertips.

"Can I help you?"

O'Conner pivoted leisurely, putting on his fresh-from-the-country expression. He recognized his interlocutor as Brad, one of the construction supervisors. O'Conner had seen him with Dale Deering in the video he'd chanced upon in the early morning. Brad and Deering were talking about an underground trolley tunnel having been inadvertently discovered during construction—waxing poetic about this symbol of a lost L.A. Seems in the 1940s, the Red Car trolley line had a stop at the Hollywood Park racetrack. For whatever reason, portions of the line out here ran underground. O'Conner had subsequently learned more about the tunnel by reading a digital copy of *Two Bells*, an old newsletter published by the trolley company. He was pretty certain a long-unused tunnel wasn't below the power plant, but rather ran alongside it.

"Just trying to take it all in, man. I mean this place is really something. You must be one of the builders, huh?"

"Sorry, but the arena's not open for sightseeing today."

O'Conner was already moving away. "Of course, sure, great place. Now all the Swash has gotta do is bring home them Ws, ain't that right?" He grinned like a goof.

Glaring at O'Conner, Brad turned, having produced an electronic fob. The door popped open.

O'Conner went to the team store, pretending to browse. Standing before an assortment of Swashbuckler swag, he memorized the layout of the plaza, in particular noting the exact location of the bathrooms in the back.

Outside again, he walked over to the staff parking lot. Joyner had hacked into the DMV and obtained Deering's license plate. Making sure he wasn't noticed, O'Conner bent and placed a tracker in the car's fender well. Straightening, he felt his phone buzz.

"Aesop," he said, answering. "I was meaning to call you."

"I've got a direct line on Oscar." Hong went silent.

"Go on."

"There's a complication."

"Isn't there always?" O'Conner said evenly.

Not long afterward, he met with Hong and another man, Ben Reynolds, at the latter's mid-century-style house in the Bixby Knolls section of Long Beach. O'Conner and Reynolds went back a ways. They talked in a converted garage-turned-mancave behind the house. The garage door had been replaced with dual glass-paneled doors. A compact lawn and a patio with a pergola over it separated the two buildings. Through the sliding glass door to the house, a dark-skinned Asian woman in a business suit, maybe in her early fifties, could be seen going about her business.

Reynolds was a year or so older than Burgess, O'Conner observed. Yet like Burgess, he moved pretty good for a man his age. With close-cropped straight gray hair, Reynolds was of medium complexion, mixed race, Black and white, though often taken for Latino. He wore jeans and a black short-sleeved shirt. A scar that began on the back of his hand traveled halfway up along his forearm, where it stopped.

"I'll introduce you two later to Rikki," Reynolds said.

Hong, Reynolds and O'Conner sat in a semicircle, Reynolds and O'Conner in club chairs. A small round table was within reach and glasses of fresh lemonade had been served. In a corner of the room was a golf bag on a roller. O'Conner had been going over with the two their roles in the upcoming heist. Satisfied, he addressed Hong.

"Okay, what about Oscar Silvera?"

"Like I said, I knew where to find him. Only it's not like I can just call him," Hong replied.

"Why not?"

"I don't have a current number for Oscar. But I drove out to the headquarters yesterday."

"What headquarters?"

"His old lady's."

"Talk sense, Aesop."

Exasperated, Hong said, "She talked about the need to keep undesirable energy from impacting one's state of being. I think that's what she said. The way she looked at me, pretty sure she didn't like my vibe."

"Yep," Reynolds agreed.

O'Conner waited.

Hong said, "Look, I drive out there and get to the gate. I

tell the guard in his little shack who I am, and I want to see Oscar. He calls them inside. Oscar doesn't come out but the queen bee does, looking all *Star Trek*, and I mean TOS, feel me? She's dressed in this kind of jumpsuit, black on one side and white on the other. Puffy pirate shirt sleeves fluttering off her arms as she kind of floats toward me."

He wiggled his fingers on either side of his head.

O'Conner asked, "Who the hell are you talking about, Aesop?"

"She who is Zelb. Ashley Armour."

"What?" O'Conner blared.

Hong ignored his confusion. "She also said that for Oscar's well-being, he should not have interactions at this time with those who are not about cohesion. Once she was done, madam turned around and went back inside. And finito, my ass was told to bounce by the guard."

"Now what are you going to do, champ?" Reynolds said to O'Conner.

At dawn the following day, O'Conner lay on his stomach among the sawgrass on the hill overlooking the Zelb compound. He took the binoculars away from his eyes. It was just past five in the morning and the cold in Apple Valley was intensified by the wind periodically kicking up. Finding out what was inside the compound hadn't been hard. The Zelb headquarters had been written about in detail in several news articles. O'Conner also read that while Ashley Armour had a home in Santa Monica, she spent a good deal of time out here. She'd stated that the ley lines of spiritual energy were particularly vibrantly aligned in the area.

Oscar Silvera was the current man in the life of Zelb's CEO. Apparently, they'd met when he was brought in to restore a vintage Rolls Royce for her. When not doing grabs, Silvera picked up legitimate work with car stockpilers, outfits who supplied vehicles for movie and television shoots. Armour, a former actor of a certain age, started Zelb as a skin care product. Now, a decade later, the goofy name was plastered on a plethora of wellness and lifestyle products. There were Zelb teachings, cookbooks, fashion—all manner of ways to fleece the suckers, O'Conner thought.

As O'Conner anticipated, he eventually spotted Silvera and the car he was driving, at about ten. What could O'Conner say to tempt him back into a life of criminal endeavor? Take a risk with his freedom or worse, his life. All for a few million? The only way to get an answer was to ask him.

O'Conner eased down the hill back to his car. He attended to the lumber and such for the Frogtown location until evening arrived. He had also checked out one of those sites that gossiped about all things celebrities, which had given him a sense of where the Zelb folks hung out in town after work.

O'Conner spotted Silvera quickly, having noted his car parked out front of the Sagebrush Bar and Grill. Silvera was sitting at a table with two others, having a beer as they conversed. O'Conner also got a beer, making sure the other man saw him. Silvera excused himself and came over. It was a weekday. The place was busy but not overly so. They easily got a table of their own, far enough from his friends.

"You don't seem too surprised to see me," O'Conner began.

"Heard about the mishegoss around Burgess, heard too it

was taken care of. Something made my nose twitch that you were involved, O'Conner."

So Silvera wasn't all the way out. "I'm lining up Burgess. Hong is in."

"Yeah, I was told afterward about A coming out here." He drank some.

"But you didn't call him."

"I did not." He tipped his mug toward him. "Didn't connect you two. Kinda assumed he'd dropped by to get to Ashley. Like proposing putting oxygen bars in Zelb stores."

O'Conner chuckled. "You don't seem to be kept on a leash."

"Maybe it's mink lined." A smile animated his face. "I mean faux fur of course."

"You're comfortable, settled?"

"Yeah, I'm pretty set I guess."

O'Conner let a silence linger. He sipped his beer.

Eventually, Silvera asked, "What kind of amount we're talking circles around, O'Conner?"

"Twenty-one million at least—but the indication is more."

"How many are in?"

"Five on the string. Ben Reynolds is part of this as well. His and Aesop's shares come out of my end. The fifth is the civilian. She has the inside dope. She, though, gets a cut like you and Burgess do."

Silvera said, "And you weren't going to walk away."

"Can't help myself."

"I see you. Four million give or take would be my end, huh?"

"Looks that way."

"You know how it is, O'Conner, is the game worth the candle? I'm a kept man these days. Kind of content."

"Once upon a time that kind of stack was a damn good payday, Oscar."

"It still is, really."

"Who you figure I can ask in on this if not you?"

Silvera considered his response. "Why do you think there might be more than the twenty-one?"

"Van Noy has a thing for threes. The scratch is in his luxe survival bunker."

"I've been in one of those," Silvera said. "A dinner party, can you beat that? The paintings this dude had on the walls would be a small country's budget for a year."

Given the other man's wistful expression, O'Conner wanted him to do the talking.

"When the big bomb drops, because of the MAGAdons or whomever bringing the apocalypse, people like you and me will be left to fend for ourselves. Gabachos like bunker boy are all save-the-whales and make sure we recycle, except when it comes to me and mine and not you." He paused, looking off momentarily. "This entitled piece of shit even had a maid's quarters in there."

"I'm sure Ashley has room for you in hers."

"For the time being." He had more of his beer, drinking slowly. "I couldn't help but think lately about the longest she's had a relationship is around three years. Always with younger men," he added. "We've been together a little over two and a half years."

As jackleg confessor, O'Conner merely nodded, encouraging him to continue.

"It was when her second marriage ended. She looked inward, as she called it. Re-evaluating who she was, what had she accomplished and what was a way to really define herself."

"You might say the same for cats like us," O'Conner said.

Silvera looked over at the people he'd been sitting with and gave them a half-hearted wave. "I'm'a get back over there." He stuck out his hand and they shook. "Good seeing you, man. I'll lay a couple of names on you who can fit the bill. Give me a number to reach you. But for me, I'm gonna enjoy this sweet ride while I can. I'm sure you can get behind that, O'Conner."

"Yes, sir," O'Conner said. Hiding his disappointment, he gave Silvera a secure number to text him.

Outside, O'Conner lingered by Silvera's Lucid, visualizing him at the wheel, Armour beside him. They were grinning from ear to ear, a picnic basket in the back, on their way up the coast to a secluded spot overlooking the rolling Pacific. Briefly, he entertained he too could walk away right now with Gwen. Better to not stick his neck out than probably to get his head chopped off.

"But where would be the fun in that?" he muttered as he walked away from the fancy car and the ordinary bar.

Before noon the next day, O'Conner was having a sweat in a steam bath, a towel around his waist. He hadn't come to luxuriate. The Dry Salt Baths was located in what was called the Arts District, adjacent to downtown L.A.—referred to as DTLA these days. The place included a juice bar. Shiatsu massage was also available. Vestiges of the area's previous industrial incarnation remained, like the Bendix building. The name was spelled out vertically atop the structure, the letters glowing neon red at night. Bendix Aviation Corporation had once been headquartered there. Now the place was high-priced lofts. The artists were gone.

The door to the steam bath opened and in stepped Burgess, wearing boxer-like swim trunks but no towel. His build was wiry, his graying hair thinning. Having worked jobs together in the past, O'Conner knew Burgess had been part of an engineering unit in Vietnam. His duties included booby-trapping tunnels used by the Vietcong, blowing up bridges and the like. Burgess eventually was assigned to bomb disposal. Had Burgess's iron nerves developed from those experiences, or had he been one of those fearless sort of kids riding his bike off a ramp high into the air? At any rate, he was rummaging in his seventies, not infirmed, and O'Conner wanted him. Like clockwork, he was steady and reliable.

The explosives expert sat next to O'Conner on the wood slat bench, which O'Conner had reserved in advance. "I appreciate you taking care of that business with the hothead," Burgess remarked, skipping past a simple hello. His one tattoo was on his bicep, the insignia of his old unit.

"Didn't want you wasting any of that C-4 you carry around in your hip pocket."

"It did cross my mind taking out Lanny would be the best solution in the long run. But there will be ripples," he said, gesturing vaguely.

Like having to kill Kanser, O'Conner noted silently. "You've been laying low in town?"

"I had other business to attend to hereabouts. Totally squaresville jive," Burgess said. He sat back, seeming to take in the warmth. "And anyway, I haven't had a schvitz in I don't know when. It sure is good for what ails you."

"This was a good idea," O'Conner admitted, allowing himself to relax. The therapeutic heat permeated his body, alleviating the soreness in his muscles. The lingering effects of his dustup with Saggz and Tyler. It wasn't too long ago he would have healed up by now, though it had only been a few days since the altercation.

His long fingers kneading his thighs, Burgess asked, "So what am I blowing up, O'Conner?"

O'Conner explained the target to him.

Burgess said, "When I was a kid in the sixties, there were still fallout shelters. You could buy a prefab one at Sears, for Chrissake."

O'Conner frowned. "Fallout shelters?"

Burgess snickered. "Not just the rich, but working folks had them dug in the backyard or converted their basements. You're too young, but back then we had duck-and-cover drills in school. If the Russkis rained nuclear missiles on us, playing turtle under our desks would protect us from the radiation." He laughed at the inanity of this notion. "All over America there'd be millions of ashen shadows in the shapes of huddled children on linoleum, fried by the firestorm alone."

O'Conner made a sound in his throat and returned to business. He told Burgess about the abandoned trolley car tunnel.

"Are you sure it's running under the hotel?" Burgess asked. "It might well have collapsed some time ago."

"That's why you and I are breaking in beforehand to find

out. The hotel hasn't opened yet. If the tunnel's been filled in, I have another way we'll get in. But it's more exposure. And we have to dope out how to smuggle in the equipment we'll need to get into the safe."

"The heart attack dodge?" Burgess said.

Burgess was referring to an old ploy. One of the crew would pretend to have a medical emergency. Arriving in an ambulance, the heisters would come in, their drills and whatnot secured under a gurney and inside a dummied-up portable EKG unit.

"Maybe. Let's see first."

"Okay," Burgess said matter-of-factly. "We won't need to lug in sandbags to muffle the blast. Got this kind of mesh blanket the black op types use when they want to do a breach and take out the next Osama bin Laden."

O'Conner added, "I was hoping to have Jeet Silvera on to handle the motor pool and assorted."

"He turned you down?"

"His getaway life is pretty sweet these days. He's going to hit me back with a couple of substitutes."

O'Conner resumed discussing other aspects of the job. A relaxed Burgess had his eyes closed, nodding occasionally.

When O'Conner was done, Burgess asked, "How do you size up the software engineer?"

"Will she fold if shit gets real, you mean?"

"Sometimes those sorts of people skate right along, rolling with the blows. Then sometimes they lose their goddamn minds when matters go south."

O'Conner told him about Joyner going undercover at the restaurant.

"She's got balls," Burgess allowed, closing his eyes and settling back.

"She comes from tough stock," O'Conner added, recalling Charlie Mack.

"She also wants to get back at this cat bad. Is she Assata Shakur crossed with Robin Hood? She might be willing to die for the cause, but some of us want to get out of this in one piece."

O'Conner said, "I'm sure she's gonna plow some of her cut into efforts training girls in tech."

"Or building laser rifles to take out the oligarchs," Burgess surmised.

"She strikes me as level-headed."

Burgess opened an eye, rolling the orb toward O'Conner. "It's been a minute, like the kids say, since you've put together a job like this."

"You worried I've lost a step or two?"

Burgess sat up, eyes fully open. "A man my age, such would be the pot calling the kettle, wouldn't it? I was just wondering if your heart was in it, O'Conner. By necessity we keep our private lives private. But it don't take no Hercule Poirot to figure out since you've been a might scarce on the scene these last few years, you too must have a good thing going out there in the civilian world."

"I do," O'Conner allowed. "Doesn't mean I'm going to be half-assin' it. As Charlie Mack used to lecture me, 'If your job is mopping the floor—'"

"Mop it the best way you know how," Burgess finished. The explosives expert sat back again, at one with the heat and his sweat. "I'll talk to Tachmann about what I'll need.

You figure to use a variation of what we did in Kansas City that time?"

"Sure." O'Conner finally settled back as well, enjoying the heat. Breathing in deep, he asked, "When do you look to hang it up, Burgess?"

"Before my luck runs out?"

"Isn't stealing the money the luck?"

Burgess said, "You ain't never lied, young fella. I'm'a keep doing this until I go out feet first putting together sparklers in the retirement home if I got anything to say about it. Send pinwheels flying across the room to liven up the bingo games. Sheet.

"What about you?" he asked.

"This could be my last go-round."

Burgess said, "That's what you're telling yourself?"

"Yeah."

"Putting the pieces together, isn't that what keeps you going?"

"I have other interests."

"What, needlepoint?" Burgess huffed. "Now I know this goes without saying, but stealing from a guy like Van Noy is not what we usually do. He's got for all intents and purposes more money than Jehovah."

"We've gone up against mobsters with all kinds of money and men. They and him still put their pants on one leg at a time."

"Until the robots take over," Burgess replied seriously. "I know you only kill if you have to, O'Conner, but what about Van Noy? Take him out once the score goes down?"

"Or is that more trouble?" O'Conner wondered. "Do the other tech gurus put up a bounty?"

"They might be busy trying to take over his company."

O'Conner said, "I assume the ex-wife would stay on the case but who knows. Maybe his board might decide to cut its losses. Anyway, you're not talking yourself out of this, are you?"

"Me? Hell no. We cover our tracks like we always do. They get wind of us, they come at us, I've long ago settled I'll blow them up along with me."

"That's the spirit," O'Conner said.

They returned to the locker room and toweled off. Buttoning his shirt, O'Conner ruminated. Putting scores together was his drug. How could he quit that? He got a text. He picked his phone up from the bench, staring at the message for several moments.

Burgess said, "Come on, I'll buy you an overpriced cleansing juice."

"You're on."

They headed out.

"Oscar is in," O'Conner announced as they walked along a short hallway.

"What made him change his mind?"

"Said he reconsidered and concluded being in on this was part of the 'cohesion he needed at this juncture.'"

"The fuck's that mean?"

"Who knows?" O'Conner said.

Plastic cups in hand at the juice bar, the two knocked their smoothies together.

"Salud," O'Conner said to Burgess.

"Cheers."

O'Conner's kale, mint and beet concoction was said to

boost your quotient of antioxidants and in general promote well-being. Seemed he was going to need an abundance of both, he reckoned, in the days ahead.

After leaving the steam baths and taking a drive, O'Conner entered the activities room of the Tulip Hills assisted living facility in Monterey Park. Through the double French doors, he could see several seniors in chairs and on the two couches watching a soap in the TV room. He paused for a few seconds, taking in the scene. The turned-up sound spilled into the larger space. Here, other residents were sitting around a long table. Some were reading, a few doing crossword puzzles, online and on paper, and more than one just sat and stared. Bora Cho was among those sitting at the table, her back to him.

Walking over, O'Conner could see she was online. She was doing a cognitive brain game meant to keep a senior's mind sharp. He watched her diligently perform the tasks on the laptop he'd bought her. O'Conner put a hand on her shoulder and gently squeezed.

"Hey," he said.

Bora Cho turned to look at him, then patted his hand. "Hey yourself."

O'Conner sat in the empty chair next to her. Her hair was snow white and she'd had cancer surgery a few years ago. So far, she remained in remission. A young Latinx worker dressed in scrubs approached them. Smiling, she leaned toward him. "Can I help you, sir?"

O'Conner was used to this from new personnel. Considering the area they were in, there wasn't an overabundance of Black residents.

"He's here to see me," Bora said, never taking her eyes away from her screen as she used two index fingers to type in a word to finish a sentence.

"Oh." The young woman straightened up. "Didn't mean to interrupt." She went away.

"How are you?"

"Old. I recommend not trying it."

"Taking your pills?"

"You know doggone well I am because you call to get a weekly report on me." In Korean, she added, "I haven't gone simple just yet. I know what's going on." Bora reached another plateau and froze the exercise, pushing the computer aside. Her eyes were alert behind the lenses of her glasses as she regarded him. "How are you?"

"Fine."

"That's jive."

After all this time, O'Conner still found it unnerving she could read him so well. "Ah, you know, business."

"Don't let it get to you, OC. You know what can happen."

Bora Cho's husband had died more than ten years ago from a heart attack while playing golf. The family had sold the Hi Hat liquor store in the early aughts and the two of them had moved out this way to nearby Alhambra. There was a grown daughter, Olivia, but O'Conner hadn't heard from her for some time. She lived in Denver and had a family.

"Believe me, I'm doing my best to handle stress." Far as she knew, he was a wheel with the Fix & Go chain.

"You say that, but I can see new worry lines on your face."

"I'm getting up there too."

"Hmm. You and the lady friend doing okay on the home front?"

"She hasn't kicked me out yet."

"You know what I mean."

"Gwen's twice divorced. She's in no hurry."The subject of marriage had come up more than once from the older woman.

Wagging a finger at him, she said, "Like you said, you ain't gettin' no younger."

He shook his head. "Not gonna have any kids. She's got a grown daughter."

"Come on, a little OC running around to give you fits." She clapped her hands together, then grasped them. "Enjoyable."

"How about we go to the rose garden again soon?"

"Mister Change-the-Subject. Of course I'm going to agree. Any chance to stretch my legs is welcome."

"Didn't you all have an outing to the zoo recently?"

She waved a hand dismissively. "Not the same thing. I can't get chili fries on those . . . excursions. That's the word, right?"

"Yes, it is. And what makes you think you're gonna get them with me?"

She chuckled, patting his hand again.

They talked more, time passed. One of her biggest complaints, aside from not enough pineapple pieces in the Jell-O, was her new roommate snored and passed too much gas at night.

"Lily died, huh?" O'Conner said, referring to her recent roommate.

"Killed herself," Bora whispered.

"What are you saying?"

"Stuck her head under the water until she drowned."

Bora Cho was mobile and allowed a walk-in tub in her suite. "She must have gotten drowsy and slipped under," he said.

She took her time replying. "Everything was getting to be too much, OC. Eyesight was going, the pain treatments weren't working. I mean she was ninety-three. She told me what she wanted to do."

As O'Conner attempted to absorb what she was saying, the young employee returned with a small tray like from an In-N-Out Burger. On it was a Styrofoam cup of water and Bora's pills in a crinkled cupcake liner.

"Time for your meds, Bora," the young woman said, holding the tray forward instead of setting it down.

The elderly woman dexterously plucked each pill from the tray. With individual sips of water, she took them separately. The caregiver went away.

O'Conner was looking at her. "You said 'wanted.'"

She was in profile to him and took in a deep breath, holding it for a moment, then letting the air out. "Yes, I helped her. She was my friend."

"Are you kidding me?" he said in Korean in a low voice. There were several Korean oldsters around.

"I sat next to her in the tub on a chair. On the phone you bought me, I put on some of that classical music she liked. We talked some, I held her hand. When she was ready, she went under and stayed there."

"You could go to jail playing night nurse. This is an

assisted suicide state, but only when it comes to an MD giving their patient the hot shot."

Evenly, Bora Cho said, "I wish a fool would try and put me in jail." Then she cackled, slapping his arm.

Despite his annoyance, he laughed too. "Okay, Moms Mabley."

"I'm not going around bragging about what I did. But she didn't want to suffer any longer. She wanted peace."

"No more playing angel of death, Bora."

"I'm not playing." This time, she put her hand on his forearm and held it there. "OC," she began in Korean, "when the time comes, I want you to help me like I helped Lily. We both know Olivia can't do it."

"You're talking crazy. Are you in pain?"

"For now, no, just the usual aches. But I ain't no spring chicken."

"Any doctor you need, you know you got them."

"I know you have the money."

"Then don't worry."

She regarded him for a moment. "How long I know you?"

"Since I was a kid."

"That's right. And do you really believe I have no idea what you really do? The cheddar you made, you invested with your lady friend's auto body shops."

Caught flat-footed, he didn't know how to answer.

Bora Cho waited for one of the caregivers to pass by before she continued in English. "It was, must have been more than twenty years ago now. We still had the Hi Hat, but were thinking about selling. Charlie Mack was still around. She had an interest in maybe buying us out. I was in the Crimson Lounge having a drink at the bar and we were talking it over. This was in the late afternoon, before the bar opened. A couple of old ladies sipping Crown Royal over ice."

"That's a frightening notion."

"Hush up," she said, smiling. She spoke in Korean again. "We talked some business and naturally, after that, we get to chatting about the changes in the neighborhood. The group home closing after Dr. Apgar disappeared and all that. Once he came up, you came up. Told her I'd recently gotten a postcard from you from Puerto Rico. She laughed, saying she guessed your leg had healed up okay."

"Hmm," O'Conner sounded.

"I asked her what she was talking about, and she tried to play it cool. That you'd had a motorcycle accident when she last saw you a month or so before. I asked why hadn't you come to see me, and she said she knew you were in a hurry, going in and out of town."

O'Conner had been limping from a bullet wound. He'd been in transit to see Charlie Mack because he'd fetched a cold piece he'd left with her. Why he'd made sure Bora didn't know he was around for just that night.

"What's shady about that?" he said, sounding innocent.

"You are getting on in age. The next time I saw you, maybe two years later, what did we eat?"

"I don't remember."

"Barbecue, Texas style," she said. "You rode in on a motorcycle with the food in a saddlebag like a cowboy."

"Okay, so?"

She smiled again. "When we were having our hot links

and beer you said you hadn't been on a motorcycle for four or five years until then."

He let out a sigh.

"Why did Charlie Mack lie to me? It's not like I didn't know the stories about her. Two plus two, or do I mean two peas in a pod?"

"Maybe I was lying to her."

"No," she said, shaking her head. "You had no reason to keep things from her."

"You figured me and Charlie Mack were in business together?"

"I figured something was between you two. But dang, they sure had a great party for her when she died."

He didn't interrupt her segue.

"There were all kinds of cars, lowriders, fancy kind, some like out of black-and-white movies filling the street that day. I stood there in the doorway, looking as all these people come to the bar after the cemetery for her send-off." As she talked, she slipped between Korean and English.

At the time of the funeral, O'Conner had been living in a man camp erected around a fracking operation in the middle of Oklahoma, setting up a score. As Bora continued her reminiscing, he wondered, was she telling him this was how she wanted to go out?

"Tables of food and drink were set up in the street. Everybody in the neighborhood was invited. Shoe Dog was there crying his eyes out." She shrugged at that. "The bartender came over to the store with a plate of food and Crown Royal in a plastic cup."

"Miss Val," O'Conner recalled fondly.

"Yeah, that was her name. So, what the heck, we toasted Charlie Mack." She paused, leveling him with a look. "And that's when I knew. One of those guys who'd been in the group home with you was there. He didn't look so good. He had the sickness, OC."

That had been their term for an addict, be it booze or drugs.

"I don't remember his name, but he was the one with the funny eye. Almost closed." She shut an eye.

"Raj," he said, the bully's face with his half-lidded eye vivid in his mind.

"That's him," she said. "He was walking by, a plate of food in each hand. His shoes were wet paper, barely around his feet. He went past, then backed up like he was Michael Jackson moonwalking. Smiling, teeth missing. He came in, staring at me hard behind the counter. One of the paper plates about to spill over with the food. Just grinning at me."

A cold anger surged through O'Conner. "He threaten you?"

She huffed. "He didn't look like he could fight a baby panda. But I guess he knew you still came to see me. He said to tell you that he had a file on you and was gonna turn your crooked ass in to the cops for a reward. That's when one of the drumsticks fell off the plate. He squatted to get it, still looking at me. He said to make sure I told you. The sick man left, eating the drumstick like he never had one before."

"How the hell did Raj know anything about me?"

"It's never been my business to pry into your life, OC. Other than I worry when I don't hear from you."

"I'll always be back."

"That's why I'm counting on you if I need to. Lily and me won't fill the streets with those come to say goodbye. But I know without knowing all about you, you've made those kind of tough decisions. I just need you." She patted his hand again.

"Oh," she said, "I had one of my dreams the other night. A chicken and a dragon talked to me."

Out from her pocket came some folded-over bills and a sheet of paper. On it would be numbers. "Play my scratchers. The pot this week is over two hundred million. Like always, if I win, I'll cut you in."

"I so appreciate that."

A man in a Pendleton too big on him began coughing violently, his hand slapping the table.

CHAPTER NINE

At the building in Frogtown that weekend, O'Conner, Burgess and Joyner worked for several hours. First, O'Conner and Burgess assembled the framework of the bunker with tape on the floor. On a ladder outside, Joyner, in jeans and a work shirt, installed hardwired cameras. The high-rises of downtown could be partially seen in the smoggy distance. Not far away was a bike path paralleling the concrete bed of the L.A. River.

Once Joyner had the cameras in place, she sat at the desk in the corner. She loaded the security app onto four encrypted phones so each could access the feed from the external and internal cameras. They took a break around two in the afternoon. To better erase their presence once they were gone, O'Conner had told Joyner not to frequent any of the eateries in the area.

"For the next two and some change weeks we're around, we need to do our best to not be recognized in local places," he said.

"Looks like we'll have our frame up in the next day or two," Burgess opined, using cheap chopsticks to grip a helping of kimchi. On the desk were the set of pseudo blueprints.

Joyner had gone to a shipping and self-service photocopy shop to print out the schematic on oversized sheets of paper. This was their guide for the build.

"We could have these on the air-gapped computers," Joyner had said to O'Conner about using physical blueprints.

"Paper burns easily and can be flushed away. And I like the idea of us seeing the whole layout together. Guess I'm just old-fashioned that way."

"You can say that again."

Burgess shifted his Styrofoam container from where it was atop one of the sheets. He tapped the drawing with a chopstick. "This panel is facing out onto the hallway, where the vault is."

"Yeah," O'Conner nodded. "I'd noticed."

"It might not exist," Joyner said. "The AI makes certain leaps, filling in gaps where the data is sketchy."

O'Conner finished his second taco. "Let's assume the panel exists. What's behind door number one if you were Palmer Van Noy?"

Burgess said, "A lean and mean Rottweiler. A robot hand comes out each hour to scratch him under the chin."

"A laser," Joyner declared.

The other two exchanged bemused looks.

Burgess said, "Is that possible?"

"Magnus-Noy has done work for the military. On the real, though, more likely it could be a variation of a sonic device. The kind used to render protestors nauseous," Joyner said.

"I'll get us some noise-canceling headphones just in case," O'Conner said.

"Since we're on the subject of rooms," Burgess added, "there's three bedrooms you figure are for the husband and the ex or the girlfriend, and one each for the two kids?"

"Or the two kids double up and the other is for Palmer's mom," Joyner explained. "His father passed several years ago, and he's an only child."

"What about the wife's folks?"

"They live in Hawaii," she said. "She has a brother who also doesn't live in California."

Burgess said, "There's another room off the kitchen that looks to be set up for more than one." He regarded the software engineer. "If you and the mighty computer's guesstimating are right, this room looks to have at least two pull-down cots built in."

"I saw that too, Burgess. What if it's in case a family member is in town?"

"Yeah, probably," the older man replied, but didn't make an effort to sound convinced.

To Joyner, O'Conner said, "Is that for Palmer's girlfriend? Or the wife's boyfriend?"

She looked askance at him. "Negro, please."

Burgess chuckled and O'Conner said, "Had to ask."

Jeet Silvera, O'Conner informed Joyner, was handling the vehicles and other aspects of the grab elsewhere, but would join them eventually.

"Jeet?" she said.

"His nickname," O'Conner explained. "Jet . . . jeet." He shrugged.

Burgess and O'Conner finished the model of the vault with fiberboard and sheetrock attached to wooden frames propped up from the rear, like how walls were faked for film sets. They had also constructed a hallway leading to the vault room, writing notes on the makeshift walls with a black marker. They were calling their headquarters Ice Station Zebra. Burgess had come up with the name.

"It's a sixties film," he'd said. "It's about being alone and relatively isolated."

Later, while Burgess and Joyner continued to work, O'Conner met with Silvera. They parked in a stolen car across and down the street from the Inglewood Water Works maintenance yard in order to ascertain the design of the seals on the service vehicles. Silvera had stolen the car the night before and switched out the plates. After taping a small camera with a long-range lens to the dash with electrical tape, they rolled by slowly to take pictures.

At the underground, well-stocked garage in Gardena where Silvera was working on the transit van the crew was going to use, he and O'Conner finished making hand grips, triggers and other 3D-printed gun parts, assembling four ghost guns. O'Conner's plan was about not using guns. But you had to be prepared for contingencies.

"I know he knows what he's doing, O'Conner, but you don't find it a bit unnerving?"

It was Monday. After a weekend of hard work, Burgess had taken up residence in a corner section of the room, where he was assembling oblong devices. He had a lined container ready for each one he finished. Joyner and O'Conner watched as he carefully nestled each one of his mini bombs in the appropriately shaped foam like they were Fabergé eggs. Burgess would then put on the top and seal the compact package with masking tape.

"If he makes a mistake, it'll happen so fast, we won't know it," O'Conner said.

"That makes me feel so much better," she said.

He clapped her on the shoulder. "I'm here to help."

Like training for an athletic contest, each member of the team rehearsed their movements over and over to form reflexive memory. They studied videos and photos Silvera and O'Conner had made of specific areas of the surrounding neighborhood. They also needed to practice carrying the weighted duffel bags.

"Why can't we just walk around with them inside here?" Joyner asked.

Flexing his arm, O'Conner said, "We need to get those triceps and calves in shape. An uneven terrain is best."

"Not for my knees," Burgess said.

"In that case I've got a place in mind," Joyner announced. "If you're not superstitious."

Later that day, Joyner took O'Conner and the others to a cemetery called Grantford in Compton. It had been in the news about half a year ago. One day, without any prior notice, the front iron gates were chained and the groundskeepers dismissed. Turned out months of back taxes were owed on the property.

"How do you have access?" O'Conner asked Joyner.

"One of Charlie Mack's relatives is buried here. I know

somebody who knows somebody and they duplicated the keys for me." She added, to his inquisitive glance, "No questions asked."

Grantford was more than a century old and contained headstones and several crypts, some of them pyramid shaped. There were several rises of land on the grounds as well. The brick walls bordering the cemetery were sufficiently tall, blocking the four of them from sight, including Silvera, who hefted the duffel bags. The crew worked out a circuit, taking them past an assortment of chipped crosses, obelisks, slanted headstones and a few constructs with the images of the deceased emblazoned in stone.

"Never thought I'd have to repeat basic at this stage in my life," a sweating Burgess said.

"I'm right here with you, grandpa," O'Conner remarked.

"You can't imagine what a comfort that is to me."

They kept at it, casting ragged shadows against the overgrown grass and weeds.

CHAPTER TEN

On a Wednesday night, O'Conner and Burgess broke into the Hilton at Del Norte hotel. Getting past a locked and alarmed side door wasn't difficult. This was easier than getting into the better fortified arena. They'd brought along a device called an emitter, which could be calibrated to a specific frequency used by the alarm company. Akin to working a safe, O'Conner fine-tuned the dial, watching the readout so as to lock on and mimic the alarm's frequency. He did, and they entered.

This portion of the building was blocked from view by the freestanding gift shop on the sprawling plaza of the arena. The park could be accessed on one side of the lot. They'd arrived in an unmarked white van. No other vehicles were parked. Propping the door open, the two unloaded three white-paneled cases on rollers and two empty nylon equipment bags.

The interior of the hotel had been completed. The lights weren't on, but there was power. O'Conner and Burgess wore headbands with lights and worked their way down to the generators in the basement. The two rechecked

O'Conner's sketch and took up a position at a juncture of floor and wall with their equipment. Using a ground-penetrating radar unit, O'Conner confirmed there was a cavity below them. He made an *X* with chalk on the lower portion of the wall.

From one of the cases, Burgess produced a thick, heavy gray tarp and unrolled it—the replacement for sandbags used to muffle an explosion.

"This is made of a honeycomb of polymers and magnesium shielding," he explained.

Burgess set his low-yield charge and they put the tarp in place over the device. Wires led to a compact detonator several feet away.

O'Conner looked at his watch. He'd checked flight times from LAX for this evening. Soon enough, they heard the low rumble of an ascending passenger jet overhead.

"Fire in the hole," Burgess said, winking at O'Conner.

Burgess set off the charge. There was a flash from around the edges of the mitigation blanket, smoke and a substantial pop. They removed the shielding, which was scorched but not rent. Then, they used a set of two-pound sledgehammers to widen the hole they'd made.

"She's still not going out for lunch?" O'Conner said to Joyner over a secure line.

Joyner had been posted up at the arena for four days watching for Dale Deering. Del Norte's personnel were working long hours to prepare for the grand opening on Wednesday. The crew needed a crack at hacking her Omnikan. Joyner had determined it was the best option to get past the bunker's door without being detected. This was Saturday. Only four days until the opening.

"No. This close to the big day, she must have a ton of work to do."

"Shit." O'Conner paused. "Okay, well—"

"Hold on," she said. "She just stepped outside to the parking lot. Tired of being cooped up, I guess."

"About goddamn time." It was close to two in the afternoon.

Using a phone, Joyner tracked the bugged car of the Swashbucklers' vice president of public relations to Pann's coffee shop on La Tijera at the intersection of Centinela and La Cienega. Pann's was one of those Googie-styled restaurants once all the rage in the Southland. Joyner could hang back given O'Conner had previously planted the tracker on Deering's car.

Joyner parked and went inside. Deering sat at the counter, as did Joyner, keeping two open seats between them. Joyner saw the Omnikan clipped to her belt.

Perusing the menu, she reached into her purse to activate an apparatus of her own design. It was made to clone the operating systems of a targeted device. The Omnikan would have built-in safeguards, but Joyner bet that her invention could overcome them. She sipped lemonade through a straw and checked her progress. Eyeing the machine's readout, she surmised closer proximity was called for. Fortunately, Deering was engrossed in something on her phone as she ate her tuna salad. Centering herself, Joyner rose, purse strapped on her shoulder, phone to her ear as if she were talking to someone on the other end.

"Girl, please, I told that fool if he expects me to come in an hour before and set up, then how can that be considered off the clock?" She stood behind Deering, her purse close to the other woman's back at the counter. "Mm-hmm," she said in her throat. "Oh hell yes." She chuckled.

Deering turned her head to the side, a half-smile evident. She turned back.

Joyner gave it more time then, went on toward the restroom, doing her best to stay calm. In a stall, she took another look at her instrument. The readout was only at 60 percent complete. Giving it a beat, she washed her hands and went back out, where she saw Deering receiving her check at the counter. A plastic bag holding the remaining portion of her boxed lunch was also on the countertop. She'd probably gotten a call from the arena to return to attend to some damn thing or another, Joyner concluded.

Having no choice, as Deering headed for the exit, Joyner looked to fall in step behind her. But two other customers, an older couple, got between them. Joyner hurried to get around the two blocking the doorway. She walked quickly and, moving close, bumped their purses.

"Oh, I'm so sorry," Joyner said, again pretending she was still on the phone. "My damn boss is giving me fits." She waved her phone around.

"No worries."

Deering used her fob to unlock her car and got behind the wheel. Joyner walked away. In her car, she once more regarded the readout. It wasn't a complete download, but it was going to have to do.

• • •

Tuesday, the last day at Ice Station Zebra, the thieves used pry bars and sledgehammers to take the model apart. The four of them loaded the wood on a flatbed truck. Silvera had made previous arrangements for disposal. While he saw to that, the other three, each wearing black nitrile exam gloves, took down schematics and drawings and pulled up the tape. Using push brooms and dustpans, they swept up sawdust, nails, screws and anything else loose. The debris was dumped in a plastic garbage bag, tied up and tossed into O'Conner's trunk for disposal elsewhere.

"Time was we'd just torch the place," Burgess remarked as he worked.

"Ah, the good old days," O'Conner gibed.

Carrying the cameras she'd retrieved from outside, Joyner grinned at them as she continued past. Her mass of hair was swept back, a scarf around the front of her head. Each man wore a beanie. They got busy with mops, both microfiber and sponge heads. Now, in addition to their gloves, they wore respirator masks and protective eyewear. Vapors from various chemical solutions composed of peroxides, bleach and enzyme bases filled the air.

"We can't leave one follicle or skin cell behind," Burgess cracked.

"I brought wine for good luck," Joyner said. She placed a bottle of red on the table. The image on the label was a woman's face in a sepia tone. She had undulating Medusa-like hair and was wearing sunglasses. Valmont Vineyards was the vintner.

Silvera now returned, the three seasoned pros drank and

ate takeout food heartily, making small talk. Joyner was off to one side, chewing slowly, her face drawn.

"It's okay," O'Conner said quietly after approaching her. "Everybody gets butterflies before a job."

"You three have a funny way of showing it."

"We're just used to it. This is a big step out of line for you. From here on in, you'll find when you walk into a damn Taco Bell or an auto parts store, you'll be absently noting entrances and exits, and the weak spots to be exploited."

She smiled thinly.

"Eat, to keep your strength up. Don't throw your body off with a change in your routine." He gripped her shoulder.

There'd been a racetrack heist several years ago with a guy named Hanaford in on the score. He too had come to that point in the life of an aging thief where he overthought the possibles, everything that could go wrong. He got distracted at a critical point in the commission of the job and a blast from a shotgun tore out part of his lower stomach. He lived, but had to use a colostomy bag for the rest of his days. O'Conner hadn't thought about that for some time. He hoped it wasn't an omen.

"Just keep putting one foot in front of the other, Mavis. We're gonna come out on the other side."

"You're so used to this. You aren't terrified?" she said, frowning.

"Sure I am," O'Conner admitted. "But I learned the hard way that you have to channel the unsureness, the anxiety into some other part of you. Acknowledge it, but store it and you'll be able to call it up when you need its energy."

She shook her head. "You sound so goddamn calm."

"It's focusing. You have one goal. Keep telling yourself that and you'll be surprised how it evens you out."

"The mantra of thievery."

"Whatever works."

Joyner arched an eyebrow. "Do I get a gun?"

"Aren't you the one who said if we did this right, there'd be no need for guns?"

"You gonna use my words against me?"

They regarded one another for a beat. He then fetched a Beretta semi-auto. "Seen one of these bad rascals before?"

"Like I said, Charlie Mack taught me how to use one."

O'Conner held his open palm to her, the gun on it.

She took it.

He walked away. She wasn't a civilian any longer, he reflected. She was part of the crew.

That evening in his hotel suite, a distracted O'Conner at first didn't notice the knock on his door. He'd been assembling and disassembling the job in his head. There was another knock. Gun in hand, he went to the door and looked out the peephole.

"Room service."

"Right." He'd been so absorbed in his ruminations that he'd forgotten he'd ordered a snack. Gun tucked away, he opened the door to let the staffer in with the cart.

"Right there is fine," he said as the man rolled the cart closer to the table.

"Will that be all, sir?"

"Great, thanks." O'Conner tipped the man and he left.

O'Conner picked at his food, surprised he didn't have

more of an appetite. Usually before a takedown, he ate too much, his psychological tachometer revving. He replaced the cover and gazed out the window. He was wired and knew it was better to take a break than plow ahead.

O'Conner left the hotel and walked along nearby Vicksburg. He headed to Sam First, a jazz spot in a building fronting onto Century Boulevard just east of Sepulveda. Gwen and he had been to the club in the past. He arrived between the first and second sets and sat on one of the couches located around the inner perimeter of the place.

The bandleader, a saxophonist, finished his introductions. His quartet started off with an instrumental version of Joe Zawinul's "Mercy, Mercy, Mercy." O'Conner vibrated to the music, letting the tune flow through him. Relaxing him.

The musicians were now playing a rendition of "Summon the Fire." He considered having a drink—just one. But he decided against it. As the music continued, he reviewed what was to come.

As was the plan, only three would breach the bunker, but the whole crew knew the layout. Violating the vault would be O'Conner's and Joyner's responsibility. They knew how they were going to get in, and more importantly, how they were going to get out. With luck, there'd be no fast getaways, no cars burning rubber through the streets of Inglewood. Though they had made those revolvers in case it came to that. If they got caught, O'Conner decided, it would more than likely be on the premises—and more than likely, that would be that.

When the set was over, O'Conner walked back to the hotel. Back in his room, he removed from a drawer a packet of THC-infused gummies.

"Listen," Hong had said when he'd laid them on him. "It'll free your mind and won't leave you with a hangover."

"Yeah?" he'd said.

"Try 'em."

O'Conner opened the packet and chewed on two of the gummies.

He didn't play any music. But, sufficiently buzzed, at some point he put on the television, letting it play on low. The light from *2001: A Space Odyssey*'s surreal ending illuminated him in the darkened room as, satiated, he lay under the thin blanket.

In his lucid dream, O'Conner was in a space suit, like the astronauts in the movie. He was at the controls of a supersonic jet identical to the ones he remembered seeing on television when he was a kid. His copilot was a dome-headed robot with a rotating loop atop its head. The thing beeped and trilled. The passengers were giant talking fish who communicated in a language of various-sized bubbles. A heavy liquid, more like glycerin than water, filled the cabin. At some point, O'Conner turned the controls over to the robot and leaped out of the jet without a parachute. A jaunty samba tune played softly inside his helmet.

He floated down to a red clay terrain resembling the Mars he'd seen in the comic books laying around Griss back in the day. This was not a barren, airless planet, but one of multistoried spires and overhead roadways where magnetic powered trains zoomed by and oxygen generators were abundant. Helmet tucked under his arm, he walked along and found himself among the denizens of the lower levels. Somehow, he knew these were the people transported in flying autonomous cars that arrived at autonomous homes where you entered your choice for dinner on a keypad and the food was created by a synthesizer. He ate with them, having a meal of real fried chicken and pasta salad. Several live two-headed chickens clucked and pecked around him as he feasted.

Turning from the mutant yard birds, O'Conner saw Dr. Apgar in ceremonial garb sitting on a throne carved into rock. He had a long gray beard and an ornate ring on each finger. Like the Mandarin in those old Iron Man comics he'd read as a kid, O'Conner knew each ring had different capabilities. The doctor wore a beatific expression as he regarded O'Conner.

Apgar said, "While I don't agree with the road you've taken, OC, it can't be argued you haven't applied yourself."

He raised a hand and from one of the rings came a beam, enveloping O'Conner. A silver substance began to coat him as he was transformed into a version of the Silver Surfer.

At five in the morning, a relaxed O'Conner was showered and shaved. He then went over his mental checklist for the day. Briefly, he was gripped with the desire to call Gwen simply to hear her voice. He didn't. He took a moment and went out the door.

CHAPTER ELEVEN

"Welcome, one and all, to the new home of the Swashbucklers!" Palmer Van Noy declared loudly with a broad grin and his arms out wide. He stood at the entrance to the Del Norte Diamond.

Applause and whoops of encouragement went up from the crowd in the plaza. They had been gathering around Del Norte since six in the morning, having arrived by bus, limousine, car service, van, rideshare, the light-rail and even on bicycles for opening day. It was now several minutes past 9 A.M. Drones circled overhead. Mingling among the gathered were the thieves.

O'Conner, Joyner and Burgess, each with the necessary guest pass on a lanyard around their neck, separated from the masses and began making their way to the still-closed hotel. While none of the arena's security detail was patrolling the hotel itself, several security guards were dispersed along the surrounding plaza. Silvera was in the vicinity.

People began filing into the arena. Traditional media, podcasters and influencers talking on their phones were there covering the event as well. It was now ten twenty-two, and

O'Conner was nearest to the hotel. He reached into his pocket and depressed a tab on a fob.

The resulting muffled thud had heads turning as members of the crowd tried to locate the source of the sound. Some locked on to the closed restrooms on this edge of the park, where water whooshed from underneath the door to the men's half. O'Conner and Burgess had dropped explosive devices into two of the toilets. Because the park wasn't officially open, the two weren't worried about the bombs being flushed away beforehand.

The few security personnel closest to the structure housing the restrooms jogged over. One of them talked on her two-way as she moved. Another pulled up a set of keys on a retractable chain. Meanwhile, the three heisters went around the hotel's far end. The diversion with the park's toilets was a variation on what O'Conner had initially planned to do inside the arena. Blow up a few toilets and, as security dealt with that, sneak into the Finale Club. An emergency, though nothing dire enough to halt the festivities. Before entering, having left the door here unlocked, they put on supple gloves. No lights were on in the hotel and the shades and curtains were drawn. They had flashlights and the lighted headbands. They paused in a darkened hallway.

From her messenger bag, Joyner removed a stingray and flicked a switch, turning on the device. Taking a knee, she put on headphones with a built-in mic, which she adjusted. The gadgetry fooled mobile phones into thinking that it was a cell tower. Calls from nearby phones were being intercepted. On a screen, Joyner could see the phone number of the caller. Scrolling, she recognized one of the many numbers belonging to the Del Norte exchanges and answered the incoming call.

"Swift Fast Plumbing and Heating," she said. The company was local and minority owned. She listened. "Yes, of course. We'll send somebody right now. Where will he be able to drive in?"

O'Conner nodded, sending a signal on a burner to Ben Reynolds. They took the stairs to the basement and headed to the hole he and Burgess had made at the base of the wall. They slipped the coveralls they'd placed there over their street clothes and into the dark they went.

Silvera drove the transit van with the city's Water Works insignia. He gave a half salute, driving past the workers out on a service call at a sewer. His burner chirped. He turned at the next block, driving toward the K-rails several blocks around the arena. Those streets had been blocked since yesterday in anticipation of today's ceremonies.

Inside the arena, Hall of Famer Eddie Harper waved and laughed along with other past and current stars, clapping his oversized hands on shoulders while he swapped stories with the fans and press.

Beneath the floors, the three made their way through the long-unused Red Car Trolley tunnel, where O'Conner and Burgess had previously left two six-foot rollaway utility cases marked with Water Works logos and flattened equipment bags. All this was retrieved. Their lights shone through this opening onto a makeshift door. They stepped out of the tunnel onto earth and then to the door, which was about ten feet away. Through the door was the Del Norte power plant.

"How come they didn't seal the tunnel up again?" Joyner said.

"Is Van Noy lookin' to build himself a new trolley line?" Burgess speculated.

They'd come prepared to blow holes in the walls, then use large pry bars to widen them.

"We got a schedule to keep," O'Conner reminded them. "We can wonder the 'whys' later."

"Got it, boss," Joyner quipped.

Once under the arena, the three halted, making sure no power plant engineer just happened to be down here checking gauges. On O'Conner's phone, the three checked their location on the blueprint. Up a set of stairs they went, lugging the rollaways step by step. They arrived in a lit passageway. Overcoming a door's locks about midway down, they entered with their gear. The three went along until a turn and a much longer passageway took them around the rear of the arena. These hallways were intended to be used by service and repair personnel to reach various sections of the arena—including the backstage to the Finale Club.

The crew approached another door, which opened onto the hallway. Two voices floated through. The three froze. The door was designed such that, for the moment, the trio were blocked from view. An unmasked O'Conner crept closer, taking one of the ghost guns in hand. Joyner also had the Beretta in hand. O'Conner was poised to strike as soon as he saw whoever was there, but the door was closed again by an unseen hand.

Joyner began to whisper. "Do you think . . . ?"

O'Conner held up his hand for silence.

The three waited. No further sound reached them through the door.

After one minute, O'Conner, who had his locksmith tools with him, put his gun away and chanced picking the lock and opening the door again. In the robbers went, taking their equipment with them. They were alone in the empty Finale Club. The low throb of celebration seeped into the space from above.

Down the corridor they traveled. O'Conner got them past the locked, alarmed door to Van Noy's office. From there, it wasn't hard to find the entrance to the bunker. It was behind a wall panel that swung outward in the bathroom at the touch of a button.

As O'Conner had anticipated, the electronic lock was merely a combination setup. They'd figured the parents would have to make it easy enough for their kids to handle in case they got ate by the zombies and weren't around. They were also certain that if the door was tampered with, Van Noy would receive an alert on his personal Omnikan. That was why they'd sought to clone the operating system from the one Deering used. Joyner hadn't been able to complete the cloning that day at Pann's. But since then, she'd been at work on her mirror device, applying her knowledge to its construction as best as possible. Now it was pass or fail, the latter meaning jail.

Joyner held her version of the Omnikan near the lock as O'Conner worked on it. He noticed a slight tremor in her hand. Like Bora did with him, he patted her arm reassuringly.

She smiled weakly. Reaching the last stage before he tripped the lock, they agreed to count to three out loud together. They did. The door popped open.

"Shit," Joyner said, rushed, staring at the device.

"What?" O'Conner said.

"The signal wasn't rerouted like it was supposed to be."

"Fix it," O'Conner urged.

"I am," she said, quickly readjusting the settings.

Van Noy was in the middle of talking with point guard Sthal Casall and a reporter from ESPN when his Omnikan beeped. He unclipped the handheld device from his belt, studying its monitor.

"Excuse me for a minute," he said, walking away at a brisk pace.

Having slipped into coveralls, the thieves invaded the survival shelter, Burgess nodding his head appreciatively as they walked into the well-appointed living room area. The walls were lined with paintings. O'Conner recognized several, including two by Basquiat and a Lucian Freud.

"These are worth a ton," Burgess said, gesturing to the art. He popped a few M&Ms in his mouth from a crystal bowl of them on an end table. O'Conner noticed that it contained only yellow and green candies.

"We came for the money," O'Conner reminded him.

They set out for the safe, which was more than seven feet high and nearly six feet wide, set in concrete.

"It's a Mosler American Century," O'Conner told Joyner as he looked at it lovingly. "Stainless steel."

Joyner was about to respond but O'Conner's face went stone.

Burgess heard it. "The elevator just settled," he hissed.

"Shit," Joyner repeated.

"Be cool, we got this," O'Conner assured her. "Hide the rollaways."

A few moments later, Van Noy entered the shelter. He looked through a number of the rooms. In the large food pantry off the kitchen, he switched on the lights, looking about as he stepped farther inside. In a corner was a stack of cardboard boxes of toilet paper and paper towels. He stood near them, checking his Omnikan. Opposite this was an industrial air purification unit. O'Conner was crouched behind the machine. He had a leather sap in hand. If he had to, he'd subdue Van Noy, and they'd bind and gag him. He estimated not too many upstairs knew of the bunker's existence. Though probably the construction supervisor, Brad, did. How long would they have if someone noticed that the boss wasn't around? Would they figure he'd stepped out to take a call, deal with a problem, and wanted privacy?

O'Conner tensed, positioning himself to spring up, grab Van Noy in one hand and crack him in the head with his other hand, hard—a couple of times if need be. Footsteps retreated and O'Conner chanced a peek over the purification unit. Van Noy had opened the door to the walk-in refrigerator to look inside. O'Conner ducked back down. Several more minutes went by and the pantry was in darkness once again. The burglars came out of hiding and got to work.

Returning to the massive safe, Burgess told Joyner, "This

model was one of the types the company made just before it went out of business."

Joyner asked, "Are you going to explode the door?"

"The amount of explosives he'd have to use would not only be noticed, it would cave in part of the ceiling," O'Conner answered while he unloaded his tools, including a diamond-tipped drill bit and a heavy-duty drill. Joyner expressed surprise that the bit was small in diameter—about the size of a dime. O'Conner also removed a frame-like apparatus, a fixed rig to steady the drill.

Burgess told Joyner, "And a torch would be too imprecise, triggering the safeguards. The goal is to see inside the safe and manipulate the tumblers until they're aligned."

O'Conner produced an endoscope that he then set aside and a dog-eared ledger book. Each page had hand-drawn diagrams on them.

"This is the bible," he said, glancing at Joyner with a wan smile.

The ledger held the accumulated knowledge of the late box man Hector Gonzales. Each diagram detailed entry points for various makes of safes. The schematics were compiled from long-gone cracksmen and the jobs Gonzales had pulled over the decades. O'Conner came to a set of drawings and paused to examine them intently. He looked back at Burgess, who was looking over his shoulder.

"That's it." The bomb man tapped his finger on the page.

Joyner watched, transfixed, as they used a tape measure, a straight-edged wood ruler from the last century and a blue Sharpie to mark off crossing lines on the door of the safe. After double-checking their measurements, O'Conner wiped away the lines on the safe, leaving only a small blue *X*. He stared at this for several moments, then got the steady rig in place. It was attached to the door of the safe.

"This is where we go in," he told Joyner, finger pointed at the *X*.

Burgess said, "If we're off by as little as a sixteenth of an inch, we're screwed. Safeguards like lock plates are built into the box. Such that trying to get past those measures we'd be thwarted even if we suddenly learned the combination."

After unfolding a canvas chair they'd brought along in front of the safe, O'Conner attached a heavy power cord to the drill and plugged it into a wall socket. As the safe door was stainless steel, he couldn't use the magnet clamp he'd brought along. But there were other ways he was able to attach the fixed rig framework to keep the drill steady.

O'Conner went to work. The drill had to operate at a slow speed. Otherwise, he was telling Joyner, the metal would get too hot and that too would trigger what was called a mouse trap re-locker and probably a couple of other obstacles. The diamond-tipped bit began penetrating the door. Fine granules of steel, like pencil shavings, drifted to the floor.

Up above, a blues band began an instrumental version of "Parchman Farm" on the plaza. Among the gathered was Aesop Hong. When the band was finished with their set, he wheeled over to a woman in Swashbuckler attire.

"How are you?" he said amiably.

"Great. You?"

As they chatted, she noticed the sparkling pirate bulldog pendant he had pinned to one side of his chest. She smiled as she stared at the pin of the team's mascot, hearing Hong's steady, soothing voice—letting her objective mind recede, allowing the emergence of the subjective mind, entering the wish-fulfillment state, opening herself to suggestions. Hong made a pass over his hand with the other. Three small orange balls appeared in his palm.

"How'd you do that?" she said.

"Want to juggle?"

"I don't know how."

"Yes, you do." He handed the balls to her. "Go ahead. You can do it."

Hesitantly, she stared at the balls and started, working her hands up and down, fingers opening and closing. "Oh, this is wonderful."

"Yes, it is," he said.

Nearly thirty minutes had elapsed and it seemed as if the drill bit was no farther in than when O'Conner had started. Droplets of sweat dimpled his forehead. Burgess dabbed them away with a handkerchief lest sweat got in his eyes and O'Conner faltered. The bit had to remain steady and true.

On it bore, the time eventually stretching to an hour. The bit was now deeper in. At some point, O'Conner got out of the chair and Joyner took it away as he took a knee before the Mosler, all the while keeping the drill in place. An hour and forty-two minutes later, all three perked up as the speed of the drill increased. He was in.

Now standing, O'Conner took the folded handkerchief from Burgess and wiped his face. The celebration above would be winding down now. They had to move. Inserting the scope, O'Conner saw that he'd missed activating the hard plate by a thirty-second of an inch. He manipulated the dial and, through the scope, was able to align the tumblers. Fingers wrapped around the handle, he clicked it in place and the safe door opened.

At the same time, the panel they'd wondered about on the blueprints slid up behind them, revealing a recess in the wall.

"The fuck," Burgess whispered.

Through the opening stepped a mechanical black orb on four stout, hinged metal legs. Its dome rose to chest level. The construct atop the legs was the size of a large beach ball, more than four feet across. The thing was made of a translucent black material. Lucite, O'Conner considered. A red circle moved beneath the surface like a roving eye. Without further hesitation, O'Conner slid across the floor like he was stealing second base, using a leg sweep to upend the spider robot. As he did, an electrical current, like from a wireless taser, sizzled from the eye. Scrambling to his feet, O'Conner got behind the robot as it too righted itself. Joyner went left and Burgess, right.

The spider contraption skittered forward and lanced a charge at Burgess which struck and sent him over, groaning. The red eye swung around to Joyner. She dove out of the way. The eye revolved toward O'Conner and unleashed another electrical bolt which he took on his back as he turned. His knees wobbled. The machine stalked toward him.

"The drill," he hollered to Joyner, who was the closest to it. "Drill this fuckin' thing."

On her stomach, Joyner was now under the robot. She grabbed the diamond-tipped drill and drove it into the robot, notching up its speed. The bit penetrated the Lucite shell.

Sparks sizzled from the hole and the robot fell over. Lights flashed inside the spider and the air became thick with the smell of fried wiring. The eye dimmed and went out.

"You did real good, Mavis," O'Conner gulped, laughing nervously. He turned to look at his back, lifting his shirt. The skin was blackened where the spider's electrical bolt had struck him.

"What he said, kid," Burgess echoed. There was a burn hole in his overalls from the spider's electrical attack.

Back on track, the thieves returned to the opened safe. Banded bills were stacked on two pallets at the rear of the vault. One of the pallets was stacked noticeably higher than the other. There were built-in shelves with gold bars stacked on them too, along with compact locked boxes. O'Conner was sure the boxes contained diamonds. Maybe cryptocurrency wallets. He took two of them.

"Too bad gold's so damn heavy," Burgess lamented.

Hefting a handful of banded cash, O'Conner said, "You do realize this is a hell of a lot more than twenty-one mil?"

"And in that, I am comforted," Burgess said straight-faced.

The thieves loaded the cash into large nylon equipment bags and the rollaways. They stuck the dead robot back in its receptacle and managed to pull the panel back down in place. The metal shavings were swept up and flushed down the toilet. The vault door was closed, the dial spun to relock it. O'Conner used a drop of liquid metal from a tube to patch the hole he'd made in the safe's door. He smoothed it out with the business end of a blade screwdriver, then scraped away the excess. The light gray color didn't match the rest of the door, but you had to look close to notice the difference.

"Let's hustle," he said. "Dealing with that monstrosity got us behind schedule."

O'Conner was limping from his encounter with the robot. Joyner eyed him.

"Don't you worry," he said, "I can run if we have to."

She remined silent.

There was the elevator used for the food deliveries. But the crew weren't going to use it, as the loading dock the elevator let out onto was in a section of the arena. They left, but not the way they'd come. They were heading toward the bunker's secondary exit that let them out in the park, not far from the bathrooms.

The three emerged from behind the bathrooms. They were dressed as before, though none of them had IDs around their necks. In the plaza, attendees were handed goody bags as they exited. Inside were a variety of Swashbuckler novelties such as the Del Norte arena snow globe and a limited-edition Opening Day moisturizer by Zelb. Joyner went in another direction, away from the other two, rolling one of the cases, topped with a nylon equipment bag. If Van Noy was outside, he couldn't be seen. A security guard was heading toward O'Conner and Burgess.

CHAPTER TWELVE

"What the heck is going on?" the guard demanded. "They sent you all out for just a backed-up toilet?"

As intended, the guard noticed the Inglewood Water Works insignia on the side of the utility cases filled with money.

"The trouble is in the lines," O'Conner said.

"Yeah, I phoned them," a new voice said.

Ben Reynolds approached in work clothes and a Day-Glo safety vest. He was carrying a toolbox and wheeling a motorized drain snake. "I've got the toilet unclogged on this end but could tell it was a more involved matter."

"I see," the guard said.

"We traced it to a valve cluster a few blocks away," Burgess added.

Silvera had parked the pretend Water Works van in the VIP section. Having a city vehicle, he was able to talk his way past the barricades cordoning off the arena—once the guard there was called over to hear about the toilets backing up. Silvera was now behind the vehicle, opening the rear double doors.

"Is there another outdoor bathroom for the park?" Reynolds asked the guard.

"No, just this one."

"Water fountains?"

"Yeah, sure."

"Show 'em to me, will ya? I might have to turn off the main line for a few minutes. If so, I'll need you to communicate with your boss before I do."

Hesitating, the guard nonetheless said, "Sure, come on."

He led the way. O'Conner and Burgess started toward the van.

"OC, is that you?" a voice called out.

O'Conner turned to see a smiling older man ambling toward him. "Keep going," he muttered to Burgess, whose jaw had tensed. Silvera was looking between them, waiting to help with the rollaways.

Favoring his bruised leg, O'Conner walked toward the man while calling up the face and body from memory. "That you, Doze?" He wore a sport coat, and under his matching Kangol cap there was gray in his hair. He had a trim, snow-white beard, thinner too, but yeah—it was him. Miss Val's old boyfriend.

The other man threw his arms wide, laughing. "None other, baby boy." He hugged OC tight, then released him. "How are you doing? You kinda limpin' there. You okay?"

"Pickleball injury," O'Conner said. "It's nothing."

Looking him up and down, Doze said, "What are you doing? Last I knew you'd left town." Noting the equipment case, he said, "You work for the city?"

"Sort of. Consulting, Doze."

"Ha, ain't nobody called me that in forever."

"Okay . . . Preston."

He frowned at O'Conner. "You know my real name?"

"Sure I do."

Doze looked past him toward the van at Burgess and Silvera. "You guys consult for the water department? But you got these cases."

"That's why we're consultants. We know what we're talking about."

O'Conner had to get out of here. There was no time for chitchat.

"I've worked for the Coliseum Commission for the last twelve years. Can you believe that?" Doze said.

"That's great, Doze." O'Conner grimaced. Deering was passing by several feet away.

Doze gestured to get her attention. "Dale, hey, want you to meet this dude."

Deering veered toward them.

"Known this guy since he was knee high," Doze enthused. "OC, this is Dale Deering, who handles publicity for the Diamond. Say, what does the OC stand for? How the heck don't I know that after all this time when you know my name?"

"Good to meet you," she said, clearly distracted.

O'Conner dared to look straight at her. "Likewise," he responded as they shook hands.

"He consults for the water department." Doze sounded like a proud uncle.

Deering frowned upon hearing this. "Consult how?" Her gaze shifted to the van and Burgess and Silvera loading in the large cases. "You need all that equipment for a backed-up toilet?"

"The backup you all had today. That's a good example of what we do. Troubleshoot." Was that the best you can come up with? he chided himself. Sweat hadn't broken out on his brow yet, but it was threatening.

Doze said, "Man, we got to get together."

"Of course," he said.

Out of the corner of his eye, O'Conner glimpsed Van Noy passing behind Deering. They exchanged a nod. She took out her phone and began to type. Was she texting Brad, asking about Water Works consultants? Van Noy glanced his way—and slowed. O'Conner met his gaze. The only time they'd seen each other before was more than twenty-five years ago. A shadow passed behind the tech magnate's eyes but was soon gone. He went on, followed by men that appeared to be his personal security.

"Why don't you come inside with me, and I'll introduce you to some of the people running this joint?" Doze leaned in. "I might even be getting a job in the front office here," he said.

"I'm on the clock, you know how it is. Give me your number, okay?"

Then Deering said to O'Conner, "Excuse me, could I get your name, sir?"

"Wonderful!" someone exclaimed.

Heads turned. Hong was in a cleared circle on the plaza. He'd taken his silk scarves from where they were tucked inside the pad he sat on. As he twirled them around, while also leaning back in his chair and this twirling too, he made several doves appear from the multicolored folds. There was enthusiastic applause as they took flight.

Doze and Deering turned back as the Water Works van pulled away. O'Conner waved curtly from the passenger seat at his friend from childhood who looked at him, confused.

Later in the afternoon, having remained in the area, Burgess and O'Conner returned to the neighborhood around the Diamond in a nondescript vehicle. The barricades had been removed. They retrieved Burgess's explosive devices from where they had been planted, like a city trash receptacle, in the event the robbers had to make a heated getaway. The IEDs were stored once again in their padded carrying cases. They returned to the hotel and the power room. With their hands, whisk brooms and dustpans, they cleaned up the evidence of their previous incursion, then tossed the debris inside the abandoned Red Car tunnel. They sealed the hole with sheet-rock and spray-painted this over. Then they rolled a service cart in place to cover the repair. Once the cart was moved, the ruse would be discovered—but not too soon, they hoped.

A single drone passed over them as they crossed the empty plaza. They didn't look up. O'Conner supposed if Van Noy ever did get a line on them, the billionaire could bomb them from the skies with one.

Toward dusk, the crew assembled in a motel room in El Segundo. Tachmann was there too. The place overlooked hills of automated oil pumpjacks. Seagulls perched on the walking arms of the jacks, slowly riding up and down. The haul from today had been divided up into neat piles on the bed and onto the floor.

"Oh my sweet Lord," Burgess said.

"Not bad, huh?" O'Conner said to Joyner.

The count was thirty-six million dollars.

"Uh-huh," she said, overwhelmed.

She'd brought a canvas bag with her and removed two bottles of wine, a corkscrew and plastic cups. O'Conner noted that the bottle was from Valmont Vineyards, the same vintner as before. She uncorked the wines and poured. She said, "A toast is called for."

Burgess and O'Conner exchanged a look.

"What?" she said.

"It's considered bad luck among some in our profession," Tachmann said. "A silent pledge is conducted by each, if at all."

"Whatever," she said. "To silent pledges."

She took a sip. They all did.

Outside, the seagulls rode up, then down.

Not long afterward, back in his suite, O'Conner rested, propped against the bed's headboard, having hidden his cut of the stash in a prearranged location. He'd rubbed the strawberry on his leg with Icy Hot while enjoying some vodka over ice.

Three days later their theft hadn't been detected—as far as the thieves could tell.

Everyone had scattered, but O'Conner had stayed in town. He decided to give it another day, then leave for home. Hopefully Gwen would be there. His secure phone buzzed. It was a text from Tachmann. The message was simple and direct:

NEW OPPORTUNITY. COME SEE ME NOW.

O'Conner texted back he was on his way. He drove to Tachmann's home in La Quinta in Riverside County, east of Palm Springs. Arranged on an acre and a half of land, the large two-story Spanish colonial revival rose on a hillock. The landscaping leading to the mansion was composed of native plants and rock formations. O'Conner had last been here when the rise was covered by a lush lawn. There was still an assortment of pygmy and bottle palm trees framing the house, obscuring some of the structure from view. The front curtains behind the large arched window onto the living room were closed. O'Conner didn't text and didn't knock on the front door. He went around back to the pool.

The patio and low walls here were made of flagstone. There were round glass tables with umbrellas, and cushioned metal chairs all about. He looked inside the pool house, staring for a beat. Then, gloves on, he opened the door and went in. Soon, he went back outside. He made his way to the sliding door to the patio. Here the curtains were pulled aside, and he could see into the house. But the way the place was designed, his view was restricted by a curved geometric room divider made of polished walnut. He discerned no movement through the holes in the divider.

O'Conner lifted one of the decorative wrought iron chairs. Raising it over his head, he used its legs to shatter the glass in the sliding door. The shards were still tinkling as he tossed the chair aside to free his hands and unlimber his gun. The door to a closet set beside the front door banged open and a man with a gun burst out.

O'Conner came in low around the divider shooting upward at the man, who returned fire, chipping the wood. Both used suppressors on their respective weapons. Only O'Conner's shots were accurate.

The man fell back into the open closet, his legs sticking out like the Wicked Witch of the East crushed under Dorothy's house, though his toes didn't curl up. There would be two of them left behind, O'Conner estimated. But the second one was clever. He hadn't shown himself. O'Conner was certain he was here, on the first floor. The plan had to have been to take him alive. The first man's job was to get the drop on him. The second would show, and together, they'd tie him and take him back to their boss, he reasoned.

The breaking glass might have been heard even though the houses in this area were some distance apart. The gunfire? He wasn't sure. But O'Conner was confident the law wasn't on its way here yet.

The other ambusher was either in the kitchen or down the hallway to a study-turned-TV room, if he remembered the layout correctly—an advantage he hoped he had. Standing stock-still, scanning back and forth from the two possible locations, he made a choice. A swing door separated the kitchen from the dining room which was also visible through an archway. Assuming there was an exit out of the kitchen onto the grounds, had the second man gone out that way and was circling back to try and surprise him? Or was he lying in wait and would open fire through the door once he heard a creak on the floorboards? Except he was supposed to take O'Conner alive. They were after the score, and the dead couldn't talk.

O'Conner knew he was walking into a trap when he received the text. He'd come prepared. If this was a chance at a new job, Tachmann would have gotten in touch with him using one of the dead drops O'Conner maintained, like he had for the meet with Joyner.

There were three names Tachmann could give up. O'Conner hadn't mentioned Silvera, Reynolds or Hong specifically. O'Conner had said he wanted someone to oversee transport but that could be any number of people he and Tachmann knew. So it was his name and maybe Burgess's. As to Joyner, Tachmann had an emotional connection to her. He'd have done right by the young woman.

More of his earlier suppositions gelled into place. Whoever was behind this knew Tachmann. They had been or were doing business together. There's no way these two would have gotten the best of Tachmann on his home turf. Was this unknown boss known to O'Conner? Time to find out. He had to flush the other hitter out.

Calling out toward the kitchen, he said, "You want a cut? I know a way you can earn it."

No answer.

"Don't know what the hell you're making, but I'll pay you to leave me the fuck alone."

He paused. Still no response. Had the second man been on his phone calling in reinforcements? Doubtful. That was a sure way to prove to your boss you were a rooty-poot. Whoever was on the other side of the kitchen door was smarter than his dead companion—or more recalcitrant.

"Look, man, I can slip away and you'll have to explain to whomever why you fucked up. But let's be real, I want to know who's coming after me and I'm willing to pay for the information. 'Cause we both know whatever bonus you was supposed get out of this ain't gonna be the number I'm talking about. Not that you got a bump coming now anyway."

"You're full of shit," came a reply through the door.

"I'm not the one on the spot. You're supposed to bring me back to your honcho. You know I'm sitting pretty on a pile of ducats. And when I'm gone today, I'm gone for good. You'll have a lot of explaining to do."

"I'm not a fool. You didn't roll up in here with money in your back pocket."

"Tachmann has to have a safe in this crib. And if you know anything about me, you heard I know how to crack 'em," O'Conner said.

"You gonna let me stroll on out and hold a gun to your head while you work the dial?"

"You think I'm a fool?"

"Then what are you saying?"

"Throw your piece out."

"Fuck that," he said.

"Yeah, I understand, sort of hard to establish trust at this stage of things," O'Conner said conversationally. "Well, I'll see you."

"Hold up."

"What?"

"I'm not comfortable being a snitch."

"You're gonna be more comfortable reporting back to the head boy after this fuckup?"

The unseen man was silent.

O'Conner said, "By the way, I gather the plan was to drive off in Tack's Jag." He was guessing the three of them had come in one car. "Me in the trunk."

The second man kept silent. O'Conner continued. "I can make a call to the sheriff's department and tell them about shots fired and this Jag was seen leaving the scene. Of course, being the good citizen I am, I'll lay the license plate number on them too."

"Whatever, man."

"Oh right," O'Conner said, "you'll switch out the plates. Seems I better just shoot out the Jag's tires before I leave."

"Hey, hey," the second man implored.

"I'm waiting."

"Look, I'm coming out with my hands up, okay?"

"Okay."

"I'm trusting you."

"That's right."

The kitchen door opened slowly. Out came a Black man around O'Conner's height, though of a slightly slimmer build. He was younger, in his late twenties, the thief estimated. He wore his short blondish dreads in a bleached high-top style. He had a tat on the back of one hand. A Japanese ideogram.

"Gun," O'Conner said, gesturing with his. "Thumb and index finger only."

He let his semi-auto fall to the carpet. "Satisfied?"

"Lift your pants legs in case you tucked a steak knife in your sock."

"You got trust issues." He did as ordered.

"All right, come on." Again, O'Conner gestured with the

gun and told the man to walk down the hall in front of O'Conner to the study that was also the TV room.

"What makes you think it's in there?" the second man said.

"A hunch."

They went into the room.

"Sit on your hands cross-legged on the floor right there," O'Conner said, pointing the gun to indicate where he meant. The other man complied once again.

"How many names did Tachmann give up?"

"Two. He talked about a Burgess and an O'Conner. You must be O'Conner."

"How'd you guess that?"

"He said you were the brains."

"Only two names?"

"Yes, sir."

O'Conner stood, looking around. He tapped a knuckle along one section of the wall, then another.

"You lookin' for a secret safe?" the second man said.

"Something like that."

Tachmann's distressed antique desk was positioned in a corner of the large room. There was also a large flat-screen set mounted on a wall and a couch before this, three different remote controls spread across its cushions. On a coffee table made of polished driftwood was wine in a wine glass. Audio and visual devices including a DVD player filled inset shelves on one wall. Additionally, Tachmann had a '70s-era reel-to-reel unit. O'Conner went over to the assortment of devices and studied them closely. He flicked on switches and turned dials, then zeroed in on the front of the tape machine.

He felt along a seam along the side of the machine. He clicked on a lever and the reels began to revolve.

"What's that?" the second man said.

Evidently, the youngster had never seen a Radio Shack ad.

"Ancient history, like sea scrolls." O'Conner worked a few knobs on the tape player and there was a soft sound of a lock releasing. He swung the face of the tape machine open, revealing a square cavity in the wall. Inside were stacks of banded cash.

"Damn." The second man started to rise.

"Stay where you are," O'Conner warned.

He plopped back down in place. "Whatever you say, my guy."

O'Conner removed the money and placed the cash on the coffee table. His quick count indicated roughly half a million. He figured there was more cash hidden around the house, but this would do. From the pile, he stacked a hundred grand and stepped back, keeping the money and the second man in his line of sight.

"What were you told about Tachmann?"

"That he was about to realize a lot of ducats."

"Nothing more specific?"

"Dude I work for ain't what you'd call chatty. He can be when he wants to be but not with his boys, if you see what I'm sayin'."

"Do you know how he learned about what Tachmann had been up to?"

Shaking his head slowly side to side, he answered, "I do not."

"But they've done business together?"

"For sure."

Fist tightening on the gun, he said, "One more question, did you—"

Throwing his hands up in protest, he cut O'Conner off. "Naw, bro, uh-uh. That fiendish shit was all Teaflake. Me and Twin Slim, the one you shot, we only tied him up. But on my grandma's head, the blessed woman who raised me, I swear, boss, that wasn't none of me."

"No shit," O'Conner said.

"You know him?"

Hearing Teaflake's name caused the fear he felt that night in the Hi Hat to return. But he quickly reminded himself he wasn't a kid anymore. Goddammit, though, he should have noted it.

"I'm certainly no damn Whoopi Goldberg when it comes to dispensing advice, but seems to me you might want to change up your lifestyle," O'Conner said to the man.

"Yes, sir, I had been thinking on just that."

"Leave your phone. Take the smaller stack and the car keys and get out of here."

"You ain't got to tell me twice. I got a lot of miles to put between me and Teaflake." Putting his phone on the coffee table, he then hugged the money to his chest and rushed out of there.

O'Conner finished surveying the room as the man's footsteps faded. The room also held a built-in bookcase. On this was a framed photo showing a younger Tachmann, Charlie Mack and a smiling teenager between. Joyner. O'Conner took the photo, frame and all. There might be other items in the house linking Joyner and Tachmann, but there was no time to do that kind of search. He did, though, pause at the desk and saw the leather-bound appointment ledger upon it. He opened it and leafed through the pages. Being of a certain age, Tachmann eschewed modern technology and wrote down his schedule and notes. He checked what Tachmann had written for the dates following their meeting at the restaurant. His notes regarding the lumber and so on were written in a coded shorthand. No sense leaving this around, he reasoned. O'Conner took it with him and left the study.

O'Conner found a soft-sided bag in a hall closet and put the calendar and rest of the money in it. Back in the front room, he was surprised to find that the dead had risen. A trail of blood across the carpet led to the open front door.

"Fuck," O'Conner said, looking outside. He didn't see Twin Slim. He wasn't about to go hunting for him and take a chance on being seen. Had the hitter he let go scooped him up?

A bottle of wine sat on the kitchen island, a cork in it. Valmont Vineyards. The wine Joyner had brought to the split, he noted. The craggy sepia face of a man who looked like a cross between Charles Bronson and Danny Trejo stared back at him.

He turned and went back out via the swing door. He wasn't worried about leaving his shell casings. He always loaded a gun wearing rubber gloves. The gun would be disposed of soon enough anyway.

In the pool house again, O'Conner took a last look at the bound and gagged Tachmann. He'd been worked over thoroughly. In addition to a puffy, discolored face, one of his pupils was slit in the middle, the halves staring into nowhere. His crooked little finger with its gaudy ring had been removed with a pair of garden snips. The severed digit lay on the floor in a circle of blood. The gold ring gleamed as if daring an observer to take it.

"Goddammit." The sweet score had gone sideways and Tachmann had paid the price. O'Conner wasn't of a mind to grieve; they both knew this way of life was likely to kill you. But still, he'd known the man a long time.

An approaching siren brought him out of his reverie. Rounding the side of the house and looking out onto the street, he didn't see anything untoward. As he drove away, making his way past residences, he pulled over as an ambulance passed by on its way to Tachmann's. Maybe Twin Slim had made it to a neighbor's house or had been seen collapsed in the street.

O'Conner supposed if he believed in signs like Bora did, running into Doze at the robbery should have made the hairs on the back of his neck prickle. Satchel Paige had said, "Don't look back, something might be gaining on you."

"Fuck," he repeated, a fist pound to the steering wheel. When he was a kid, Tachmann and Teaflake had been running buddies turning over hot cars. All these years later, and they'd remained crime partners. Well, hell. The only thing to be done was to deal with this shit. He compartmentalized and focused. Car back in gear, knowing he still had to alert Burgess, he called Joyner, simply telling her they needed to meet and to be prepared to hack into a phone. He'd give her the bad news in person.

CHAPTER THIRTEEN

Mavis Joyner put a hand to her mouth after O'Conner told her Tachmann was dead.

"They tortured him."

"Yes," he affirmed.

Joyner turned away from him, wiping a palm across her wet eyes.

Hand on her shoulder, O'Conner said, "I know he meant a lot to you, Mavis." They sat on a park bench, birds chirping and toddlers laughing and stumbling about in the nearby playground. "But he went into this business with his eyes wide open."

Joyner kept her hands pressed on her knees, looking at the ground. "Doesn't change the foulness they did to him."

O'Conner waited. Anything else he had to say would sound trite.

Eventually, she turned to look at him. "I assume you have a plan?"

"And you're part of it."

"I damn sure better be."

"We start with this."

O'Conner handed her the phone he'd taken off the second

man at Tachmann's house, explaining who it belonged to. She plugged in the devices she'd brought and soon overrode the phone's security protocols.

"What do you want as the new PIN?" she asked.

"I'm dumping this thing once we scroll through."

Together, they looked though the phone. There were numerous texts between Teaflake and Boris—the owner of this phone, they determined.

"He was Russian?" she asked.

O'Conner described the man he'd encountered at Tachmann's. He made notes of the texts. Several times, Teaflake mentioned he was at Grace's.

"Sounds like a restaurant, not a woman," O'Conner reflected.

When they were done, he said to Joyner, "Wherever you're laying your head, stay put."

"That's it?"

"You're just getting started."

A tight smile came and went on her face.

Once O'Conner had discussed her next task, they parted ways. Heading toward his car, he dropped Boris's phone onto the asphalt of the parking lot and stomped on it, obliterating the device. What he needed was now on his legal pad and in his head.

Teaflake Strock had, like O'Conner, funneled his monies into legitimate enterprises. O'Conner didn't know this directly, but mentions of Teaflake had surfaced over the years when criminals gathered, engaging in their own kind of shop talk. While O'Conner followed up on Dimitri "Teaflake" Strock,

Joyner was doing a deep dive into all things regarding him. She hadn't confirmed it, but O'Conner was sure she'd reach out to her contacts in the hacktivist community A Minus One for help.

O'Conner left a message for Gwen on her secure phone. "There's been a complication. Though not from the direction we'd worried about. I'm going to handle it." He felt being terse was the best way to go. There was nothing to argue about or discuss. He had to eliminate the threat. Maybe she'd make peace with that or not. Either way, he didn't expect to hear back from her now.

A few days later, checking one of his dead drops, O'Conner found a parcel someone had left for him. It bore no address or any other markings. Inside was a thumb drive. It was from Joyner. On his laptop he opened the file. Not only were there Teaflake's various investments listed with addresses and phone numbers, but his tax records as well. Several businesses were scattered around various municipalities. There were the usuals, including exotic car dealerships. His attention caught on a coffee and sweets shop in the Ladera Heights section of L.A. Grace's.

O'Conner looked at pictures of the coffee shop online. From what he saw, Grace's was a neighborhood hang. There was a shot of what he took to be a spoken word event as well as people playing chess on tables on a patio out front. In one photo, a smiling Teaflake posed for the camera with a group. O'Conner hadn't seen him in more than two decades, but as with Doze, he instantly recognized Teaflake. He was heavier in the middle than when O'Conner last laid eyes on him. Seemed having a joint that sold baked goods meant you got to sample your products for free. Adding up the years, he calculated Teaflake was in his late fifties. There was some gray in his hair, but his face was not heavily lined. Larceny agreed with him.

O'Conner extended his stay at the Presidium Hotel. So far it seemed their theft hadn't been detected by the civilians. That might change when the next food swap was done. Though, even when Van Noy figured it out, it wasn't like the robbery would be publicly acknowledged. Conversely, Tachmann's torture and death had made the news. The local newspaper that usually covered the mundane doings of city council meetings and profiles of local businesses highlighted the deaths on its digital front page. Local TV news had also picked up the story, adding that the identification of the younger dead man was pending and that the investigation was ongoing. Which meant the cops knew who he was, O'Conner reasoned.

"It's our understanding the man found shot near the house may have been alive when he was rushed into surgery. He expired on the operating table," the newscaster added.

The following morning, O'Conner drove to Grace's Coffee and Fresh Baked Goods. The enterprise was in its own building at the Centinela Shopping Center, which also included a Vons supermarket, a Pasta Desoro chain restaurant, a cigar lounge called EXP and a Gold's Gym. A Maybach registered to Teaflake was parked in a designated slot at Grace's. Casually, O'Conner walked inside. If Teaflake was around, he figured, unlike Doze, it was unlikely he'd recognize O'Conner all these years later. He was just some smart-mouth kid who soon had been dismissed from his memory. Tachmann might have given up his name and maybe a quick description, but so what?

The coffee emporium was spacious. Art lined the walls. There was also an enclosed side patio upon which was an art piece, a freestanding, undulating slab of burnished copper. He ordered a medium coffee with a shot of espresso. The barista asked him if he wanted to add a chocolate croissant to his order. He was tempted but then he recalled Teaflake's expanded waistline and declined.

He sat at a table beside one of the large windows. As was usual in today's coffeehouses, several people were typing away on their laptops, earbuds in place. A woman in her yoga togs and a bookish-looking white man with round-lens glasses read hard copies of the newspaper.

There were a few gray heads in there as well, O'Conner observed. Some sat at a larger table talking to each other while two others were at another table playing chess. The overall feel of Grace's was of comradery and community. Two characteristics he would never have associated with the cut-throat Teaflake. There was a rack stacked with local newspapers including the giveaway *Wave* newspaper, which O'Conner remembered from his youth. He took a copy.

Sitting there pretending to be reading the newspaper while he had his coffee, O'Conner idly considered how best to kill Teaflake. Despite the Maybach in the parking lot, O'Conner wasn't positive Teaflake spent much time here, but he would reconnoiter the place for a few days. Tomorrow he might post up in his own car in the parking lot, keeping Grace's in view.

Some minutes later, two men entered and walked past the counter. One was Black, the other Latino. The Black guy was taller, substantial build with a pirate-style hoop earring in one ear. From this drooped a teardrop diamond. His partner was shorter, toned in a slimmer fashion. O'Conner clocked his fancy sneakers. The two appeared at ease with one another. A neon arrow didn't have to flash over them for O'Conner to understand these two weren't here to sit and sip. They entered the only hallway in the shop and disappeared from view.

O'Conner folded over the newspaper and remained sitting for a few minutes. He got up and, at the counter, asked another barista for the code to the bathroom. He glanced down the hall on his way to the bathroom. There was a door at the end. It was unmarked but there were two locks on it. Could be the two were in the office discussing with Teaflake the news from La Quinta. Up till now, had they considered Boris and Twin Slim were both in the wind? Did they think O'Conner had taken Boris prisoner? Torturing him, for all they knew, about the doings of Teaflake, like they'd done Tachmann?

Stepping out of the bathroom, O'Conner paused as the door at the far end opened. Three men stepped out. O'Conner lingered at a display case, seemingly considering a bottle of infused water or some other damn overpriced item. Passing behind him with the other two was an older man. Teaflake.

"Get over there and talk to the girlfriend again. We got to get out in front of this. This here ain't done by a damn sight."

"On it, Tea," the Latino said.

Standing outside on the front patio area of Grace's, O'Conner scrolled on his phone, watching the two underlings. They walked along an aisle of parked vehicles toward the Vons. Teaflake got in his late model gray-on-black Maybach and departed. The other two got into a black Aviator and also drove away. From O'Conner's angle, he couldn't make out their plate.

O'Conner walked to his car and got on the roadway to head back to his hotel room. By his side, in the lane across the double yellow, came a driverless Overland taxi. He regarded the near silent empty robot car as it passed.

Back at the hotel, he worked out in the gym with weights and got in some cardio on a stationary bike. He could simply tail Teaflake one evening and put a bullet in his head. But would that stop his two henchmen or whoever else his bruisers were from coming at him? Also, he needed to know how the gangster had tumbled to the score. What else hadn't he accounted for? He was certain Teaflake had put money on the street in an effort to find him. So far, he was only a name and he intended to keep it that way.

The next day, O'Conner returned to the shopping complex. To change it up, he parked nearer to the Pasta Desoro, which nonetheless offered him a view of the comings and goings at Grace's. The place was designed exactly like the rest of them. Here, he could sit at the bar and, through the window framed on either side by shelves of wines and hard liquor, see the front entrance to the coffeehouse. Teaflake's Maybach was back in its reserved slot. This confirmed for O'Conner the man spent time at this office rather than two others Joyner's spreadsheet had indicated. He'd made a circuit of the parking lot and hadn't seen the Aviator driven by the other two. There were several black Aviators about, but the one of interest had red piping, and he'd also noted the vehicle's distinctive aftermarket rims.

From Boris's phone, he knew their names. The larger individual was Paul Blackwell, nicknamed Glide. Ecks was Saul Escobar. Perusing the menu, he ordered the lunch version of the chicken parmesan and the zuppa Toscana.

"Would you like a beer with that?" the bartender asked him. She was a pleasant-faced middle-aged woman with dirty blond hair.

"Just seltzer from the tap with ice."

"Very good."

Several minutes later, as O'Conner enjoyed his soup, he saw Teaflake walk from around Grace's—apparently exiting a rear door. He was dressed in slacks and a pressed shirt. He entered the Pasta Desoro and sat down at the bar, two stools away from O'Conner.

"Afternoon, Dimitri," the bartender greeted.

"How you be, Abby?"

"Like this and like that," she answered.

"I hear you."

"The usual?"

He briefly rubbed his hands together. "Feel like a change is due, ya know? Let me get the chicken and shrimp carbonara."

"Salad, not soup, and a taste to accompany your lunch?"

"Why the hell not?"

The bartender produced a bottle of Hennessey Black from below the bar. She poured a healthy draft for Teaflake and placed it before him. O'Conner continued having his soup. While Teaflake had his cognac, he scrolled through his phone, occasionally stopping at something of interest on his screen. More than once, he chuckled at whatever he was viewing. O'Conner's meal came and he ate leisurely. He kept his eyes on one of the two silenced flat-screens behind the bar. The one he watched had on a replay of a Swashbucklers game from last season. Teaflake's food arrived.

Another person entered and sat at the far end of the curved bar. Teaflake's phone announced a call by playing music. O'Conner recognized the tune. It was an instrumental track of an old J.B.'s number, "Pass the Peas."

"What's going down, baby girl?" Teaflake answered. He listened for several moments, a shit-eating grin on his face. Then, Teaflake responded in a low voice, hand cupped over the phone and his mouth. Lascivious promises were being exchanged.

O'Conner activated the cloner he'd gotten from Joyner. He placed the phone on the bar, pointing it at the other man. O'Conner made sure to finish before Teaflake, leaving an amount of food on his plate. He paid in cash and left a tip. The two men shared a brief look and O'Conner left.

He walked around the parking lot looking again for the particular Aviator. He didn't spot the vehicle, but did see a white guy sitting in a too-clean Jeep Cherokee. He was parked along an aisle from which Grace's could be seen at the far end. The man had fawn-colored hair and he appeared to be studying a sheet of papers. Various people were about, leaving the store, walking to the Gold's Gym. O'Conner wasn't worried about being conspicuous.

Teaflake emerged from the Pasta Desoro working a toothpick between his teeth. He went directly to his car and got in. O'Conner was taking a circuitous route, but now quickened his pace to get to his Cadillac. He'd concluded in the restaurant that he might as well kill him today. He could handle any fool from Teaflake's men, post his taking out their jefe. Behind the wheel of his car, O'Conner moved out, contemplating his coldly arrived at decision.

Teaflake's Maybach turned onto La Cienega, heading south. The light was red, and he came to a stop at the intersection with La Tijera. The Jeep, which had pulled out of the lot, was two car lengths behind the Maybach. The light changed and the two cars went on. O'Conner purposely hung farther back. Was the man in the Jeep following Teaflake too or was it merely a coincidence? This dude might be a cop, he assessed. The killings had gone down in Riverside County. The sheriff patrolled La Quinta and would be the one handling the case. Twin Slim had likely been identified and Teaflake was on his rap sheet as a known associate. Ladera was also patrolled by the sheriff's department, though this was the L.A. County version. It could be that a call was made and the local deputies had been enlisted by their colleagues in the east to keep eyes on Teaflake.

O'Conner got in the lane to the right and, increasing his speed, got closer to the Jeep to the left of him. He eyed its plate, repeating the numerals and letters under his breath to lock them down. At the next opportunity, he turned right to leave Teaflake and the Jeep's driver.

It didn't take O'Conner long to confirm that the Jeep's plates were protected under the DMV's exempt category. A sure sign the car was a cop's undercover vehicle. O'Conner ventured it was a sheriff's department investigator behind the wheel. Teaflake Strock had been around a long time, managing to avoid prison or the grave, the fate of several of his contemporaries. Over time, there had to have been at least one, if not more, task forces tailing him, comprising personnel from various police agencies assembled to catch slippery dudes like Teaflake. It made sense he'd be an ongoing person of interest as far as the law was concerned. O'Conner couldn't ignore this. Eliminating the man was going to require an awareness of just what kind of eyes were on him.

Joyner had supplied O'Conner with Twin Slim's real name and record. Joshua Johnston had been a standout basketballer at Manual Arts High School in South L.A. He'd gotten a partial sports scholarship to a college out of state. For whatever reason, or set of them, he was gone before his third year. Reading through his record, O'Conner saw only two arrests and those were for minor infractions. He did note that at some point Johnston worked at one of the sport rims and tire shops Teaflake owned.

O'Conner checked the cloner he'd used on Teaflake's phone at the Pasta Desoro, which had captured the number of the person who called him. He didn't need Joyner to find out who the number belonged to. O'Conner was able to find a name and an associated address by using a reverse telephone directory using a different IP and a firewall. The address was tied to a location in Denver.

People often kept their old numbers long after they'd moved elsewhere. He entered the woman's name, Dolly Rand, into another app. Several addresses came up, in and out of California. Comparing those to the addresses associated with Teaflake from Joyner's information, including ownership through holding companies, he found two matches. More searching and he learned Rand was a noted sculptor. That was her piece in Grace's. Another surprise about Teaflake. He and an artist were intimate.

"Amazing," he muttered.

Leaving the hotel, O'Conner drove to the Fox Hills Mall to do some clothes shopping. Not long afterward he was clean and neat in suburban attire back behind the wheel of his car. He arrived at the address of the condo in Brentwood. The condo was on the bottom end of a curved street with residential homes farther along. It was permit parking on this street and the others nearby. A few of these signs allowed two-hour parking from 8 A.M. to 6 P.M. As Brentwood was still pretty much a white area of town, O'Conner reflected, his Black ass sitting in a car for any length of time was going to garner unwanted attention. He parked at a meter several blocks over on San Vicente and walked back. As far as he could tell, there were no cops sitting on the condo building.

He intended to pick the lock to the front door leading to a short foyer and the elevators of the six-story structure. Before he could go to work, the elevator doors opened and out stepped an older woman in a big floppy hat with her dog on a leash. This was no purse-sized bug-eyed pooch but a panting Labrador. As she got the door open, which swung inward, the dog strained at the leash. It was lunging at a bird that had landed on the upper part of a potted plant in the corner of the foyer.

"Asimov, easy boy," the lady said.

O'Conner held the door open for her.

"Thank you, young man," she said, tugging the dog out the door. The bird flitted away.

"No problem," he said, stepping inside.

O'Conner took the stairs down to the garage. There, he spotted Teaflake's car in what he took to be an assigned slot. The space next to it was empty. Dolly Rand must park her vehicle there, a 1970s-era Chevy pickup registered to her.

Going through a door with a crash bar let O'Conner out to a short set of steps leading up to the sidewalk. He considered his options for staking out the building when another idea occurred to him.

Back in his car, he called Silvera. He'd already alerted him and the others about what had gone down regarding Tachmann. He filled him in on the new developments.

"This is gonna be playing into stereotypes, but hear me out."

"Not like you to be all SJW, O'Conner. Go ahead," Silvera said.

CHAPTER FOURTEEN

Tachmann's graveside funeral service was attended by an assortment of people. A handful O'Conner recognized, including a one-handed bomb man named Spicer. He was the only attendee in a checked sport coat. Tachmann's sister was there. O'Conner had never met her, but Joyner had provided a picture. Joyner wasn't present. She'd wanted to go, but O'Conner had convinced her otherwise.

Dressed in camo and, like at the Zelb compound, using his binoculars, O'Conner watched the watchers from hiding. After the slipshod episode when he'd shot Twin Slim and wandered off, O'Conner was determined to be as detailed as possible. Taking his cue from the cops, he surveilled the proceedings—you never knew who might show up at a funeral. The cemetery was larger than Grantford, its older graves marked with headstones as well. Swaths of land swelled toward knots of trees, and there were a few mausoleums on the grounds too. He was more than a football field's length away from the service, nestled among the tree line up along one of the rises.

O'Conner spotted the man with the fawn-colored hair. He wasn't in a Jeep this time, but a more sedate vehicle parked along a roadway that wound up a hill above Tachmann's grave. Nearby, two groundskeepers in matching green-colored khakis had just arrived on a golf cart.

O'Conner had also spotted another man viewing the attendees from afar from his vehicle. A disturbance caused him to look around, hand moving to his gun. It was a deer. The animal and the man regarded one another for a few moments. Then, the animal wandered down the hill, pausing now and then to nibble at the lush grass.

The service ended. Several mourners surrounded Tachmann's sister. One of the two groundskeepers lowered the coffin into the earth using a mechanical winch. O'Conner recognized a woman in slate gray and diamonds. She'd invested her ill-gotten gains into building a real estate empire. She tossed a rose into the hole as the mourners departed.

O'Conner watched as the man with fawn-colored hair and the other man surveilling the service got out of their cars and were met by a third man. The one with the fawn-colored hair was medium build. That he weight trained was evident by his heavy chest and upper arms. One of the other men was also white—in his late forties or even fifties, O'Conner estimated. He was over six feet tall, his salt and pepper hair cut bristly short. He had a full trimmed mustache—a copstache, O'Conner thought, grinning. The last member of the trio appeared to be Latino, likely also in his forties. He wore sunglasses. A big watch decorating his wrist glinted in the sunlight. They seemed to be talking out of earshot of the two groundkeepers, who were busy filling the grave from the mound of previously dug earth. The three soon departed in two vehicles.

When the grave was filled, one of the groundskeepers handed several folded-over bills to the other. They spoke a bit in Spanish and the man who handed over the bills headed toward the trees. O'Conner descended to meet him. He'd stripped off the camo, carrying it rolled up under an arm. The other groundskeeper was below, evening the dirt using a handheld tamper.

"Got some shots of them," Silvera was saying to him, grinning. "They're with the sheriff, as you suspected."

"You overheard them?"

"Nope. But I grew up in the Gardens in Pacoima, homes. The older gabacho with the 'stache got a bracelet on. See, not all the time do deputy gang members have tats. Old school like homeboy here has a bracelet you can take off and on. This gang's been around more than a couple'a generations. They're called the Interceptors."

Silvera removed the camera he'd rigged to his belt buckle and plugged it into the monitor.

"These bad hombres go back to before when I was a kid. Some of them were shot callers at substations, let cartel members move their product through town for a cut, planted guns. You name the shit, and they did it."

As Silvera talked, he swiped to a picture.

"The Gardens was in L.A. County, not Riverside," O'Conner noted.

"Don't mean him and a few of his boys didn't transfer." Silvera enlarged a section of the picture. "Here's the bracelet."

O'Conner saw what at first appeared to be a medical alert bracelet. Taking a closer look, he could see the oblong-shaped tag on it was engraved with a capital *I* inset in the middle of a skull with flaming eyes. Like others in the Southland, he was aware that over the years there had been various investigations about deputy gangs. These cliques went by various names, such as the Executioners and the Vikings, operating out of several L.A. sheriff substations.

"The cliques are patrol, aren't they? These boys are plainclothes."

"They had to start on patrol," Silvera observed.

"And maybe beefing with another clique, they got pushed out of L.A.," O'Conner said.

"Who knows?" Silvera acknowledged. "So now what? Gang or no gang, they've got the scent somehow, and are gonna keep birddogging."

"Great, two sets of greedy assholes to deal with," O'Conner drawled wearily.

"If I didn't know better, I'd say you were being ironic."

Thumb to his chest, O'Conner said, "We worked for the swag. We put in the work. We took the risks."

"I'm on your side, brother. I wanted a nest egg. What choice do we have but take these fools out?"

They discussed next steps and Silvera departed. O'Conner took a few minutes to stand next to Tachmann's grave. He meant what he'd said to Joyner about thieves like them—they knew the deal. He wasn't going to get all weepy, dredging up memories of the man. They didn't have that kind of relationship. But still, he'd been a stand-up guy. Played straight and didn't cheat anyone he did business with. Damn Teaflake.

"Think and grow rich," he said, quoting Reverend Ike.

O'Conner returned to Grace's. Teaflake's car wasn't there. He went shopping for food at Vons, as there was a kitchenette in his suite. Back outside, Teaflake's car still wasn't there. Now, though, the Aviator was parked near the coffeehouse. O'Conner deposited his groceries in his trunk and walked inside Grace's. Ecks and Glide were at a side table playing a game of chess. He got a coffee and, back outside, did a circuit of the area around Grace's. He didn't spot any of the deputies from the funeral.

Off the freeway and on the streets nearing his hotel, he spotted a parked lunch truck offering Japanese Mexican fusion food. He stopped and waited in line to order. He had them box his food, which included two beef sukiyaki tacos.

"We only use Japanese A5 wagyu," the young woman taking his order informed him. She seemed quite pleased by that.

"Righteous," O'Conner said, having a vague knowledge of what she was talking about.

Back in his suite enjoying his meal after reheating it in the microwave, he sat, the Theme Building behind him out the window. The newscaster had said Twin Slim was clinging to life when he'd been taken to the hospital. On the ambulance ride to the hospital, a deputy must have accompanied the wounded man, rattling questions at him. O'Conner envisioned Twin Slim lying on the gurney. In between calling for his mama and the Lord, Twin Slim muttered a few names, perhaps mentioning the millions. The diligent deputy followed up with his department's investigators.

But there was a piece missing. Was it just the idea there could be millions involved that made the Interceptors interested in going after the loot? Surely there'd been other hoods bleeding out, hallucinating about them stacks waiting for them in heaven along with a few big-booty video vixens. When O'Conner was younger, he certainly believed such would be his reward. Why had these veteranos believed Twin Slim?

He was resolved bumping off Teaflake was still the way to solve his problems. Yes, it was cold-blooded murder, but this was kill or be killed. With him dead, the sheriff's gang would assume it was one of Teaflake's rivals who did him in. Possibly someone else looking for the loot. He knew how to rig a car to make it look like an accident. But a civilian might get hurt. No, the simplest was the best. Shoot him.

The best time to take out Teaflake was at night. He couldn't very well tail him all over town. Getting a tracer on his Maybach was dicey. When parked at Grace's, the car could be seen through the windows. He could try the condo but again, to know his comings and goings involved sitting on the place and that was a no-go. One of the residences listed for Teaflake was in Westchester, which wasn't far from his coffee shop.

The split-level home was built into a hill in a tony neighborhood overlooking the Ballona Wetlands. The first night O'Conner was there, no sign of Teaflake. The second night, the same result. He'd give it two more tries. On the third night, Teaflake's car pulled into the driveway a few minutes before eight. The garage was such that it was below this part of the house but Teaflake didn't put the car inside. From where O'Conner was perched, he saw the arrival through his night vision binoculars. He started to move out, one of the ghost revolvers in hand.

A black van roared onto the driveway, right behind the

Maybach, bumping the rear end. The car's alarm whooped. Out of the black van came three men in dark clothes and balaclavas.

The gangster cursed, taking a couple of swings, but a crack to his head from a Maglite got him wobbling. Apparently Teaflake wasn't strapped. The men threw a dark sack over his head and hustled him inside the van. The sliding door clicked shut and off the van went.

O'Conner, who had stepped back into the shadows where he'd been hidden, emerged again to watch the vehicle reach the end of the block, then turn. As he returned to his car, a door opened behind him, a neighbor looking out to see what had caused the commotion. He kept walking and the door closed to his back.

Those goddamn Interceptors black-bagged Teaflake and O'Conner had no idea where they were taking him.

They might go at him like Teaflake had done with Tachmann. Or maybe, O'Conner considered clinically, they would use the iron fist in the velvet glove approach.

Returning to the park, O'Conner and Joyner had subs and chips from a sandwich chain. They sat at one of the bolted-down picnic tables. Like before he'd chosen a spot affording him a panoramic view of their surroundings. Joyner may have turned in her gun, but he'd come strapped. No more mistakes, he'd admonished himself.

"I was able to put names to the Interceptor faces," Joyner said, her air-gapped laptop open before them.

He studied the information on the screen.

"The one with the copstache is Bob Winslow. He's got a

boat if you're interested. The three of them enjoy going on it on weekends to fish, drink beer and talk about how lesbians are ruining this country."

He raised an eyebrow at her.

"Except for the fishing part, the rest is conjecture. He has a presence on a fishing blog. But it's accurate, I'm sure. There's also internal reports tracking these three and others suspected of being in their gang, or another."

"What else you got?"

"I've got home addresses for them, vehicles they own, divorce records and more."

"You do good work."

She grinned.

O'Conner ate heartily as they continued to discuss the Interceptors.

Later, at the hotel, O'Conner listened to a multipart podcast Joyner had recommended. It was called *Badge Life, Gang Life* and documented the nefarious activities of deputy gangs, including the Interceptors, the Cavemen and the Wayside Whities.

A pillow under his head, he lay on the couch, fingers laced over his stomach. Somewhere around the third episode, he dozed off as one of the victims of a deputy gang talked about being held at their black site. He wasn't beaten but doped up, he'd said. The podcast's host stated their researchers had been told by an anonymous source that, allegedly, the chemical used was derived from the enhanced interrogation techniques conducted by the CIA. Used at Gitmo in particular. The location of the black site, the host added, had yet to be determined. By then, O'Conner was sleeping peacefully.

CHAPTER FIFTEEN

The cloth sack was removed from Teaflake's head. He blinked hard. Two construction work lights on poles with tripod bases were angled on him, shining harshly into his eyes. He was lashed to an aluminum chair by heavy cable. Handcuffs were clasped around his left wrist.

A baritone voice spoke to him from beyond the lights. "It doesn't seem you have your hands on the money yet. But who are you looking for? Your main wonder twins, Glide and Ecks, have been all over the place shaking the trees. We know it's someone associated with the late Tachmann, who you fellas did in."

"Go fuck yourself."

A low chuckle. "Look here, playboy. You do understand the position you're in, don't you?"

Teaflake didn't respond.

The voice continued. "Far as we can tell, this mysterious O'Conner, the mastermind according to the late Mr. Johnston, is an alias. And he's done his best to not get on any kind of criminal justice databases. Not like the homies running bragging about their crimes on Instagram, videoing themselves committing larceny and shit." The voice chuckled.

"The name does come up a few times but none of those studs fit the bill. Hell, one of'em is eighty-five and living in a trailer park in Boca Raton."

"What can I say?" Teaflake replied.

"Indeed," the man behind the lights drawled. "Where was the heist pulled? Been nothing like that on the wires. Wires." He scoffed. "I'm dating myself, ain't I?"

"If you say so."

The Interceptor continued. "Now Tachmann, he'd shown up in a few 'known associates' from over time. Going back to the days when he was a go-between for a hot car ring hanging out at the Crimson Lounge."

Recognition flashed behind Teaflake's eyes.

"Yeah, homeboy, I remember that place. You and Long Box Tolles were vying for the dope king title of the 'hood and you won out. Long Box got put down one night damn near right in front of the bar and nobody saw nothin'. Some heavy ducats were recovered at the scene. It was assumed he'd probably had more on him. For sure, his bar was one among several places he used to keep his loot. Just like you had spidey holes before you washed your ill-gotten gains into legit businesses."

"You seem to know a lot about Tolles."

"Don't I though?"

"Anyway, that's old, stale news, man. Long Box had a lot of enemies."

"True that. As you do too. But a few days before Long Box met his demise, a body was found in the Athens area. Heart attack resulting from a hell of a lot of cocaine he'd ingested. Looked like this older gent dropped dead beside a

Newberry's at night. The day before he'd returned by train from a visit to family in Kansas City. Still had the stub of his ticket in his pocket. Blanking on his real name but he was called Prof, or Professor X, like in the comics."

"Yeah, so?"

"So this cat had a photographic memory. Eidetic is what it's called. The talk on the street was he worked for you. That you were smart not to write down facts and figures but had this walking, talking computer at your beck and call. Taught over at El Camino at one point. But he liked his vices which you also parlayed since he didn't mind keeping company at the Crimson Lounge. Even with his drink on, what he saw or heard stayed in his head. Whispered back to you, I suppose."

"Where you going with this?"

"That there's been eyes on you a long motherlovin' time, player," he gibed.

"'Cause of the Prof?"

"Think about all them chippies he liked to party with, throw money around and play the big man."

"One or more of them hos gets got on a humbug and would say anything to get out from under," Teaflake said. "So you're a cop, huh? You were on one of them cooperation of agencies taskforces always getting put together back when to nose around."

"About the mastermind."

"Like you said, I got no idea who this O'Conner is. Big dumb white guy it sounds."

"Like me, huh?" the other one snorted. "Anyway, we figured you tortured the hell out of Tachmann and got him to spill on the deets of the robbery—a heist of a buttload of cash, the dying Mr. Johnston said before departing this world. The late Tachmann gives up a name or two. You get him to put in a call. Your boys lie in wait, but you didn't hang around for the top dog. How come? Something more important to take care of?"

Receiving no response, he went on. "Well, you were gonna have him bagged and gagged and brought back to you to pull his fingernails out at your leisure."

Teaflake took a deep breath.

"Man, I gotta say the old fella was tougher than Ajax apparently. I mean, whowee, I've seen some nasty shit, but what you all did . . . my, my."

"I got nothin' to say to any of that."

His interrogator continued. "Look here, one of your other boys, Boris Chalks, was Johnston's running buddy since they was in juvie together. Only seems he ain't around lately. The only blood at the house was Tachmann's and Twin Slim Johnston's. Did you speculate this O'Conner snatched Chalks to make him talk?"

Teaflake glared straight ahead.

"Now, post the dustup at Tachmann's crib, you're making moves to find the slippery O'Conner and so are we. And for reasons of greed, you were willing to turn on Tachmann, a dude you've done business with for years. Probably going back to those Crimson Lounge days, ain't that right?"

"You the one tellin' it."

"I like that you're able to keep your sense of humor." His interrogator paused at the buzzing of his phone.

"Yo," he answered beyond the lights.

Teaflake heard him walk away, a door opening then closing. He couldn't tell if he was more angry or scared at this moment. Either way, if he lived, he was going to fix these mutherfuckahs. Soon the door opened and again closed. His interrogator's footfalls came toward him.

"Where was I? Oh yeah. Tachmann's had his hand in all kinds of nefarious shit. What about this time got your nose open? Is it more than cash? Gold? Jewels?"

Teaflake responded, "Guess you was always busting high rollers but it finally occurred to you, you wasn't gonna be one."

"Oh, I've had a taste now and then, don't you worry. Sad to say though, we all get old," he said softly. "I'm fuckin' due. I'm owed."

"The fuck you talking about? That your reason for a trip down memory lane?"

"Just tryin' to get my head around what went down, my guy. Guess you figured you was owed too. Or was it a deeper, Dr. Phil kind of thing? Like did it eat at you? Why does this old white dude get them stacks when it should be me? Or was it you wanted in on the score and he froze you out?"

Teaflake said, "What do you think you're going to get out of me? You know I know only what you and your boys have. Which ain't shit."

"This O'Conner can't be no kid, he's clearly been around awhile. He's not on anybody's radar which means he takes care of the details. There's no doubt there is more than one stud taking the dirt nap 'cause he's had to chill 'em. He and Tachmann went back a ways too, I'd wager."

Teaflake's brow furrowed as he considered his interrogator's speculation.

The interrogator was quiet, then he said, "Sure glad we had this talk as we get our ducks in a row."

"The hell you talkin' about?"

Now the man stepped in front of the intense lighting. He was wearing a Hawaiian shirt and cap, his mustache tidy and lush. He held a syringe. "As we want to get our association off on the right foot, we decided beating the living shit out of you would be getting off on the wrong foot."

"What is that?" Teaflake muttered, eyeing the needle.

"Truth serum."

"There's no such thing."

"Close enough. Let's just say it relaxes your inhibitions. Allowing you to possibly babble something useful. To mutually benefit us . . . partner."

"That's right," a new voice said. He appeared from behind the interrogator. He was older, looked like a bean counter to Teaflake with his large, round owlish eyeglasses and short, graying hair. He came over and, using a butterfly knife he unfolded with a flourish, cut away a section of Teaflake's shirt at the crook of his arm.

"Got a nice vein right here," he said, tapping the arm.

The man with the mustache inserted the needle and depressed the syringe's plunger.

Teaflake shifted, wincing. He started to squirm and sweat even though the room was cold.

O'Conner returned early the following morning to surveil Grace's. He'd come today in the fake Water Works van. Inglewood was about a ten-minute drive away. People could assume whatever they liked regarding the van's presence—a municipal worker playing hooky, for instance. Sitting behind the wheel, he worked a variation of the dodge the deputy had perpetrated. He pretended to study a clipboard of paperwork leaning against the steering wheel. Behind him in the cargo area, he'd brought along a pistol grip shotgun hidden under the trick floor Silvera had rigged, as well as a few other items he thought he might need. In the glove box was his leather-bound lock-picking kit.

The Aviator arrived less than an hour later. Ecks and Glide exited and went inside the coffee shop. Was this a normal morning for them, or were they aware Teaflake had gone missing? As far as he was concerned, if the Interceptors worked Teaflake over then killed him, great. The bent deputies had no fix on him. But experience had taught him not to be complacent. He'd better know who was doing what, even if Teaflake was dead.

To vary his routine so as not to be conspicuous, he got out of the van and went into the Vons. He did need coffee and was desirous of obtaining an avocado. After making his purchases, he walked around again, then returned to the van. A woman with a toddler walked by, staring at him. Maybe she was a resident of Inglewood and would report him for lollygagging, O'Conner considered, amused. Around ten, the two came out of Grace's, got in the Aviator and drove away. O'Conner followed them. He was sure they were heading to the house in Westchester. He took a different route.

The van would be out of place parked on Teaflake's street. He parked several blocks away and walked to the house. By the time he got to the block, the Maybach was heading in his direction. He maintained his stride. At the wheel of the car was Ecks and beside him in the passenger seat, Glide. Sitting in the back was a lumpy-faced Teaflake.

"Goddamn," O'Conner muttered as he continued on.

The car proceeded, making a left at the corner and then disappearing from view. O'Conner went to the gang lord's house. Like a lot of these mid–last century homes, it had a side door to the half basement along a passageway between the house and a retaining wall cleaved onto the hillside. In this way, he was unseen from passersby.

The side door, like the others and the windows in the house, was on an alarm. He used the emitter like he'd done at the hotel at the Del Norte arena. Once the alarm was tricked, he picked the lock and got inside, gloves slipped on.

On a dining room table there was an open laptop, a short stack of papers next to it. The papers were of a general nature. He considered taking the laptop and asking Joyner to crack it. He wasn't worried about making Teaflake even more suspicious with its absence. Teaflake's shotgun marriage to the crooked deputies was doomed from the start. When they put the snatch on him, O'Conner reconstructed, they'd made it understood they could get to him any time they wanted, kill him any way they wanted. Then came the proposition—we're going to be partners. They'd work together to run O'Conner to ground. That way, they'd get to the money and split the take down the middle, fair and square.

O'Conner almost laughed out loud. Naturally neither side believed such an ending was going to happen. Teaflake had been put on his back foot and he needed an advantage. O'Conner could use this to his favor. He continued probing the house. In a large living room area was a geometric sculpture composed of various types of rusted and stressed metals. This must be Rand's piece, he concluded.

Searching farther, O'Conner found a gun strapped to the underside of a coffee table and another in the base of a lamp in the master bedroom. There was a hidden catch, and the weapon was revealed once a section of the base swung outward. There were also several bowling trophies on a shelf. Fuckin' Teaflake was a bowler. It just got stranger.

O'Conner paused at a wine alcove in the kitchen with racks of merlots, cabernet sauvignons and what-have-you. He wasn't much into wines but did enjoy sitting and talking with Gwen while sharing a bottle. Idly, he gazed at the bottles, suddenly wrapped in memories of domesticity. Would he have those times again with her? She hadn't called him back after he'd left his message. He wondered, what would Dr. Apgar make of him at this moment, desirous of domesticity yet lured back to risking his freedom and life?

O'Conner took a few wine bottles off the rack. Some were the Valmont Vineyards brand. The bottle in his hand had a rapper's sepia-toned face on the label. This was the third time he'd encountered the brand. That was no coincidence. The vino couldn't be that goddamn good. He returned the bottle to the shelf. O'Conner looked in the refrigerator and, spying a plastic bottle of orange juice, removed it and poured himself a glass.

He sat at the dining room table with his refreshment. Not wishing to be petty and leave a wet ring on the wood, he folded a paper towel into a precise square to use as a makeshift coaster. He weighed several options, the next moves to make. A bluebottle fly buzzed around his face, then ear. He didn't swat at it. The insect flew about some more, finally landing on the papers, rubbing its front legs together with enough friction to start a fire. The bug walked about on the white expanse, stopping now and then as if deciphering the words. Eventually the bug took off, for some reason ignoring the sweet allure of the sugary juice.

As if an automaton with his motor switched off, O'Conner sat unmoving in the chair he'd angled from the dining room table. His hand lay flat on the table, the glass on the square of the paper towel at the crux of his thumb and index finger. Nearly twenty minutes ticked by. Then, as if a signal had been received from a remote source, his hand closed on the glass. He brought it to his mouth and almost drained the contents. He got up and, taking the paper towel and glass with him, went back into the kitchen. He placed the glass with the small amount of juice left in it on the countertop. Once more the folded paper towel was underneath. He found it comforting to leave this for Teaflake to see.

O'Conner left the house by the front door, not particularly concerned whether a neighbor might see him. He doubted any of the Interceptors were babysitting the pad. They'd put the squeeze on Teaflake, so they'd hang back for the next few days, see what developed. O'Conner knew the Interceptors operated out of the La Quinta substation. He'd already enlisted Ben Reynolds to make inquiries through third parties and confirmed Teaflake had offered a bounty for information regarding him. This also meant the bent deputies were rousting their confidential informants trying to surface him as well. Burgess's name had come up, Reynolds learned.

"From the way I understand it, neither Teaflake nor the deputies were onto him like they are with you," he'd told O'Conner.

Tachmann hadn't given up Burgess when he was tortured, O'Conner concluded. Saggz and Tyler and Kanser and Lanny Murser knew O'Conner had been looking for the explosives expert. He was of the opinion the first three hadn't ratted, but he was sure Murser had for a few thousand—and no doubt was resentful after getting threatened by O'Conner. If he made it out of this alive, he'd fix that motherfuckah. O'Conner's plan now was salting disinformation amid the underworld grapevines tended to by all manner of low-level snitches. Keep the chumps searching for him off-balance, he thought, strolling toward his car. He was going to make sure something developed to winnow down his opposition.

O'Conner and Joyner met at a different park this time. Still, as this was another weekday afternoon, the children present were either babies in strollers or toddlers with their mothers or nannies. There were a few men here with the kids, along with old-timers fishing at one of the county-stocked ponds. O'Conner and Joyner walked around.

"Pretty sure I know why Teaflake killed Tack," Joyner began.

"Something to do with wine?"

"Damn, you do know your shit."

That night in the Hi Hat replaying behind his eyes, O'Conner said, "Teaflake's a hyena. Been feeding on the spoils of others a long time."

"Valmont is a vineyard Tack owned."

"A vineyard?" O'Conner said.

"I checked Santa Barbara county records today."

"Why?"

"Since we last talked, Tack's sister got in touch with me." Joyner held up a hand at his questioning look. "I'd given her the number to one of the encrypted lines. Given she's his next of kin, naturally she assumed she would inherit the Valmont winery. In fact, it's so stated in his will. Yet one of the subsidiaries controlled by Dimitri Strock has taken out papers to quitclaim the land. She tried to resolve the matter, but no dice. She turned to me hoping I might have knowledge she didn't possess."

"Knowing you were an investor," O'Conner concluded.

Joyner nodded.

"That's why Teaflake didn't wait around for me," O'Conner declared, remembering the cuffs only around one wrist of the tortured man. "Once he forced Tack to sign the vineyard over, he left to transfer title."

"Motherfuckah," she muttered. "I assumed Tack was killed over the robbery."

"In a way, he was," O'Conner said. "He must have tried to barter information about our takedown to save his baby, the winery. It's the damn confluences," he said, recalling Dr. Apgar. "Is there gold or oil under the land?"

They stopped before another pond. Around the curve, a kid was being held back by an adult, laughing with delight as ducks flapped around her.

"The wine business is huge. Tack bought the place way back, when he was young, when California wine came in a box. It was a joke. Now, despite droughts, the pandemic, continuing wildfires, the wine business generates some eighty billion of the worldwide total."

"Tack saw that happening all those years ago? That's why he bought the winery?"

"Hell if I know. He always had a different story as to what interested him in buying it."

Several ducks waddled ashore near the giddy toddler and her caretaker.

Continuing, Joyner said, "Slowly but surely, Tack built it up from hundreds of acres to thousands."

"And you were looking to invest more with your cut of the haul."

"Tack was about to take the label national. He was planning to leave La Quinta and live up there. Change his name and whatnot. Finally, away from thieves like you."

"Teaflake owns several exotic car lots. Tack used to be involved with a hot car ring way back. Pretty sure that's how they first got connected."

"I could find out," Joyner offered.

"Doesn't matter now. Because whatever their ties, Teaflake not only wanted in on the winery but being the greedy fuck he is, he wanted it all."

Looking out past the water, O'Conner said, "I ain't mad at Tack for giving up my name, Mavis. How much pain can any one person take?"

She regarded him as they continued to walk.

"I've got more in mind for you to do," he said.

"Good."

Like a miniature Frankenstein's monster, the squealing

child chased the ducks stalking around the edge of the pond. She stomped about, rocking from side to side gleefully. The birds flapped their wings but didn't fly off.

"Okay then," O'Conner said as the two watched the kid having fun.

CHAPTER SIXTEEN

Teaflake took the elevator to his car parked at the condo building in Brentwood. Walking toward the vehicle, he noticed the loop of a wire in the front tire well on the driver's side. He bent and removed a tracking device.

"Those motherfuckahs," he said, stomping the device into useless pieces.

Bob Winslow guided his catamaran toward the shore. On board were his partners, Harvey "Hache" Hemsworth, who wore an Angels cap on his fawn-colored hair, and Gaige Avilla, in his prescription sunglasses as usual. The three had spent the day fishing and drinking beer on Lake Perris. As Winslow got within deboarding distance, the other two waded onto land. Avilla then backed up Winslow's F-150 pickup, guiding the trailer down the slope toward the boat.

"A little to the left." Standing next to the trailer, Hache signaled to Winslow. The latter made the corresponding adjustments as he straightened out the bow and brought the craft forward. There was a definitive sound as the boat snugged into place on the trailer.

"Tighter than a nun's coochie," Hache pronounced decidedly.

"You would know," Avilla cracked, now out of the truck.

Winslow joined them on shore. Lowering the tailgate, he opened the back of the truck and paused. "G, was you looking around for something?"

"No, what do you mean?"

"Check it," he said, pointing.

The other two looked at the bed-over toolbox straddling the opposite end of the cargo area. The heavy-duty combination padlock securing the box was in place but the lock hadn't been fully pushed back onto its shackle. Winslow took the lock off and opened the lid. He rummaged through his tools, as such were kept in orderly fashion. He stored a gun in there. It was still present.

"Not a goddamn thing is missing," he muttered.

"You think the thief got interrupted?" Hache said.

"You?"

"Fuck no." Avilla pushed his sunglasses atop his head.

"Don't seem like internal affairs style," Hache added.

"No, it doesn't."

Idly, Winslow shifted a wrench and, frowning, reached for the object the tool had covered. He held a baggie containing white powder for the other two to see.

"Coke?" Avilla wondered.

Winslow parted the ziplock. Wetting his little finger, he dipped it into the powder and withdrew the granules. He then dabbed the stuff on his tongue to taste it. "Fetty, I'd say."

"The fuck?" Hache looked around as if prowl cars on silent were rolling up on them.

"A setup," Avilla intoned. "Teaflake."

"Oh, that motherfuckah," Winslow said, a sardonic twist to his lips.

"Man, I'm telling you, I know that motherfuckah," the bleary-eyed individual claimed. "Or I did, but I got a line on him."

"That right?" Glide looked at his partner, Ecks, winking. Both sat in a corner booth by the window overlooking a strip mall. They were at the Silver Spoon restaurant in Inglewood having their lunch. A number of framed pictures of players from the Swashbucklers and Barons, the pro football team, were framed and mounted on the walls.

Ecks regarded the man who'd come over to their table. Slightly stooped over, he was dressed in a shapeless polo shirt and flared checkered slacks from some long-gone era. Forties to maybe even sixties, Ecks estimated. The hard living evident on his whiskered face made his age range hard to pinpoint. One of his front side teeth was missing. This guy said he knew they worked for Teaflake, which was common knowledge, and had information on the dude. Money had been promised in exchange for his whereabouts.

Ecks said, "What you got, homes?"

"Me and the stroke you looking for, we was practically raised together. Well, that is we was in the same group home for a few years back in the nineties. Griss," he added, his face taking on a downcast look. "I only realized later how good I had it there," he added softly. "Doc just up and drove into the desert one day and never came back."

"Uh-huh," Glide said, over a mouthful of fried catfish. He

hadn't looked up at him and was only nominally paying attention to what he said.

"That's right, and the one I'm talking about, his shit didn't stink then neither." He snorted. "We all called him OC in those days, but it's him. He was always studying up on how to be a thief. He could pick locks, I mean."

"How do you know that?" Ecks asked. "The part about this kid you knew being the one Teaflake is interested in?"

"Saw him back in the old 'hood over the years after we was both grown. Riding his motorcycle bold as you please down the street like he was Action Jackson. Come back to see his Ko-re-an mama at the Hi Hat."

"He's Korean?" Glide interjected.

"Naw, bro."The stooped man waved his hand impatiently. "He's a negro."

A burst of laughter from Glide. "But his mama is Korean?"

"Play mama, they sort of adopted each other. He speaks their language. I heard him. He called hisself OC once upon a time. OC . . . O'Conner, understand?"

Ecks asked, "Where's he now?"

The stooped man looked over his shoulder as if sensing a wraith had penetrated the walls, its clawed hand reaching out for him. He returned his gaze to them. "He got a motorcycle shop out there in Altadena."

"And you know this how?" Ecks said.

The stooped man straightened, holding his arms out wide. "The place is called Connie's Dirt Bikes. That's a nickname for O'Conner. Saw it online using the library's computer. Heard about the bounty, knew I could find his ass."

Exasperated, Glide narrowed his eyes on him.

Ecks reached into a pocket and withdrew a twenty, which he handed across. "Go on now."

He shook the folded-over twenty. "I gave you all valuable information. Just look up them records from Griss. It burned down, but there has to be records at the county. Or the Hi Hat. It got sold but again, there's ways of tracking down what happened to Mrs. Cho."

Ecks was standing, hand on the stooped man's shoulder. "Go on about your business and leave us to ours, okay?" He underscored his message with a hard squeeze to the other's upper shoulder.

"Awright, ya big sumagun. But I know what I'm talking about."

The man once known as Raj turned and left the restaurant.

Glide and Ecks resumed their lunch, having dismissed the destitute man's ramblings. Afterward, Ecks was driving the Aviator, Glide in the passenger seat. Over the immersive sound system played a song by Megan Thee Stallion, "Cognac Queen." Glide nodded his head to the beat as he checked out a video on TikTok. It was an influencer extolling the virtues of the new fur-lined suede boots she'd just unwrapped. The young woman wore a string bikini with the boots, showing off by the pool of a mansion. Glide smiled at the pretty woman who was going on about how the boots fit in with her lifestyle, all fast fashion and selective clubbing. He knew it was bullshit, but as far as he was concerned, wasn't nothing wrong with getting your hustle on.

Ecks's phone buzzed. He tapped on the familiar number. "What's up, Tea?"

Coming through the vehicle's speakers, Teaflake said, "Need you two to come get me. I need to go up to the recorder's office in Santa Barbara. Today, right now. I got to straighten some shit out."

"How come?" Ecks said.

Teaflake said, "Some kind of fuckup has happened with the transfer of title. And the winery's account has been hacked. A what do you call it—a ransomware has infected it and money demanded to turn it off."

"By who?" Ecks said.

"Bastards call themselves A Minus One, whatever the hell that's supposed to mean. A group of wild-ass computer geeks. They seem to mostly fuck with sieg heiling tech bros."

"This those nasty-ass deputies' doing?" Glide asked.

"Don't seem like," Teaflake allowed. "Nightstick upside your head is more their style."

"True that, but money has been demanded, right?" Ecks said.

"Not exactly," Teaflake replied.

"What exactly?" Glide asked.

"I'm supposed to give out at least three million to charities and then the account will be freed."

Ecks said, "Then one of the charities is behind this."

"None were named. Dealer's choice, the message told me."

"Where you at?"

The call was interrupted before Teaflake could answer. "I hear you've been looking for me."

"Somebody else in the car, Glide?" Teaflake yelled.

"It's on the phone," Glide said.

"This is O'Conner."

"How are you doing this?" Teaflake demanded.

"You and I have a mutual problem. The Interceptors."

"That's a you problem," came Teaflake's voice from his end of the phone call.

"I know their names," O'Conner said. "And I know more."

"You're full of shit."

"I'll give you one for free. Bob Winslow."

O'Conner disconnected the call, took off the headphones, and nodded at Joyner, who sat across from him. They were sitting before an array of electronic surveillance equipment she'd set up.

Not long afterward, back at the hotel, he worked out on weight machines and spent time on the stationary bike, then swam back and forth in the hotel's heated pool until he was exhilaratingly exhausted. Laying on the deck on a towel, he was as prepared as he was going to be.

CHAPTER SEVENTEEN

The fog lay heavy amid the rows of ripening grapes of the Valmont Vineyard in Santa Barbara County. A number of similar estates could be found along this part of the California coast. Gaige Avilla wasn't wearing his prescription sunglasses, which were tucked away in a pocket of his windbreaker. It was early morning, still overcast and misty. His sensitivity to light had developed a decade ago. He used to get migraines from the condition before he got the proper diagnosis. At this moment, as he stepped along an earthen column bisecting the rows of vines on either side of him, his bigger concern was ensuring his vision was in no way obstructed.

Crouched, the deputy continued forward. His gun was on a belt holster, and he had an earbud in place. Its spiral cord trailed to the two-way clipped to his upper chest. He couldn't see the main buildings off to his right, in the near distance, but he knew from the detailed map they'd studied that they were there. They included a processing and bottling facility, a warehouse and a tasting room for the tourists. A voice crackled in his ear.

"Anything, G?" Winslow asked.

Avilla touched the earbud. "Nothing so far, but this goddamn pea soup ain't exactly making it easy to see diddly," he whispered back.

"Same here. We keep to the plan."

"Don't we always?" Avilla said.

"Yeah, we do." Winslow clicked off.

Avilla kept moving between the rows of vines crawling up staked posts. His other partner was closing in on the buildings from a different angle. The fog hadn't relented. If anything, he had the impression the pall was thicker here, as he got nearer to the buildings. A crunch caused him to stop and produce his gun. Straining to penetrate the gray veil, he gritted his teeth, frustrated he couldn't tell from which direction the sound had originated. No choice really, he started off again, doing his best to be as quiet as possible. He was almost at the end of the row when again there was a disturbance. This time, he was certain it had come from his left.

Scanning what little he could discern in that direction, he secured the suppressor and piston in place at the end of his weapon. Not that he was too worried about the sound of gunfire carrying that far on the wind to another winery, let alone to anyone nearby at this time of the morning. But old habits, he reflected. Veering off the path, he stalked through the rows, stepping over horizontal crossbeams of PVC piping and trellises used to help support the growth of the vines, as well as wires used to keep those vines in place.

Something whooshed out of the fog and clipped the side of Avilla's arm. He was knocked to the side, tripping over his own feet. As he fell, tearing through a cluster of the wooden stakes and vines and wire, he shot his gun in the direction from which he was attacked.

"Shit," he blared, sideways on the ground now. Avilla was wearing a bulletproof vest. His bicep was bloody, but the wound wasn't deep. Whatever had struck him had torn the material of his shirt and scored his upper arm. Back on his feet, he glanced around, trying to discern where his attacker was.

"Show yourself, bitch."

Avilla started off in the direction the blow had come from. He heard a soft shuffle ahead and strained to see a form in the gray. He perceived hurried movement. His attacker was now running. He could hear stakes and crossbeams being torn loose, snapping underneath the runner's feet.

"Got your ass now." Avilla also ran, following the other's footfalls, which indicated that the man was heading away from the complex of buildings. Shifting to his left, he could now make out a darker form within the murk. He shot at this. The form dropped. Avilla grinned as he closed in on his presumed kill. But he slowed as he scanned about, at first not seeing a bulk on the ground amid the gaps where the gray-white gloom shifted. Then.

"There you are," he declared triumphantly, rushing forward.

The man on the ground reared upward, swinging a bat wrapped with razor wire on its business end. The bat made contact with Avilla's bulletproof vest, impaling the material. The deputy's progress was briefly halted. The bat man, balaclava covering his face, was also wearing a bulletproof vest. The man yanked, causing Avilla to lurch awkwardly and not get off his shot. The bat man, holding onto the stuck bat, pulled himself to his feet. He ripped the bat free, both hands on the hilt. Avilla fired his gun twice more, aiming at the lower regions of the bat man, who dove aside into gray murk.

"Fuck me," he said.

The masked attacker was momentarily swaddled in the fog. The Interceptor wasn't sure if his bullets had struck the intended target. Momentarily frozen in place, he turned, firing the gun again as the bat man came at him on his flank. He was bent forward and rammed his shoulder into the deputy. Both went over, grappling, each attempting to get the advantage over the other. The masked one punched Avilla in the jaw and rolled off. Gun up, Avilla started to rise. The studded bat was brought down on the forearm, the spikes driven into his muscle.

"Goddammit," Avilla wailed. His hand spasmed and his gun dropped to the earth. As the bat was pulled free, Avilla swung and his fist connected to the side of the other man's head. He grunted and, using the small end of the bat, stamped it against the deputy's body, rocking him backward. Gritting his teeth, Avilla countered by moving in close like a boxer, doing his best to pummel his attacker.

"Back the fuck up," the bat man said, blocking and ducking and slipping in punches of his own.

"Been at this forever, homeboy," Avilla replied.

"Me too, ese." His jab came under the side of the vest, catching Avilla in the ribcage between the straps.

Avilla gasped, the bat coming at him again. He turned, the razor wire raking the upper portion of his back. Head down, he could see the butt of his gun laying amid a tangle of broken PVC pipes, wire and smashed grapes. He dove forward and got it back in his hand. He flopped onto his back, preparing to shoot the masked man, who he expected to be looming over him. He wasn't.

Scrambling upright, Avilla looked around. He didn't see the man or hear him running in any direction. He'd lost his earpiece, his communication with Winslow and Hache disabled.

Bloodied and bruising, he set out again toward the buildings. He made no effort this time to be quiet in his approach.

Hache arrived outside the wine tasting room and offices. The damn fog was thinner here than out on the fields. He spoke into his two-way. "Still no G?"

"No," came Winslow's reply. "Stay on point."

"Copy that."

Hache tapped off. Crouching forward with gun in hand, he came around, near the end of the building. Here, the fog had settled, hovering over the ground at knee level. He approached the steps leading to the front doors, which were obscured. He looked over his shoulder toward the fog shrouding the seemingly endless rows of vines. Out there, the fog was more of a pale wall of mist. Staring, he noted a dark shape emerging from the pall. The figure was getting closer. Hache crouched beside the building, ready to fire.

"It's me," Avilla said as he came over. Both of his arms were bloody, the shirt material torn.

Hache lowered his gun and went over to him. "What the hell happened?"

Avilla told him about the man in the balaclava. "There's

probably more than one of those would-be Ohtanis running around."

"O'Conner or Teaflake, you reckon?" Hache asked.

"Or are they working together?"

"Guess we'll find out." Hache tucked the cuff of a pant leg behind an ankle holster to be able to retrieve his second gun quicker.

Together, they walked toward the main building. Each glared ahead and at the ground, wary there might be a trip wire. They mounted the steps and paused at the entrance. Each examined the doorframe. Satisfied, Hache tried the glass double doors. Locked. With no need to be subtle, he freed the short pry bar from its harness on the side of his utility pants. Inserting it between the lock and frame, he popped the door open. Guns at the ready, the two went into the gloomy interior, Hache in the lead. He'd put the flashlight attachment on his pistol, the light on.

"The hell?" Avilla murmured.

Revealed in the sweep of the light were large plush toy animals that resembled prizes at a carnival ring toss or shooting gallery. After snapping the overhead lights on, they cleared the adjoining rooms, then returned to the area with the plush toys. The stuffed teddy bears, pandas and so on were upright, some on the floor and some elsewhere. Toward a corner of the wine tasting room was a four-sided bar, an island where a column rose from its center to the exposed beams of the ceiling. Behind this, and built into where the two walls came together, was a substantial wine rack stocked with numerous bottles. Furnishings included freestanding tables, padded mid-century-styled chairs and couches as well.

Hache stared at one of the stuffed animals, a dragon. "They're trying to get in our heads." Frustrated, he knocked the mythical beast aside.

Regarding his wounds, Avilla said, "They're doing more than that."

Hache called Winslow on his two-way. "We're inside. G was attacked but he's here with me now. We're gonna keep checking the premises. Stay put."

"Roger that," came the reply.

Hache set his gun aside as he took hold of the dragon. "What if there's nanny cams in these things?" He didn't wait for a response. Digging his fingers into a seam along the side of the dragon's neck, he tore it open, exposing the cotton stuffing. He proceeded to rip the plushie apart.

"Nothing," he declared.

"Fuck that," his partner said. "We're wasting time." He shot a few of the toys, sending plumes of cotton exploding from them.

Avilla picked up another stuffed animal, a cuddly looking lion, giving it a squeeze. The toy exploded, releasing a plume of sparkling green gas, causing both men to cough and wheeze.

"Christ." Avilla dropped what remained of the lion. His hand was burned. Bending over, hands on his knees, he said between coughs, "The fuck was in that gas?" His damaged hand was blackened and already the skin was blistering.

Hache vomited. "Must be some kind of shit made for riot control."

The deputies spun around as two men wearing gloves and respirator masks with plexiglass shielding rushed into the room. The thinner one hefted a heavy-duty crowbar. The other one, who was bulkier, had the bat he'd previously used on Avilla in the fields. Avilla, who was closer to them, swung his pistol toward the two. The larger of the newcomers was quicker and brought the razored bat down on Avilla's already-injured forearm, wounding him deeper.

Hache fired but the man who'd struck Avilla shoved him into his partner, spoiling his aim. Bullets shattered racked wine bottles, spilling their contents. By then the second masked individual was on Hache and clubbed him with his crowbar alongside his forehead. Bone cracked as he wilted to the floor. Avilla was struck on his jaw, and he too sank to the floor. He lay on his back. He wasn't out like Hache, but his unfocused eyes indicated he was having trouble with misfiring neurons.

The attacking duo, still wearing the respirators and face shields, bound the deputies using aircraft cable with eye ends. After looping the cable around the downed Interceptors, they padlocked the bindings.

"G, Hache, come in," crackled Winslow's voice over the latter's two-way. "Hache, Hache, what's happening?"

The thinner man removed the radio unit and destroyed it with his crowbar. Together, they duct taped their captives' mouths and wrapped tape around the heads of the two so-called law enforcers, covering their eyes. Hache remained limp. Avilla breathed heavily, offering no resistance. Both were bleeding from head lacerations and bruises, and lumps were already forming on their heads.

Jeet Silvera and Ben Reynolds pulled off their gas masks, wiping their sweating faces with paper towels obtained from underneath the wine bar. They left the captured men face down on the floor.

The slimmer Reynolds signaled silently to Silvera. Into the kitchen they went. Reynolds placed his crowbar near the swing door as did Silvera with his bat. Reynolds withdrew the gun he had stored in his cargo pants pocket and placed this on a metal table. Opening the industrial refrigerator, he saw several prepared charcuterie boards and other light refreshments under plastic wrap. He took a board out. Removing the wrap, they sat at a metal table and ate, waiting for word from O'Conner.

"I guess we better not leave anything uneaten," Reynolds said, snacking on a piece of hard cheese inserted between a folded slice of salami. "Teeth prints," he added.

"You mean bite marks," Silvera corrected.

"Yeah, that." He plucked more salami free from the board.

"That's proven to be a lot of bullshit. Innocent dudes who got sent to death row were later freed. It's junk science."

"How come that doesn't surprise me."

"But better to finish what you start eating. We don't want to leave our DNA around."

"I heard that." Reynolds ate with gusto.

Some five hundred yards away from the rear of the cluster of buildings, Winslow was stationed with a Winchester rifle and scope. He had his holstered sidearm and a pair of binoculars. He was hunkered down among a stand of maple trees with lush, fanned-out foliage to better cover his presence. Less than a mile away, where the land and greenery ascended, was a trailhead. Winslow used his binoculars to individually sight each of the buildings, but there was no further movement. He'd seen his two partners enter the wine tasting room several minutes ago. Then came the radio silence.

Winslow remained where he was. He decided he'd give it another few minutes before moving in. The fog was starting to dissipate as the sun rose higher in the morning sky. Scanning the buildings again, he spotted movement. A figure moved in the murk from around the warehouse and, running, covered the space in a handful of seconds, scooting around the side of the two-story processing plant. Winslow had reached for his rifle, but was too slow to fire.

"Shit, shit, shit," he uttered. Rifle in hand, he exited the tree line. There were no plantings on this side of the vineyard's expanse. He had to cover open ground. Warily and steadily, he soon reached the cluster of buildings and headed toward the processing plant. The fog continued to clear.

Cautiously, he approached the prefab steel structure. Pausing at the corner, crouching low, Winslow poked the barrel of the rifle around first with him following, tensed and ready. The main door was closed. Next to this was a roll-up door. This too was closed.

Winslow put a hand on the front door's latch, then withdrew his fingers to listen, paying close attention to the second sense that had saved his bacon in more than one dicey situation. In a few beats, feeling as reassured as he could given the circumstances, he turned the latch and the door opened outward silently. Back to the wall, he used the toe of his boot to further open the door, but only by an inch or so. The design of the entrance was such that there was a raised threshold a few inches off the ground. Placing his foot over the rise, he knocked over empty soda cans. They skittered over the concrete floor.

"Fuck me," he whispered as he rushed inside, flopping onto the floor, sliding some.

The interior was partially gloomy, the only light let in through the windows. Winslow took it in. There were all sorts of machinery and vats. The man he'd spotted ducking in here could be hiding anywhere. Winslow got off the floor and proceeded forward cautiously, head on swivel.

O'Conner had assumed one of the deputies would keep watch as the other two moved in. Baiting them here hadn't been all that complicated. They were greedy fucks. Them not knowing details about the robbery was part of the lure. O'Conner's catnip for the deputies was supplied by Reynolds, who spread the word on the underworld grapevine, knowing such would reach the ears of the Interceptors' CIs. O'Conner had them believing the money was salted away on the winery. Yes, they'd suspect a trap. But the lure of all that lucre was too much to ignore.

The finances of the winery had been compromised by Joyner bringing in A Minus One—the group would be paid. When Teaflake had been here previously, O'Conner had been keeping watch. Ecks and Glide had escorted visitors out of the wine tasting room and thereafter the staff left, too. They'd been furloughed until the money could be straightened out. The buildings were shuttered. O'Conner broke in after everyone left. He'd discovered the panic room where Reynolds and Silvera had hidden in wait for the deputies. Probably, he figured, installed by Tachmann.

In the front part of the facility there were stainless steel pneumatic presses and grape crushers. From his brief research, O'Conner had learned about destemmers, a term winemakers used for the machinery that removed the stems from the fruit. There were also tall metal tanks the freshly crushed pulp flowed into. This was where the mixture would reside and begin the fermentation process. The tanks, supported on metal struts, were tall enough that to reach the top there were steps built onto their sides. It wasn't yet harvest season, so everything still shined from having been cleaned when last used.

The second half of the plant contained rows of stacked oak barrels. The barrels were used to finish the fermentation process, turning the wine into merlots and cabernets to be bottled later. O'Conner located a gap between two rows to hide in, which also afforded him a view into the first half of the building. He rested his gun on a cask and waited.

It wasn't long before he heard the soda cans he'd left being knocked over. Winslow wouldn't withdraw now. He was in too deep to turn back. O'Conner knew it was him from Silvera's photos and Joyner ID'ing them.

"Hey," Winslow called out. "Why don't we make a deal? Stop all this fuss and sit down like two pros, huh?"

"Don't need to," O'Conner called back.

"That's a disappointing outlook, my friend. I'm guessing here, but you and Teaflake ain't all buddied up, are you?"

O'Conner didn't bother to answer.

"What I'm saying is me and my boys take care of him and his boys and you give us a cut in gratitude."

O'Conner understood he was trying to find out what happened to his partners. "Let me talk it over with my crew."

"Go ahead."

"I need to do it face-to-face."

"I gotta think about that."

"Take your time."

Winslow was up to something, O'Conner determined. But it was better to have him in the open. He was certain Winslow's voice was closer. Several minutes dragged.

Winslow finally called out again. "Hey, O'Conner—it's O'Conner, right?"

"That's right."

"I'm coming out, hands up, okay?"

"And . . . ?"

"And don't shoot me. We have a mutual problem we can solve by working together."

"Okay, we got a temporary truce, but I better see that rifle." He figured he must have brought one along.

"Of course."

"Come on." He rose.

Winslow stepped from around one of the stainless steel tanks. He held the rifle aloft in both hands and walked forward slowly. He had on a duckbill cap. O'Conner moved out from where he was, also stepping forward, but not as much.

"You can stop there," he told the crooked cop as he got close to the archway.

Winslow said, "I'm gonna put this down on the floor."

O'Conner imagined him swinging the rifle around to shoot him as he pretended to comply. He said, "First, slide your right hand over to where the left one is holding the rifle's stock."

"Kinda awkward what you're asking for, playboy."

"Isn't it though."

Winslow changed his grip, holding the rifle by the stock. He started to lower it and his body to the ground.

Too late, O'Conner saw that he'd been tricked. The rifle flipped over so that it was on its side but parallel to the ground. Winslow had taped a compact canister to the side of the stock away from the other man's view. It was a flash-bang grenade and it went off.

O'Conner fired his gun, but he was already blinded by the intense spray of white. He bulled ahead, having a mental image of where Winslow had been standing. O'Conner collided with Winslow, and the gun Winslow had pulled from concealment went off near O'Conner's ear. Motivated as he was to fight for his life, he lashed out with a series of blows even though his vision was a swirl of sparkling pinpoints of light.

A sock to his jaw rocked him. Winslow's hot breath was on him. He managed, though, to latch his hand onto the other's arm. O'Conner drove his legs while twisting his upper body. Together they fell into a stack of barrels, sending several rolling across the floor. They also rolled off, separating. O'Conner's vision started to clear. He saw that Winslow made to fire his sidearm again. O'Conner threw the spigot he'd plucked from a barrel, striking the other man in the eye. The deputy's round clipped a lunging O'Conner along his back, but he nonetheless got his arms around Winslow's upper body, temporarily pinning both his arms.

The cop kneed him but to little effect. Winslow tried to wrench his arms free and O'Conner struck him in the kidneys twice. The other man buckled. Abruptly, O'Conner accelerated upward, butting the underside of Winslow's chin with the top of his head. Wine had sloshed onto the floor from the barrel without a spigot. O'Conner shoved him and back he went, his boots in the red liquid. Winslow momentarily lost traction. The deputy's balance upset, O'Conner drove a foot into his chest to send him over once more. He cracked the back of his head on the edge of a barrel. Now O'Conner held the rifle on Winslow.

"Toss it aside," he said, blinking hard.

Winslow hesitated.

"Go on and try me."

Winslow let the gun go. He touched the back of his head, coming away with red-stained fingers. "I suppose it would be too much to ask for medical attention."

O'Conner gestured with the rifle. "Let's go."

"What are you going to do with me?"

His thin smile was not reassuring. "It ain't gonna be 'Ring Around the Rosie'."

O'Conner let Winslow walk in front and he followed behind him. They reached the front, the door ajar. O'Conner stepped back a length to allow Winslow to pull the door open. As the sheriff's investigator went through, he turned to the right. Part of his body was momentarily blocked from O'Conner's sight. Winslow spun around and threw a knife underhanded at the thief. On its hilt trailed the duct tape he'd used to secure it near the door on the outside of the building.

The blade sank into the upper portion of O'Conner's shoulder as he got off a shot with the rifle. But Winslow was running, already going around the rear of the utility shed.

O'Conner took off after him, yanking the knife out and dropping it and the rifle. As he crashed through the rows of staked grapes diagonally, he burst though the PVC piping and wiring, pulling out several trellises. Briefly, he became tangled in wires and posts but tore himself free.

Still running, Winslow shot over his shoulder without looking back. It didn't surprise O'Conner that the devious cocksucker had a backup to the backup piece on his person.

Silvera and Reynolds came out of the main building, masks back on, guns out. O'Conner signaled for them to hold back. No sense having even more gunfire going off. He gained on the running Winslow. As the deputy veered left, O'Conner ran to the right. He stopped, his gun held outstretched in both hands. Taking in and holding a lungful of air, he took one shot. Some eighty yards away, Winslow went over, the bullet passing through his head.

Reynolds and Silvera came over. "Huh," Silvera said, noting the revolver in O'Conner's hand. He'd used one of the ghost guns. The end of the barrel was split and had mushroomed from the bullet traveling through it. O'Conner put the ruined gun in his waistband.

Regarding O'Conner's wound, Silvera said, "Better get you patched up." He pointed at Winslow. "Should we bury him?"

O'Conner said, "No, we leave him like this. All the better to hem up the other two."

O'Conner crouched down and repositioned Winslow's hand. His body was sprawled across the rows, broken posts and smashed grapes beneath him. O'Conner took a picture of his bracelet. He also removed the dead man's phone, holding it by his thumb and forefinger on the edge of the casing to preserve Winslow's fingerprints.

Given the mineral-rich soil for growing grapes, and DNA being hard to extract from dirt anyway, he wasn't too worried about trace evidence being extracted from the field. Bleach was applied to sanitize the area where the knife had been dropped in the processing building. O'Conner used his binoculars to see if there were any vehicles approaching the winery.

"So far, so good," he announced.

Back in the wine tasting building where the other two Interceptors were bound, the three went about several tasks. The two captives were lying on their sides, aware but unseeing. Hache muffled words but he was ignored. O'Conner found a small tube of superglue in a drawer in the kitchen. Finding no rubbing alcohol, he took a bottle of vodka from behind the bar. He stripped down to his undershirt in the bathroom. Jaw tight, he used liquid soap, the vodka and folded-up paper towels to clean his wound and dry the skin. He then applied the superglue to seal the tear. He applied tape and gauze found in a medical kit over this when the glue had fast-dried. He washed out the sink and flushed the pieces of gauze, tape and used paper towels down the toilet. After wiping off the tube of glue and booze, he returned both to their respective locations.

While he did this, Silvera and Reynolds removed the various hidden nanny cams. The cameras had been shut off. But they had fed videos of what went down in the main area when Avilla and Hache had come inside. The feed went to an off-site computer overseen by Joyner. O'Conner texted her. At a previously set time, she was to stream selections from the videos to various online destinations. He asked her to hold off until they could meet later that day. After that, he figured he had a long drive out to Temecula coming.

After taking a last look around, the three left. Silvera drove them away in a four-year-old Ford Fusion, O'Conner in the passenger seat. There was little small talk among the three, each tending to his own concerns. Reflecting more on the podcast he'd listened to, O'Conner suspected that some of the cliques had demanded and gotten a bribe from a cartel to move its contraband unmolested through the part of the Southland they patrolled, as Silvera had said. The missing piece occurred to him as they rode along—why the Interceptors were interested once they knew about Tachmann's murder.

"Those deputies must have been 'taxing' Tachmann," he announced.

Reynolds said from the back seat, "Exacting tribute, you mean, to let him operate."

"Who knows how," O'Conner answered, "but he got hemmed up by them and rather than bust him, they bled him."

"The golden goose," Silvera added.

Once they were back on the 101 freeway heading south, O'Conner produced an old flip phone. He waited until he had a signal, then made a call to 911. He got a recording that told him not to hang up and his call would be answered by the next available operator. O'Conner stayed on the line, staring stone-faced through the windshield.

"I don't know what's going on," he began, sounding frantic when the call was finally answered. "But I was driving by on this road, see we'd gotten turned around off the highway. Anyway, me and the missus saw a man running through a vineyard. I mean just tearing through. And we heard gunshots too. Maybe it was an ICE raid, but me and the missus don't think so. This guy was white."

"Where was this, sir?"

He didn't want to sound too precise, but he needed to provide enough information to guide the authorities to the winery.

"Can I have your name if you would?" the operator asked.

"Oh, my," O'Conner said, sounding flustered. "I can't do that. The wife wouldn't want the bad people you have here in California coming for us. No sirree, Bob." He snapped the phone closed and threw it out the window.

"You missed your calling, Denzel," Reynolds cracked.

He got comfortable in the seat, conserving his energy.

The Ford hadn't traveled eighty more yards when a family van drove over the phone, pulverizing it.

TALES FROM THE CRIMSON LOUNGE

There was a knock on the rear door to Charlie Mack's office. "Yes," she announced. It was just past two in the morning. She held an efficient Beretta.

"It's us, Tachmann and Doze."

Recognizing the voice, Charlie Mack undid the two dead bolts and swung the metal door outward. Standing there were the two, a parked U-Haul rented pickup behind them. The bed of the truck was filled some five feet high with stacked cardboard boxes held down by bungee cords. Doze stood next to a hand dolly.

"All good?" Tachmann said to Charlie Mack. His mane of premature gray hair was combed back from his forehead.

"Don't stand on ceremony," she answered.

Doze undid the bungees and began placing the boxes on the dolly. Tachmann carried in two boxes. Soon they had transferred the cargo from the truck to the office. They put the dolly in the pickup's bed and Doze shut the tailgate. The back door was closed and locked again.

"Fresh off the boat," Tachmann said, smiling proudly as he tapped one of the boxes. The restacked contraband took up a good portion of one wall.

"We came straight from the docks," Doze said.

Tachmann continued, "These won't be on the market for at least the next two months."

"What the hell is a Game Boy?" Charlie Mack asked. The boxes were detailed with Japanese lettering but the words "Game Boy" distinct in English.

"All the kids want one," Tachmann answered as he pulled the flaps open on one of the boxes. He removed a smaller, slim rectangular box with a coated finish. On its front were the manufacturer's name and other graphics including the title Charlie Mack had read on the shipping box. In bold multicolored type was the word "Color" partially superimposed over the image of the electronic game console. Tachmann opened this box and took out an electronic device made of plastic. Tachmann handed her the thing, which looked like a calculator to her.

"Yes, ma'am. That one's in Atomic Purple."

"What does it do?"

"You can play Po-ke-mon on it," Doze said, as if stating the obvious. "You try to become a Po-ke-mon Master."

Charlie Mack looked at Tachmann for clarification.

Smiling again, he said, "There are different games. They all have obstacles and enemies to overcome to make it to the end."

She asked, "What's this thing cost at a Radio Shack?"

"Eighty bucks," Tachmann answered. "'Cause this comes with a cartridge. We'll sell 'em for ten dollars less, cash money."

Charlie Mack whistled, tabulating the number of the individual boxes inside the larger boxes.

Tachmann shook his thumb in a northerly direction. "Those dorm rats at 'SC are our target market. Once Wayland, my connect on campus, puts out the word, we won't be able to keep enough in stock."

"This the only shipment?" Charlie Mack asked.

"Doesn't have to be if these move like I think they will," Tachmann said. "Hell, even when Nintendo starts distributing them, we knock off another five dollars for the Game Boy, we'll still be selling."

"Can't be having them little shits dropping by here," Charlie Mack said.

Doze chuckled. "We just need to park these here until later this afternoon. Got a storage room of my own in my boy's fish fry place over on Adams. They'll come there or buy from the Wayland kid direct."

Tachmann checked his watch. "Let's finish up. Got an early drive to make tomorrow to see a winery."

"A winery?" Charlie Mack said.

"Guy I've known since grade school says they're a good investment, like computers."

Charlie Mack puffed out air. "Ain't nobody gonna be lining up to buy California wine, Tack."

He smiled, hands outstretched. "Whatever."

Soon Doze and Tachmann were gone. Rather than leave, Charlie Mack put on an Ella Fitzgerald CD and poured an amount of Crown Royal. Sitting at her desk, she figured out how to manipulate the movements of the little fella on the screen. It was slow going initially as she haltingly maneuvered the digital avatar through its paces. But soon she was deftly controlling the character. After five in the morning Charlie

Mack yawned one more time and rose. She tabbed off the device and placed it on her desk. Lights off, she too exited by the rear door.

In the darkened office, the screen on the handheld flashed on and there appeared a squat, pixelated, hunched-over dinosaur with wheels. The jagged-edged creature made its way along a rolling roadway, dodging or jumping over obstacles to a never-ending soundtrack of low-level fuzzy arcade-like electronica. The creature reached the plateau of a mountain. An orange and yellow ball of fire came from the sky and exploded on the wheeled dinosaur. As the flames crackled around it, the pseudoreptile transformed into a humanoid shape. The screen went dark.

A few days later, Charlie Mack gave the Game Boy to OC when he was cleaning up.

"Oh, wow. Thanks, Miss Charlie."

"My pleasure."

When he was done, OC took a circuitous route through the neighborhood. He arrived at an abandoned house next to a lot overgrown with grass and weeds where tires and debris were regularly dumped. Layers of graffiti were sprayed on the walls of the house and plywood was nailed in place where windows once were. Underneath the house was where he'd hidden his grocery bag of cash. But he was becoming more and more worried as squatters, addicts and the homeless continued to occupy the house. At one point, a fire had been started in there. And what if a cigarette was tossed onto those tires, he considered.

OC walked along the lot beside the house. He crouched

beside a planked-over window. There were holes in it. The youth heard motion inside. On he went to a crawl space blocked from view by the junk from the street. He'd repaired the broken screen that had lain aside the opening. It was still in place. A good sign, he thought as he took the screen away. He went into the crawl space, using his elbows to help propel him across the dirt like he'd seen soldiers do in an old war movie on TV. His treasure was still there. Relieved, he turned around and went back the way he'd come.

"Hey, what you doing down there?" somebody said as OC poked his head out of the crawl space.

He looked up to see Shoe Dog. He hurried out from beneath the house. "Keep your voice down, dude."

"Why? What you got under there?" He had his wagon with him.

"You know me."

The rheumy eyes gained focus. "You work at the Hi Hat."

"Yeah, Mrs. Cho gives you food from the store."

"Twinkies," he said derisively.

"She gave you some crackers last week."

"Right, right," he said, bobbing his head.

"What about a hamburger?" OC said.

"What about it?"

"I'll buy you one."

He shook a finger at him and asked again, "What you got under there?"

"Come on, let's get a hamburger." OC beckoned to him as he backed up toward the front of the house. Shoe Dog followed, tugging his wagon.

When they had nearly gone, the front door creaked open.

Once it too had been boarded over but the plywood had been removed some time ago. Out stepped a barefoot woman wearing a sheet like it was a toga. Her big hair haloed her unwashed face. She blinked hard in the daylight. "Who said something about a hamburger?"

"It's mine," Shoe Dog proclaimed.

"Fuck it is, bitch," she said.

"Who you callin' a bitch, you ole' fish-eyed fool?"

The woman stomped down the steps and got in his face. As they argued, OC ran and got back under the house. He retrieved the bag and crawled toward the other side. A rat dropped on him as it skittered along a length of pipe over his head. He shook the creature loose and kept going. It didn't take much effort to push out the screen over this part of the crawl space. He got out from under it. The two were still arguing.

"Take your nasty ass on, fool," the woman yelled.

"I got a right to be here," Shoe Dog yelled back.

OC ran. Shoe Dog called to him, "What about my hamburger?"

The young man continued slapping the soles of his sneakers onto the sidewalk. Running toward a goal beyond being stuck in Griss until he aged out.

CHAPTER EIGHTEEN

The video of the fight between the Interceptors and the masked men went viral. Hache, Avilla and the dead Winslow were soon identified by news outlets. Joyner made sure their names were also circulating on the web. The high sheriff of Riverside County rushed in to give a midday televised news conference assuring the viewers and voters his department would do all in its power to get to the truth of what happened in what was already being called "Murder in the Vineyard." Questions were naturally raised by reporters as to what his office's detectives were doing there, and what about the allegations they were part of a gang called the Interceptors with roots in the L.A. Sheriff's Department? So-called branches of the gang were rumored to be operating in other Inland Empire cities, some said.

By the time the sheriff finished the press conference an hour later, he was drawn and exhausted. Two hours later the governor also went on the air, promising the justice apparatus of the state would be looking into this matter.

"For too long," the governor said, "the cancer of these secretive gangs in our policing agencies has gone untreated. There's been documentation of some of these cliques going back decades. They must be stopped, and they will be stopped."

Teaflake, Glide and Ecks sat watching the press conference on a flat-screen in Teaflake's Brentwood condo. The attorney general took his turn at the lectern. Teaflake turned the set off.

"Motherfuck," he exhaled. "I already got the police on my left nut. Whoever the hell this O'Conner is, he's managed to screw with the paperwork transferring ownership of Valmont. Which is also bringing up Tachmann."

"For sure," Ecks said.

"They ain't got nothin' hard to sweat you on, Tea," Glide said.

Teaflake, who was sitting forward, showed gritted white teeth. "The winery is now radioactive. I'd backdated the quitclaim just in case so, yeah . . . but still this stink can't be camouflaged with no Air Wick."

"He went right at these fools, too. Killing a cop. A crooked one, but still."

"Damn sure don't seem like he's sweating any of their friends coming after him," Ecks added.

A glum Teaflake said, "He's put the spotlight on the gang. Got Sacramento involved. Them motherfuckahs sneeze, they coming under scrutiny. This bastard is playing Mr. Spock chess while everybody else is playing after-school checkers."

"Like he's working his way down a list?" Glide wondered.

Teaflake slumped in his chair.

A key turned in the lock on the front door and Dolly Rand entered. Her dark blue Dickies pants were smeared in places with a mixture of substances. She had on a worn work shirt and hair partly contained within a decorative scarf tied around her forehead, like a modern-day version of Rosie the Riveter. She held a bulging leather tool satchel at her side. "Y'all looking kinda down," she remarked.

"Complications," Teaflake said. "Dude who's giving us the blues is not one of the ganged-up deputies. But his circling out there is a major problem. Too many ways he can come at us."

"And he will," Ecks added.

"Tea put out snitch money," Glide continued. "That looked to have gotten mouths talkin' but it was just bullshit. Taking us all over the place chasing down what turned out to always be a whole lot of nothing."

"Then you need to draw him out."

"Don't I know. Except there's nothing to fancy him," Teaflake said resignedly.

"Not money?" she wondered aloud.

Teaflake said, "Naw, looks like he's got plenty of that."

"He wants you?" she said flatly.

"Oh yes," Teaflake confirmed. "I can't shake this feeling about this cat. Is he that bold or he just don't give a fuck."

O'Conner having broken into his call had unnerved him. Did he have a background in black ops?

"Guess you said no," Rand said.

"Even if we did go for it, he'd eventually turn on us," Glide proclaimed.

Teaflake nodded assent.

"What are you going to do?" Rand asked him.

"For the time being, hunker down," Teaflake said. "Somebody knows something about this guy."

"You figure to use that space across the way from my studio?" she said.

"I was considering that. Ready-made to be a fort," he said with a hollow chuckle.

"Okay then." Rand walked on with her bag.

Glide was alone as he navigated the Aviator into the parking slot at the Centinela Shopping Center. Instead of Grace's, he walked into the EXP cigar lounge.

From accessing his credit card records, O'Conner knew Glide was a member of the establishment. O'Conner had previously scoped out the place. It was outfitted with oversized comfy chairs and couches, big-screen televisions, a well-stocked walk-in humidor and a full bar in the rear. Too, from further studying his credit card purchases, O'Conner had determined the big man frequented EXP at least once every two or three weeks. There was no set day, though a Wednesday or Thursday seemed more likely. This was the second time this week he'd posted up after the events at the winery. But this afternoon, Glide did drop by.

O'Conner had looked to put Teaflake and his men back on their heels. The fallout from the exposure of the duplicitous deputies would put them in a defensive mode. They'd go to ground for a period to regroup as they also redoubled their efforts to gather any and all they could about him. Tachmann's sister went by a different last name. That didn't mean they couldn't find her and sweat her too. She was now on a cruise ship for a week thanks to O'Conner's money and Joyner convincing her to take the trip.

O'Conner watched as Glide went inside the cigar lounge.

He was stationed once more in the transit van. He'd removed the Water Works insignia. He figured Glide wouldn't be inside too long. If he'd calculated correctly, the big fella would be stocking up. Not a cigar smoker, he did know those who did partake could take their time making selections of their "sticks." They had standbys, their favorites of course, but invariably there was some new cigar that came in. Such had to be discussed with the shop's sommelier—or whatever the hell a cigar salesclerk was called.

Now walking past the Aviator, he paused and bent over, placing a magnetized airgap-like tracer inside a vent opening that was part of the front bumper. On he went. Soon enough Glide was back outside, an assortment of cigars in protective plastic held in his large hand. Activating a phone set in a holder, O'Conner tailed the dot of Glide's vehicle on the digital map some car lengths back after he left the lot in the Aviator. The other man made two more stops on his errands and finally wound his way to his apartment. O'Conner knew where he as well as Ecks lived. In Glide's case, it was a newish building overlooking Overland in the Mar Vista area. Glide parked on the street and not below the building, signaling he was going in there to return soon.

Cars and pedestrians passed by as O'Conner went to work on the driver's side door of the Aviator, the roadway to his back. Given the size of the vehicle, he had a certain degree of privacy as pedestrians passed by along the sidewalk. His mechanical skills aided by another type of emitter to fool the alarm, he overcame the lock. A fob was usually used to remotely open a car door. But vehicles were designed so that if the fob's battery was dead, a key could be used in an emergency. Usually this meant part of the door handle could be removed to reveal the old-fashioned lock, and that's what O'Conner had done.

Sitting in the driver's seat, gloves on, he planted the ghost gun he'd killed Winslow with under the SUV's passenger seat. Back outside, he relocked the door and reassembled the handle. At the rear, he crouched down as if inspecting the tire. He remained crouched down for several moments. As he began to straighten up, Glide stepped out of his apartment building's entrance, looking at his phone.

Crouching again, O'Conner duckwalked to the SUV's rear end. He had no other weapon on him. Sadly, it had crossed his mind when he first saw Glide, who was bigger and younger than him, he'd lose a fight with the roughneck. So he damn sure was not going to get got.

Glide had a luggage type of duffel bag strapped over his shoulder. As he came around the SUV from the front end, O'Conner snuck onto the sidewalk from the rear. He walked away at a brisk pace as the Aviator started and drove off.

The vehicle hadn't reached the end of the block when the back end blew up. O'Conner had attached one of Burgess's explosive devices he'd collected after the heist to the differential, the gear housing into which the rear axles were attached. The rear wheel on the driver's side spun free into the street. The back end of the Aviator dropped onto the roadway, sparks flying from underneath as the car skidded along. Glide must have overcompensated at the steering wheel because as O'Conner watched and others videoed with their phones, the big vehicle rent sideways violently, colliding with another car. This caused the car to jump the curb, sheering off a hydrant. The rolling hydrant cannonballed the door of a travel bookshop, knocking it off its hinges. Water shot into the air, cascading onlookers as Glide got out of the wrecked Aviator. He was wiping a nosebleed with his hand.

Around the corner O'Conner approached the van parked in the street. There was a ticket under the windshield wiper. He walked up, frowning. He'd put enough coins in the parking meter but its lights were blinking red. When he'd arrived, he'd paid enough but hadn't paid attention to the meter. Now he put in another quarter. The meter didn't flash green. It was broken. If he were any other John Q. Citizen he could go to court to argue his case. But he damn sure wasn't. The plates on the van weren't hot. As far as the traffic division's computer was concerned, the vehicle was registered with the Inglewood Water Works. Taking the ticket in hand, for a moment he considered mailing in a money order to pay it, to further bury it in the system should there be any nosing around.

"Sheeet," he said aloud. O'Conner crumpled up the ticket and tossed it in a trash receptacle. He might be a thief, but he wasn't a litterer.

Teaflake didn't show up at Grace's for the next few days. The ghost gun O'Conner put in the Aviator was quickly found once the street was cordoned off and the SUV was searched. Possessing an unregistered weapon was enough to have Glide arrested.

A bullet had been dug out of the dead Winslow's head. O'Conner was familiar with current forensic practices as lab techs sought to establish protocols when dealing with

3D-printed guns. The plastic residue left on the fired bullet was a telltale sign. Whether spectrometry could match the material on the bullet with the gun, he had no idea, but he wasn't dwelling on the science. It was enough that his actions caused further headache for Teaflake.

O'Conner broke into Glide's apartment. He wanted to see if he could find a clue as to where Teaflake would be holed up—probably with extra men added for security. The gang lord owned a number of properties but that seemed to be too obvious. He would be concerned about the cops keeping watch on him now as well.

Searching the place, careful to put anything he moved back, O'Conner came upon a catalog for a recent showing at a gallery. On the cover was a substantial metal piece like what he'd seen at Grace's. He opened the catalog to a picture and profile piece about Dolly Rand and this exhibition.

Court proceedings being public, O'Conner knew when Glide was getting bailed out of Men's Central. He was there late in the afternoon when the big fella walked out of lockup. A man was there to meet him. They embraced and kissed. He too was of a certain size, so if the macho types also here being released to the happiness of their homeboys had something to say, they kept their opinions to themselves. O'Conner walked some distance behind them as they got into the boyfriend's vehicle, a Corolla. He made a note of the car's license plate. Was he going to keep his distance from Teaflake? The cops might be watching him, but so what if they were? It wasn't breaking the law should the big man likely be called in to do guard duty.

O'Conner didn't attempt tailing them but did make a call

to find out an address associated with the plate. When he got there, he found a fourplex in what was called the Arlington Heights. He drove around the block, parked and returned. Spying no cars in the driveway of one house, he walked along it to the home's backyard. There were lemon and orange trees back there and a wooden fence bordering the rear of the fourplex. On that side was all concrete. He climbed over the fence and crossed to the fourplex. Creeping about, he listened beside more than one window. At a curtained one, he heard Glide's bass in one of the two ground-floor apartments. He left and returned to his hotel room, taking a chance they were in for the night.

Pacing, O'Conner considered how to proceed against Teaflake. It did occur to him their paths weren't likely to cross should he embrace civilian civility. He'd cleared a significant sum from the steal. He wasn't broke to begin with. Yet if it was time for him to call it a day, he just couldn't leave a troublesome loose end like Teaflake around. For surely one sunny day, standing in line at a Chipotle, some ragtag mufu with barely two dollars to rub together would sneak up on him to collect a bounty and he would get his brains blown out all over his chicken bowl.

O'Conner'd fucked up Teaflake's money. He's got a hard-on for payback, O'Conner reasoned. He might be laying low now, but he was scheming. O'Conner needed to keep applying the pressure. This business was going to get finished. Bemusedly, he noted he would have the opportunity to be all he could be as a Hemitian, as the lowlanders were called. Or maybe not. Could be there'd be no townhouse for him to return to if him and Gwen were quits.

Exactly at two minutes to five the following morning, O'Conner returned to the fourplex to keep watch. Around half past seven, Glide and his boyfriend were in the latter's Corolla driving away. Having run the plate, O'Conner knew the man's name was Tyson Murphy and he worked at an agency specializing in "elevating your presence" on social media platforms, according to their website.

Glide was driven to his place. After his goodbyes with Murphy, he went in and not long after was back on the street. He had a rolling suitcase with him. Given his car was a wreck, O'Conner was curious if he was going to be picked up by someone else, perhaps a rideshare driver. A van arrived. On its side was the name of a car rental chain. Glide got in and was taken to one of their facilities for his replacement vehicle.

In his plain sedan, O'Conner tailed Glide several cars back in the slow-moving traffic of the morning drive-time slog. From the way they seemed to be heading, O'Conner had a hunch where he was going to end up. He turned off and took a different route to Dolly Rand's studio bordering South L.A. He'd gotten info on her, including a look at the studio's lease in her name. By the time he arrived, the rental car Glide had driven was parked near her workspace. This was on a side street with a dead end. The studio was housed on a lot, one of five stand-alone single-story buildings bracketing an open area where Glide's car was, among others. Occupying the open area was also a trio of dumpsters and a stack of wooden pallets to one side. There was a low wall bordering the lot on two sides but no gate. Next door was a large building housing a printing plant. They were in a partial industrial section near East Slauson and Woodlawn Avenues. Not far away were modest homes, a shoe outlet, pupuserías and so on. The pup tents and lean-tos of the unhoused were also about. The area was designated a redevelopment zone. But for now, this was where an artist like Rand could afford a large space, certainly much cheaper than in the so-called Arts District.

Posted up on the lot were two men sitting in a ceramic gray SUV, clearly on guard duty. O'Conner had surveyed the surrounding neighborhood. He bet he wouldn't be noticed by the two as there were a number of people around, some of them the unhoused. He followed several homeless folks walking together, heading farther east on Slauson.

Soon they queued in a long line at the Lasting Light food bank. Plastic bags containing food were given out. Staff of the pantry was keeping order. An older Black man in short sleeves and khakis stepped out, smiling and greeting the hungry.

"This is a good day, isn't it?" he said, addressing the gathered and shaking hands.

A bedraggled individual answered, "When we eat, yes it is, Brother Hamlin, yes it is."

Brother Hamlin voiced agreement. You could tell from the expression on his face he knew how hard it was out there.

O'Conner stood nearby for a few minutes, hands in his pockets, a studied cast to his features as the giveaway took place. He turned and walked back to where he left his car. He went to the Dry Salt Baths to have a steam while he considered his options.

Comfortable in the general room of the sauna with others,

O'Conner reviewed. There was no way to stake out the studio without being noticed. The other lots in the vicinity used for parking belonged to specific businesses, and more than one was fenced in, anyway. There were also several buildings for lease in the immediate area. But a car parked alongside one such structure wouldn't remain unnoticed for long. He had to draw out the ones inside. Ultimately, he needed to isolate Teaflake or be able to get the drop on him for less than thirty seconds—kill him and be in the wind. He could study the right blueprints and, using the sewer, plant one of Burgess's bombs underneath the studio. Once it went off, as everyone poured out, shoot his target. But there was no place to hide. He could try and get on the roof of the printer but once he did the deed, it was too much exposure to make his getaway. Though a nighttime hit might work, he amended.

He assumed Teaflake was sending out one of his guards to fetch takeout. He wouldn't take a chance on delivery should the driver get waylaid and O'Conner take his place. For all he knew, the studio might have a kitchen as well. He found it amusing to picture Teaflake at the stove preparing a big pot of spaghetti and meatballs for the gang. There was the poison angle to consider again. Even if he could get access to their groceries, it would mean wiping them all out. Could he rationalize such a drastic measure? Naw. He wouldn't go that far.

Eyes closed as the invigorating warmth seeped into his pores, he shifted to Rand. She would be the only one coming and going regularly from the studio for the next few weeks or so. Her pickup wasn't there earlier. Was she going to get in any work with them hardheads hanging around? What if he did kidnap her from the condo? Pulling it off wasn't the problem. That it was a federal crime wasn't a deterrent, given he was already plotting cold-blooded murder—contemplating dropping several bodies before he was through.

Now a move like that was getting desperate, wasn't it, he determined. You had to keep your captive way the hell out some damn where, keep them fed, bathroom facilities and whatnot. A cabin in the woods. Keep Rand on a length of chain so she could go about and do for herself at the stove and bathroom. But what about her yelling her fool head off? Fashion a clamp around her lower face? Let it get back to Teaflake on the sly where to find her. Have his traps set when he and his crew arrived to bust into the cabin.

O'Conner chuckled at the fancifulness of such a plan. Right out of an *X-Files*, a show his grandma loved. Entwining his hands over his stomach, he continued his therapeutic indulgence. O'Conner floated along, weighing various options to accomplish his goal. He did know better to get this done sooner than later. The more this situation with Teaflake festered, the more chance he was going to get tripped up.

On an overcast day the four food trucks rumbled onto the street where Dolly Rand's studio was located. According to the various graphics painted on the sides of each vehicle, they offered a variety of foods from fusion to traditional, soft drinks and cold-pressed juices. Two of the trucks parked diagonally toward the dead end. The other two parked on either side of the street so no driveway was blocked. Out from the trucks came personnel who opened up the sides as their respective grills were fired up. Doing guard duty on the studio's lot were Glide and Ecks. The latter got out and walked over to one of the trucks.

"Why y'all setting up here?" he asked, stepping under the truck's overhang to talk to the people inside. He checked his phone for the time. It was past three in the afternoon.

"This is where we were told to be," a beefy man in a tight T-shirt with tats covering his arms said. His back was to Ecks as he began cooking a number of hamburger patties flecked with chunks of cheese.

"By who?" As Ecks asked this, he heard footfalls and turned to look at an assortment of people entering the street. Some were the area's homeless, some were dressed in work clothes and more than a few were clad in office attire.

"Are you the guy?" a woman missing two of her front teeth asked Ecks as she closed in. She had a leopard print sweatband around her forehead.

"What guy?"

She produced a folded-over neon-green flyer. Unfolding it, she showed the announcement to him. "Well whoever you are, thanks, huh?"

Holding the flyer, Ecks read that on this day and time, and at this location, free freshly prepared meals would be given away for the next hour and a half. Further, each order would come with a coupon for another meal from the individual truck good for twenty dollars. The benefactor named on the flyer was Dimitri Strock, Teaflake's real name.

"Fuck," he muttered as he hurried back to the SUV he and Glide were in.

A crowd of people were already milling about the lot as

the street continued to fill. At the open end of the block, music from a tuba band filled the air. As people got their food, they lingered and ate, some gathering around the band to dance in the street.

"Look at this," he said to Glide. The big man stood outside the vehicle.

Glide regarded the flyer and was talking on the two-way with Teaflake.

"That motherfuckah is obviously behind this," Teaflake was saying. "Stay on the door. I'll send out Butch and Rainey."

"Good," Glide said. He put the two-way in his back pocket as he and Ecks took position. The other two came up and Glide directed them closer to the entrance to the lot. They moved through the crowd to do so.

A thinly disguised O'Conner blended in with the people milling about. Among Aesop Hong's talents were stints in his twenties learning various theatrical skills working Renaissance fairs. He was disguised in threadbare clothing with his hair now salt and pepper. He also had prominent gray whiskers to add to the effect.

"Thank you," the transformed O'Conner said, taking his order of carne asada fries in a paper basket from the truck. He ate, milling about. He seemingly wandered past the first two of Teaflake's men stationed at opposite sides of the opening. Any number of people were standing around eating and talking and generally having a good time, on and off the lot and up and down the street. He worked his way closer to the studio. As no one was paying attention to him, he quickly pushed back his buttoned cuff. He wanted to see what time it was on his obviously expensive Breitling Gwen gifted him last Christmas. He then smoothed the cuff back in place. He wandered around more, making sure to engage others in conversation.

A few minutes behind schedule, the stilt man appeared. His getup was a cross between a Transformer and a Power Ranger. The entertainer was a hookup also through Hong. The stilt man's head was framed in an open cowling that included a built-in mic, the circular mesh of a speaker on his chest.

"Is this the shiznit or what?" he boomed through his speaker with its bullhorn resonance.

Shouts of approval went up from the gathered despite the use of the dated slang.

"Ain't no party like a Slauson Avenue party," the stilt man said, arms upraised, waving from side to side. Whoops of approval increased in intensity as the stilt man started to dance. Moving and grooving, bobbing and weaving, he too stepped onto the studio's lot. Teaflake's men tensed. O'Conner moved farther toward the door. Among the weapons he'd brought were pepper spray and a collapsible baton. If he had to, he'd shoot Glide and Ecks, dash in and take out Teaflake. He was certain it was only four of them on guard duty. He was ready with his diversion.

In position behind Ecks, O'Conner was about to strike when a gun was pressed into his back.

He turned his head, regarding a slender white man in owlish glasses. He was medium height and dressed in dingy work clothes. Where had he seen him before?

"Just be cool, O'Conner." A slight smile creased the other man's features. Softly, he intoned, "Let the pepper spray go while we keep walking out of here." He jerked his chin indicating the direction.

"Whatever you say."

O'Conner did as directed. Any sound the canister made when it dropped to the macadam was swallowed by the boisterousness of the crowd. They kept going, the slender man close behind the taller O'Conner, a gap of a few inches between them.

The woman wearing the leopard print sweatband was spinning around, chewing on what was left of her torta. She collided with one of the legs of the stilt man and careened into O'Conner.

"Dang, sorry mister."

O'Conner grabbed her by the shoulders and swung her into the other man. Even whipped around, she managed to hold onto her sandwich, plopping the last of it into her mouth. O'Conner didn't try to flee. He lunged at the slim man as he brought his gun up. He deflected the gun hand as he fired. The retort of the bullet brought instant silence. Meanwhile O'Conner used his sap and struck him viciously on the head, grabbing for the gun, but the other man evaded his grasp as he staggered back a step.

"Gun, the teacher-lookin' dude's packin'," somebody yelled.

"He's a mass shooter," O'Conner hollered, working his way backward, getting bodies between him and the man in the owlish glasses. The panic building among the gathered erupted and people began yelling and running every which way.

"Get back,"The man in the glasses blared as he started to go after O'Conner. "I'm a cop, this is official business." Gun in one hand, he now held a badge upright in the other.

"Bullshit motherfuckah," Glide said, gun on the bespectacled man.

"Fuck off," Glasses said, shoving Glide with a strength belying his size.

People rammed into the stilt man's elongated legs and over he went onto the top of a car, denting the roof and bursting the rear window.

Glasses darted about, trying to get a fix on which way O'Conner had gone. He heard feet approaching to his side. Turning, he was whacked in the face with a flat of wood, breaking his glasses. His attacker, the one called Rainey, hit him again over the head, cracking the piece. The struck man staggered and was hit one more time on the head. He plopped to the ground in a sitting position. Satisfied, Rainey tossed away the slat he'd broken free from a pallet.

Glide and Ecks were there. From a pocket, Glide took hold of the barely conscious man's identification. As he did this, he said, "We better get Tea out of here. Go get him."

Ecks and Rainey jogged toward Rand's workshop.

"He *is* a cop?" Butch asked.

"Sheriff's department. Must be one of them," Glide said, referring to the Interceptors, as he dropped the badge and ID in its leather holder onto the downed man's lap. The parking lot had cleared. The stilt man was nowhere to be seen. People were still milling about on the street, a number of them having hunkered down behind the lunch trucks. The lunch truck crews had slammed the sides of their vehicles shut. So far, no police were on scene. There seemed to be an uncertainty on what to do next.

The Interceptor was left where he was, holding his head.

Out rushed Teaflake. He was hustled into the SUV the guards had been sitting in and off they went, Ecks and Glide in the front seats. This vehicle was followed by the one containing Butch and Rainey. The end of the street was still clogged. The tuba band was on break but no one had dispersed. Evidently they hadn't heard the gunshot or the commotion over their music. The cars had to slow. Horns honked and Teaflake yelled at the crowd.

"Get the fuck out of the way." This earned him the finger from more than one person.

O'Conner, still in disguise, appeared. He pressed the muzzle of his gun to the rear passenger window next to Teaflake. He hadn't been noticed by him or the drivers. The SUV eased forward. Before he could squeeze the trigger, brakes screeched and Rand's pickup skidded and slammed into the rear quarter panel of the SUV.

"Fuck," he blared. She'd tried to pin him and he'd dived out the way. Very quickly, three guns were on him and he was pulled upright.

"Get his ass in the car and let's get out of here," Teaflake ordered.

O'Conner's gun was taken and into the back of the SUV he went. The vehicles were still operable and Ecks sat next to him on the back seat of the SUV, his gun on O'Conner. Teaflake rode in the pickup with Rand, and the other two in the third vehicle.

As they transported O'Conner, the SUV passed a rec center designed in a modern style. Young men and women were playing basketball outside. This particular facility, the Matthew Henson All-Purpose Athletic Association, also put on midnight basketball leagues for what was termed at-risk youths, and other such programs. O'Conner knew this because through a corporate veil, he oversaw the Apgar Initiative, which annually donated money to such efforts across South L.A. Morbidly, O'Conner clocked that it was best to concentrate on his current predicament.

The vehicles arrived at a one-story building south of the airport, a few blocks east of Aviation Boulevard. Around here were a tow truck facility, freight forwarding concerns and a strip club. There was a construction area as well, part of the extension of the Metrolink, including to Del Norte arena. Though for whatever reason, there was no worker activity on-site today. Rolling along an alleyway, they parked behind the building. O'Conner was hustled inside through a rear door Teaflake keyed open.

Overhead fluorescents came on. O'Conner was marched past freight containers stacked three high. Some were the rigid type for cold storage and others soft-sided, the collapsible kind. He was marched into a smaller room, sparsely furnished with more of the freight containers along one wall. O'Conner was lashed to a chair with a series of bungee cords stretched tight around his upper and lower body. So far, he hadn't been beaten. Teaflake studied him for a few moments. Glide and Ecks hung back. The other three weren't there.

"We know each other?" Teaflake finally said.

"Hardly." That much was accurate.

"Something about you, man."

"I got one of those faces."

"Sure you do. How you gonna make me whole, huh, O'Conner?"

"Sorry to disappoint you. But you started this shit."

"You and Tachmann go back a ways? He had his finger in all kinds of pies."

"You tell me."

"This about revenge?"

O'Conner didn't respond.

Teaflake pointed at him. "No, you got snake blood in your veins, you ain't the sentimental type. Yeah, Tachmann was done in, but this is about safeguarding the snatch y'all pulled off. He was part of that." Teaflake paused, head slightly cocked as if listening to a faint beat. "Those ducats you made away with. This is how we square matters up."

"Keep dreamin'."

Teaflake signaled to the other two and together they all left the room. O'Conner didn't suppose the gangster was trying to make him any more anxious than he already was. They were weighing how best to come at him. What sort of torture to unleash on him, he coldly concluded. Such hadn't been the situation with Tachmann. Teaflake had been heated, taking it personally Tachmann wasn't going to bring him in on the sweet deal of the winery. Sitting there in the gloom, O'Conner suffered from no delusions. He was quite aware of the grim reality that if he gave over where his stash was, he'd be shot in the head. Don't say boo and he was still going to wind up on the slab. Considering those options, the relatively positive side of the ledger was the quick death route.

After a few minutes, the door opened again. Glide wheeled in a portable oxyacetylene rig on a dolly. Teaflake followed, carrying protective goggles, asbestos gloves and a striker for lighting the torch.

"Make no mistake, brah," he was saying, "you're gonna talk. It's a simple equation of how many body parts you can stand to lose before you blabber like a little bitch. My girl works wonders with shaping steel and iron and all kinds of metals. Her pieces sell for long green, baby." He patted the twin tanks of the torch. "It's amazing what she can do with this bad rascal. I mean, I watch her for hours doing her thing."

Teaflake fixed the prisoner with a glare. "Dig what I'm laying down?"

O'Conner steeled himself, wondering morosely how much he could take.

Teaflake turned valves on the tanks and put on the gloves and the goggles, placing them above his eyes. The rig was moved closer to the bound O'Conner. Glide then stepped farther back. Teaflake unhooked the torch and delicately turned knobs on the body of the nozzle.

"Gonna start on your toes and work my way up," he explained with the calmness of a physician informing a patient about a pending surgical procedure. He put the goggles in place. "Sucks to be you." He sparked the torch to life and adjusted the flame to a fine precision blue. Bent slightly over, downward came the cutting flame at O'Conner's shoe.

Yet rather than reflexively rear back as the flame cut from the little toe toward the big one, teeth and jaw clenched, O'Conner lurched forward. He and the chair collided with the torch and Teaflake.

"What the fuck?" the gang lord blared as he fell over, still holding the lit torch.

O'Conner's arm was on fire. So were some of the bungee

cords being used to tie him up. He rolled, partially putting out the fire as well as getting his arms free, wrenching and twisting at his binding. Glide was helping Teaflake to his feet.

"Fuck it," Teaflake said. "I'm gonna roast your ass like I should have from the beginning. You're too much damn trouble."

Teaflake scooped the live torch off the ground. Underhanded, O'Conner rolled one of Burgess's mini bombs at them. He'd strapped them to his ankle. He slid beside two sets of containers for cover. The device went off, blowing up the torch's twin tanks. One was for oxygen and the other contained fuel in gas form. The explosion rocked the small room with a boom and concussive force. Glide was the closest to the tanks and was set on fire.

"Aw shit," he said, hands up, part of his face burning. He panicked at first, running around, the flames intensifying. It finally occurred to him to drop to the concrete floor and roll to extinguish the flames. He came to a stop against one of the collapsible freight containers, covered with insulation material. A number of them started to burn.

O'Conner was back on his feet. Apparently Teaflake had managed to get out of the room, as he wasn't around. Momentarily O'Conner crouched beside Glide, who was sprawled on his stomach, trails of smoke rising from his burned face. He pounded his fist twice onto the back of the downed man's head to keep him out of his way. The fire spread to the other collapsible containers. O'Conner retrieved Glide's weapon.

Ecks and Rainey rushed in through the open door. They

shot and O'Conner shot back, dropping both of them with the speed and accuracy of an Old West gun hawk. Maybe, like Twin Slim, they still breathed, but they wouldn't be trouble. Gray smoke from the burning containers filled the doorway, drifting into the main room. The smoke rose toward the ceiling, setting off the automatic sprinklers. Warily, O'Conner entered the main room. It wouldn't be too long until fire trucks arrived. Yet as the fire burned, the sprinklers sputtered, intermittently stopping and starting. The glitching sprinklers helped to stop the spread of the fire but could not fully extinguish the already-burning freight containers. Toxic smoke occupied the ceiling area of the rooms. His upper arm was severely burned. O'Conner was also worried he was leaving a partial shoeprint in red from his damaged foot. Fuck it.

Focusing, blocking the pain, he figured Teaflake and Rand might well have exited the premises. He also assumed Butch had been left behind to take him out. They'd come through this way, a forklift not far from the rear door they'd exited. It was parked somewhat parallel to the far wall there. Enough to obscure a man hiding behind it.

O'Conner shot out the overhead lights illuminating the area where the forklift was. If he was hiding, Butch was smart enough not to react. Crouching low, eyes on the now-dark bulk of the forklift, O'Conner circled the other way around in a wide arc. He then cut diagonally toward the machine. It took effort as his foot bothered him, but he couldn't slide his shoe along, as that would make too much noise. Closing in, he sensed then was able to recognize an object before the wall to his left—a freestanding, chest-high metal shelf with tools and plastic containers on it. O'Conner kicked it, as if he'd bumped into the shelving.

Butch rose from beside the forklift, rattling off gunfire in O'Conner's direction. The latter had gone flat on the greasy floor and, aiming upward, released several rounds from that position. A stifled gurgle indicated one of his bullets had struck Butch. As quickly as he could, O'Conner covered the distance. The hoodlum was sprawled backward against the forklift, arms outstretched as if he'd been crucified. The front of his shirt was soaked red from his leaking fatal throat wound.

O'Conner backtracked. As he did this, he used the flashlight on his phone to see where his blood was on the floor. There were traces of crimson but not as much as he'd surmised. He concluded the torch had both cut and somewhat cauterized his flesh. But where he spotted any blood, he used his good foot to smear it on the grimy floor. He sought to contaminate the samples—make it as hard as possible for the law to lift his DNA and file it in one or another damn federal database. He retrieved the key fob to the SUV from Glide's pockets. The downed man made sounds in his throat, but his eyes didn't open. Sirens approached. Teaflake and Rand were in the wind, and he needed to be as well.

O'Conner paused by the two he'd killed. He and Ecks were roughly the same size. He stripped off what was left of his shirt. He regarded his burned arm. The skin was red and blistered. Flexing was painful but he could do it. Second-degree level, he estimated grimly. There was a neat red hole over Eck's shirt's front, but far less noticeable than O'Conner's burned-away sleeve. Briefly he considered taking off the other man's shoes, as his right one had been sliced into, though not all the way.

"Naw," he said, buttoning up. Maybe a couple of his toes were severed and maybe not. For now, he was going to leave well enough alone. He tossed his shirt onto a still-burning cargo container.

Outside, O'Conner got in the SUV and took off. Pressing the accelerator, he was happy to see his foot had stopped bleeding. The fire department rolled into place out front. O'Conner made a turn and headed along the backstreets, avoiding the main throughfare of Aviation. Traffic was light in this area.

O'Conner was driving near the construction area, K-rails and temporary cyclone fencing bordering most of it. The street he was on was blocked at this end and he turned to take the detour. That's when he saw a column of steam rising from behind a mound of earth in an area of the construction site. He slowed and saw the crumpled front end of Rand's pickup. The smoke was rising from its ruined radiator. He pulled over, turned the car off and got out. He had Glide's weapon with him.

Laying on the ground near the pickup was the fourth Interceptor. He was on his back, unseeing eyes behind his lenses open to the darkening sky. Must have had a second set of glasses, O'Conner noted. Powder burns were on his shirt over his fatal wound. He'd been shot up close.

A drizzle started. Two fingers on the big vein in his neck, O'Conner confirmed the man was dead. He surmised that the sonofabitch must have followed them here. Droplets of water dotted the corpse's glasses now. The car he'd come in, a Prius of all things, was parked nearby, right in the middle of a roadway that curved away to the east. Teaflake and Rand were on foot. The cops didn't seem to be coming, but just in case O'Conner placed the dead man under the pickup so he'd be less conspicuous. He left the Prius where it was and went in search of the other two. He didn't imagine they'd be waiting at a bus stop. They could have taken off using a rideshare but those services kept records. If it was him, he wouldn't have summoned that kind of transportation. Now calling and waiting for a crime partner or friend of Rand's, that made sense.

The SUV had a dashboard monitor. O'Conner pushed the ignition button to turn on the battery. He called up a street map of the area and gave it a brief study, concentrating on feeder streets into the main throughfare. Some of the businesses in the vicinity were also indicated on the map. Thereafter he turned off the car and wiped the steering wheel and other areas of the interior he'd touched with pretreated disinfecting wipes. There was a pack of them in the glove box. He also wiped down the fob, which he left in the SUV, and the exterior door handle. He tucked a few wipes in his back pocket and searched for the duo. The drizzle had stopped but the sky overhead remained gray.

Sure enough, as O'Conner got to the corner of a boom lifts for rent outfit, he spotted the two about a block away from where he was. They were moving, each looking around for him and their ride, he figured. He couldn't run up on them given his injured foot. The block was short and narrow and they were at the far end. He could shoot at Teaflake from his vantage point. But if he missed, there'd be return gunfire. These buildings were occupied at this time of the business day. If the police hadn't been alerted before when the fourth Interceptor was shot, they would be now if a gun battle was taking place. O'Conner was aware that often when people called the emergency number, they'd reach a recording. It might be some time before the law came—or not. Either way, he'd be a fool playing those kind of odds. He had to wrap this up as quickly as possible.

O'Conner took a moment to assess. Where would Teaflake be heading? To get the equivalent of his go bag and bolt out of Dodge. Teaflake hadn't heard from Butch, so he had to conclude O'Conner was still alive. His plan had been to go to ground and, by upping the price on his head, flush O'Conner out. Now, though, his men were dead or wounded and he had a dead sheriff's investigator to answer questions about. Teaflake was going to leave town, but not empty-handed.

Heading back the way he'd come along the side of the rental outfit, O'Conner walked as fast as he could around the back end of the building. On the opposite side of the street were several crisscrossing freeway overpasses. Under the overhead loops of concrete was an expanse of dirt and gravel where an earth mover, allocations of rebar and so on were stored as part of the ongoing construction. Stationed at the end of the street, at the corner of another building, O'Conner again put eyes on Teaflake and Rand. A car was slowing as it neared the couple. Teaflake lowered his raised arm.

O'Conner waited until the car had stopped and the rear door was open. There was a woman at the wheel. As Rand got in, talking to the driver, Teaflake stood outside of the vehicle, looking about over the roof. Once Rand was settled inside, he too began to enter the car. Emerging from hiding, heading diagonally across the street, O'Conner exaggerated his limp and held his burned arm with his other hand. He was taking a risk that Teaflake would start shooting, but he sought to lure the gangster to him. Make it appear he was worse off than he was, an easy kill. O'Conner made it to the other side of the street and hurried his pace under the shadows of the overpasses. The sky had darkened once more. The drizzle had started up again. He heard the car zooming away as well as footfalls on asphalt. He was sure Teaflake wanted him dead but had likely concluded that O'Conner was armed too.

It occurred to O'Conner that, like all those years ago when he'd seen him gun down the injured Long Box, history might be repeating. He hoped for a different outcome.

"How you want to do this, homeboy?" Teaflake called out. "Showdown like in the cowboy days? How about a duel like in *Hamilton*? Start back-to-back, walk off twenty paces and turn and fire. Or we take potshots at each other until the law rolls up?"

From his position, O'Conner answered. "However you want to settle it, Teaflake. Don't make me no never mind."

A short burst of laughter from Teaflake. "Since you the one swinging a set, O'Conner, what about we handle this like from back in the day?"

"Cold rockin', you mean."

"You called it."

O'Conner stepped into view, the gun tucked in his waistband.

Teaflake held his weapon. "Yeah, that's right. Man-to-man shit. Survival of the strongest and all that he-man yakety and blah." Leaning near him were two shovels. There was a freshly dug trench some yards away, its purpose unclear. He too put his gun in his waistband and, taking hold of one of the shovels, tossed the other one toward O'Conner. The drizzle steady and continuing, O'Conner picked it up. Both of the shovels were pointed for better digging.

Each with both hands holding their respective handles, the digging ends upright, Teaflake and O'Conner began their showdown. A thrust by Teaflake was blocked by O'Conner. They separated, circling each other as cars and trucks rumbled by on the freeways. O'Conner swept the shovel toward Teaflake's lower legs and he jumped back. As he did that, O'Conner pressed his assault with a swipe of his shovel. The business end nicked Teaflake's jaw.

"Huh," he murmured, back of his hand to his fresh cut.

Warily, Teaflake backed up, the shovel propped on his shoulder like a rifle at rest. O'Conner stalked toward him, eyes intent on the other man's hands. Then, in a flurry akin to the kung fu films both had seen as young men, the metal ends of the shovels banged against their twin again and again. The wooden shafts crossed and uncrossed, sending splinters into palms. O'Conner pushed back hard against Teaflake, his damaged arm bleeding, leaking fluid into the shirt sleeve.

"Back the fuck off me, motherfuckah," Teaflake growled, stomping on O'Conner's injured foot.

He yelped, countering with a jab using the end of the shovel's handle, causing Teaflake to backpedal. Yet, as O'Conner came at him, Teaflake was ready and the flat of the shovel's blade whacked his burned upper arm. O'Conner stumbled backward, sweating and breathing hard. Teaflake brought the shovel up and over, down toward O'Conner's head. He moved aside, slipping on a patch of gravel. He plopped onto his belly, rolling out of the way just in time to not get the back of his head cleaved in two. Flopping onto his back, he was able to block another attack from Teaflake. He got to a knee as they parried and thrust with the shovels as if fencing.

O'Conner was upright once more. The combatants continued swinging the shovels violently at each other, metal clanging against metal melding with their grunts of exertion. O'Conner made to turn to avoid a blow, but as he put pressure on his damaged foot a lance of pain had him coming up short. The edge of Teaflake's shovel ripped into his pant leg just above his knee.

Gritting his teeth, O'Conner was able to backpedal this time, continuing to swipe and block with his shovel. Teaflake brought his shovel around at waist level, meaning to slice into O'Conner's stomach. Bringing his shovel up and under the swing he deflected the attack. His motion had him off-balance and Teaflake kicked him in the shin, causing O'Conner to grit his teeth.

"Damn this jousting bullshit," Teaflake said, and reached for his gun.

Like a big-league batter, O'Conner twisted his upper body around, swung the shovel in a blur of speed. The edge of the blade sliced into an artery in Teaflake's neck. Both men gaped in surprise as the blood spurted.

Teaflake's gun fell to the ground. He followed, at first

falling to both knees, his mouth hanging open. He slumped over onto his side, his blood staining the gravel red. The light went out of his eyes. O'Conner blinked hard. He looked over his shoulder. Their battle had been in and out of the shadows and light of the overpasses. Drivers passing by on the street had certainly seen them. Had they been videoed? Would one or more digital records of what went down find its way to the cops?

Hell if he knew. He still had the makeup on his hair and face. He didn't want to remove the stuff for fear of leaving any more of his DNA around.

O'Conner looked up at the steel-gray sky, used the shirt-tail to wipe down the shovel's wooden shaft and dropped it beside the man he'd killed. He took a last look at him, remembering that night in the Hi Hat and how much he forced himself not to shake when the gangster faced him down. How that moment taught him about using his fear not to turn his guts to jelly, but as fuel. O'Conner went farther under the freeways, knowing he'd find some way out—or make a way. His limp due to his injured foot now wasn't an exaggeration. In a gloomy area under a roadway, not far from the LAX Airport Police Lost and Found building, he called Gwen on what he'd called her Bat Phone.

"Hey," he said. "I could use a ride."

"You done?"

"Almost. One last detail to take care of."

"Isn't there always?"

On the freeway, O'Conner lay in the reclined passenger seat while Gwen drove her Mustang Bullitt coupe. He'd walked to a CVS while waiting for her. There were two teenagers out front with their skateboards—taking a break, it seemed, and scrolling on their phones. He gave each one a hundred-dollar bill and told them they could keep the change if they went into the store and got him some rubbing alcohol, gauze and such, including superglue to seal his wounds. They gladly accepted the task.

Patched up and resting, O'Conner turned to look at Gwen.

"Jeanie, they called her," he began.

"Your grandmother, you mean?" she said, looking straight ahead.

"Yeah. Her friends at the restaurant called her that."

O'Conner let some of the night traffic go by, then continued. "The way she died, Teaflake rearing up . . . all this time I guess it was in me, but I hadn't seen what it was. But I know now, Gwen. I know why I do what I do."

She turned briefly from watching the roadway to regard him, then turned her head back.

"It's my door I want to go through, not carrying dirty plates of other people. If I am carrying a plate, it's food for me on it or someone I love."

O'Conner placed a hand on her thigh and gave her a squeeze.

By the light of other cars, he could see her smiling.

The Swashbucklers were playing at home and were up five due to a three-pointer Sthal Casall sank. Palmer Van Noy raised a fist, yelling, "Yeah, baby, way to go." Directly behind where he sat courtside, O'Conner took a seat and leaned forward to be heard clearly.

"Don't look around," he stated casually. "By now you've discovered you've been robbed of not an unsubstantial amount of money. You've no doubt employed personnel who have proven track records at hunting down people. Maybe they'll turn up a few leads or maybe they won't. But should anything happen to me or one of my associates, there will be consequences."

"Incredible," Van Noy replied. "You steal my money and have the nerve to threaten me?"

"Motherfuckin' right I do. And yes, I know who the hell you are and who you hobnob with. None of that will stop us from coming right at you, no matter how many Maltese cross–tatted yahoos you have on your payroll."

Joyner had used her computer skills planting breadcrumbs indicating the Interceptors were behind the theft. Including traces of the Omnikan hack on Bob Winslow's phone, which O'Conner had taken at the vineyard. He'd returned the phone to Winslow's house in Temecula after breaking into it. Which was why he'd had Joyner hold off releasing the incriminating videos. He didn't want the authorities sitting on Winslow's house before he had a chance to plant the faked evidence. Maybe Van Noy would find out the truth eventually or maybe not. But for now, there was no better set of assholes for him to go after.

Van Noy breathed in and out measuredly.

"Enjoy the rest of the game."

O'Conner left Van Noy staring straight ahead. Walking away from the arena, O'Conner checked his watch. Right about now, Lanny Murser should be getting booked by the authorities. He'd named Burgess for money when Teaflake was looking for O'Conner. He'd planted evidence Murser stole proprietary information related to that which is Zelb. A few years in prison was what a punk ass like him deserved, the thief mused. Hell, he was lucky, O'Conner further reflected. If it was up to Burgess, he would have blown him up.

Later that evening, the Swashbucklers won a close game.

The following day at the Lasting Light food bank, Brother Hamlin and his staff were giving out prepared bags of food to the needy. For years, he'd been addicted to all manner of dope and alcohol, living on and off the streets. But one time, Charlie Mack had given him a hundred dollars, extracting a promise from him he'd do his best to get his life together. Naturally, he'd lied to her, saying he would make the effort—as he'd done several times before. But when she unexpectedly dropped dead the following week, he took that as a sign when he attended her fabulous send-off. He couldn't lie to a dead woman, for surely her ghost would haunt him. Roger Hamlin shed his identity as Shoe Dog and since then had been sober and of service. It was what he did, what he would continue doing, until he could do it no longer.

ACKNOWLEDGMENTS

Writing as Richard Stark, Donald Westlake's hard and spare novels about an amoral professional thief named Parker left an imprint on a whole bunch of crime fiction writers, including me. In particular, part of the architecture, as it were, of this work was inspired by two of the Parker scores, *The Seventh* (filmed as *The Split*) and *Deadly Edge*.

Here's also to master safecracker David McOmie and the segment on *This American Life* where in spellbinding detail he recounted how he was summoned to break into Prince's vault—and did. You can check him out commenting on what's realistic and what isn't regarding various heist films on the *Vanity Fair* website.